"Now we have two places the killer had to be. At two specific times. But we've only narrowed the suspects to twenty thousand students, ninety-four teammates, the coaching staff, and anybody in Georgia on drugs or with a thousand dollars bet on a football game."

"Do you really think it's someone we haven't met?"

"No chance," said Morris. "No one ever kills a stranger...on purpose."

REPLAY: MURDER

Also by John Logue
Published by Ballantine Books:

FOLLOW THE LEADER

REPLAY: MURDER

JOHN LOGUE

BALLANTINE BOOKS • NEW YORK

To Johnny, Mac, Joey

"...*free from smallness, 'a grand, ungodly, god-like man.' He is our hatred ennobled, as we would wish to have it, up to heroism.*"

Newton Arvin,
on Ahab

Harry Carr did not live. He is *not* Bud Wilkinson, Bobby Dodd, Bowden Wyatt, Johnny Vaught, Abe Martin, Woody Hayes, Andy Pilney, Frank Howard, John McKay, Matty Bell, Bear Bryant, Peahead Walker, Tommy Prothro, Darrell Royal, Murray Warmath, Scrappy Moore, Ralph Jordan, Wallace Butts, Ears Whitworth, Jim Tatum, Duffy Daugherty, Frank Broyles. But if Harry Carr *had* lived, he would have been of their generation, and they would have feared him.

Prologue

Morris could not hear it. Not from this height. But he knew the *grunt* the shoe made against the football, sending it in the air like artillery. A clutch of players hung under the descending ball, one of them catching it easily, twisting, pantomiming desperation with a burst of speed. The kickoff was still ten minutes away. The noise of the crowd had not yet gathered momentum. Morris looked across the rows of reporters, opening note pads, arguing, using telephones, hands feeding cigarets and sandwiches. He propped himself out of his seat, turned his back to the field, careful to keep his balance, and walked into the press-box elevator. He got off at ground level without speaking to the operator and made his way carefully through the field of abandoned automobiles. A sudden noise rolled behind him. He turned on his cane to see the stadium. The noise seemed impossible without Harry. Who could be Harry for the next thirty years? It was Harry's game.

Chapter 1

The newsprint had gone brittle and turned the color of an old nicotine stain. The man in the photograph had aged with it. He was taking a cigaret from his mouth with his left hand. He had broken the cigaret between his fingers and was about to backhand it into the camera. Even then his thick, black hair was running to gray. His eyes were cut into one dark, horizontal line above his broken nose. His mouth was shut tight. His jawline was heavy but firm, even shot from below. An old Speed Graphic camera had stopped all that anger and spread it across six columns of newsprint twenty-one years ago. John Morris felt the stiff age of the clipping between his thumb and finger. He smiled in the empty room. Nobody could hate like Harry Carr.

Morris slid the clipping back in the folder and dropped it on the bed. He reached over and switched on the radio. The instant music surprised him. It always did if you grew up on vacuum-tube radios, he thought. He kept switching channels, looking for the news. You could hear anything in New York on the radio. Somebody was being interviewed in Spanish. He kept working the dial. The drapes were closed, but there was enough light in the room to read the clock. It was 10 A.M. He found an announcer going on about the international balance of payments. "You should have been here last night," said Morris, "to pay our way out of La Groceria."

He propped his head higher on the pillow. His bulk under the spread was like a rowboat on its back. He patted his upper body, which was massive but not soft. He would have to swim an hour to lose the veal Parmesan. If he was lucky the Sunday sports would follow the news. It did.

The announcer said the word *barbarian* cheerfully, as if he had invented it. "We will be back in thirty seconds for the story of the quarterback and the barbarian." It was a fun word to say here in New York, eight hundred miles from Georgia. Morris waited. When the announcer came back he almost got the incident right. He seemed to know Harry Carr. He even said the quarterback's name, Trapwell, with a certain confidence. But he blew it identifying Harry's school. He called it Georgia Tech. What could you expect from a radio announcer? Harry Carr coached at Georgia A&M. He hated the ground Georgia Tech was built on. Morris switched off the radio. If the kid, Trapwell, hadn't used that particular word *barbarian*. Or if Harry's football team hadn't been unbeaten. The whole thing would have been only a twenty-four-hour newspaper virus.

The telephone rang. Morris thought it had probably rung before in his sleep, but he had been lost in his dreams.

"Are you alone in there?" Sullivan's voice seemed at home in the room.

"I don't know. There's a lot of us under this spread."

"Why aren't you in church, asking forgiveness?"

"They only take sinners," said Morris. "I'm too old for all that."

"That's why I stay out here in Colorado. Life is so clean you can be bad as long as you live." Her voice was remarkably low in her throat.

Morris could see her sitting on her deck, having her morning coffee, looking out at the mountains, her slim legs crossed, her brown hair almost blond in the early sun.

"Your nose is too long," said Morris.

"They killed a man in Carson City who said that."

"My vacation's been cancelled. For at least a week."

"Morris. How can you tell? When you're on vacation?"

"I can't put it on my expense account when I pick up nitwit brunettes. Damn Colorado," said Morris. "We don't have a mountain. But you can climb the World Trade Center."

"Morris. Are you sure that's a spread you're under? And not a net? You've run out of golf tournaments this year. What do you have to cover, the Van Cliburn competition?"

"Harry Carr. Remember, seven or eight years ago? The Sugar Bowl. You met him."

3

"Not the big, dark one. Who asked me up to his suite?"

"That's Harry."

"Can I still have him?"

"You will have to get in line. There's been a decade of girls since you've seen him. My God, Harry must be . . . sixty-four years old." Morris couldn't believe it. He missed what she said. "What?"

"That's not too young," she repeated. "When do we leave for New Orleans?"

"He doesn't *own* the Sugar Bowl," said Morris. "His team was playing in it."

"We can go by the Royal Orleans and hear Armand Hug play the 'Rinky Tinky Waltz.'"

"Armand's dead."

"I'm sorry."

Morris could feel her touching him on the shoulder. "Nobody could play piano like Armand. You know, he never spent but one night of his life outside New Orleans. He could have made it anywhere. But Harry Carr doesn't play piano, and he lives in Sparta, Georgia."

"John Morris, you couldn't get me in Georgia if you promised me Sparta, Athens, and the Greek Islands."

"I'll have you arrested in Colorado and extradited."

"What's happening in *Sparta*?" She said the word as if it were an infection. But there was an edge of curiosity in her voice.

"Harry's still going strong. His team's unbeaten. Ranked Number One. That sort of thing. He probably has a new harem."

"Do you have to go all the way to Georgia to find out?"

"His best player quit Saturday. Called him a barbarian. On national television."

"Wonderful," said Sullivan. "Why?"

"Harry told him to 'get his ass back on the field.' After Alabama broke the kid's nose. He had a nice nose."

"I like him."

"Who?"

"Harry Carr. Give me a barbarian every time."

"You're hopeless, Sullivan. I'm leaving Monday morning. Harry's speaking that night, and I want to hear him." Morris propped the telephone against the pillow. It was true. He loved to hear Harry speak. Harry had been coached by an old Notre Dame man, and all of them could speak. Rockne sent them south carrying his formations like letters of introduction. Rockne never coached in the language Harry used, but the rhythms were the same. When Harry spoke, you expected to hear horns sound. All of the old Notre Dame men, and the players they coached, could drink, too. But none of them could drink with Harry. God couldn't drink with Harry. That's why Harry's still alive. They don't have a cup in the hereafter deep enough to toast him. Morris laughed aloud.

"What are you laughing at?" said Sullivan.

"God."

"He's funny all right. But he could use some new material."

"I'm going to save you a room in Sparta. In the old Georgian Hotel. You'll know it. All the floors slant from east to west. The bar's in the west, and when you're drinking, there's no way to walk east."

"Morris, the best thing I like about you is you are completely crazy."

"You can tell by the funny calls I get. I've got to make a plane reservation. You better call, too."

"All the planes are grounded in Colorado. We can't get a weather report. The Associated Press is hung over."

"Sparta is about sixty miles from Atlanta. You can rent a car."

"I can't drive. My nose is too long."

"I'll be waiting for you in the west."

Her telephone clicked twice. "Operator. I don't know this man on the phone. Please reverse the charges." She hung up.

Morris reached for his cane, to prop his stiff left knee out of the bed. It was the cane Sullivan had ordered to be made nineteen years ago from Monty's two-iron, after the wreck that killed him. And ruined Morris' own knee. Somehow it was the right thing for her to do. She had been married to Monty, and God how they both loved him. Monty, "who was born with the gift of laughter and a sense that the world was mad." Monty, who would have won the U.S. Open twice except for Hogan. The only man whose golf swing Hogan stopped to admire. The sound of the cane, riding solidly in Morris' hand, always seemed to keep Monty with them. But not between them. "Monty could stand anything except phony guilt," said Sullivan. So they never practiced it.

Morris looked at the walls of the single room, bare except for a black-and-white poster from the British Open at Sandwich, the year Palmer slashed at the winds as if he would beat them back across the channel. Morris looked at the homely poster and remembered the sight of him almost lost among the gorse. It was all he had to show for twenty-three years of work with the Associated Press. Moments out of time, alive only in his own mind, except for that one place and date printed in ink on poster board. Well, it was time to write his own mind, to see if he had anything to say after nearly a half century of being alive.

No regrets, thought Morris, not even for the days and nights and years lost in unknown motels. Only when he had been drinking and was tired did he think of the children he never had. What would Sullivan say when he told her of his resignation? Some wisecrack. Then she would be afraid of her block of downtown Denver that Monty had failed to lose at gin rummy. As if it could come between them. God knows he couldn't afford to give up his old expense account; he'd never miss the AP salary. Morris laughed in the empty room. He picked up the stack of newspaper clippings. Well, he had come into the newspaper game writing about Harry Carr, and who could have guessed he would go out writing about him?

God love Harry, he was going to win forever.

Chapter Two

Morris swung his stiff knee forward, working his cane on the slick floor, careful to guide his bulk between the unseeing travelers in the Atlanta airport. All of them pressed forward in separate directions, some breaking into an awkward jog down the long passageway. It was like a moving camp of displaced persons. Their lives seemed broken down into flight numbers. The expressionless planes carried them or stranded them without passion. Morris felt no sense of being home. The Atlanta airport of his youth would always be an old army-surplus hangar and the thirty-degree climb into a reconditioned DC-3. "Jesus, I'm an antique." No one turned a head at hearing him.

The push and shove for rental cars did not fluster the U-Drive-It girl at the end of the counter. She was all patience, but no smile.

"Do you need a map of Atlanta?" Her careful voice carried directly to him.

"I'm going to Sparta."

She held the keys in both hands, as if weighing whether to trust him with them. "That's my home town." She seemed surprised to hear herself say it.

"Do you have a map of Sparta?" Morris couldn't keep a straight voice.

Finally, a smile. "I can draw you one with a straight line," she said. She looked again at his charge card. "What's the Associated Press doing in Sparta? No football games on Monday."

"This is Monday? I knew I lost a week there somewhere."

She handed him the keys. And his papers. And turned her patience on the next customer.

Morris could have taken the perimeter road around Atlanta; instead, he took the expressway straight through it. It was like an aircraft runway, banking along at the bottom of a deep cut of clipped grass. The midday traffic was as heavy as he could remember it during the rush hours of twenty years ago. The skyline was a fantasy of buildings that would never be familiar to him. The city was behind him, and he was moving north and east. Office parks leaped ahead of him where acres of trees had been. Still familiar were the cuts through strata of granite that froze sometimes for two weeks straight in the winter and in summer trickled with the sweat of false springs. He left the city in a last, concrete spasm of shopping centers and motel chains, then thirty miles to the east, he turned off the expressway. He cut his speed as he entered Winder, the birthplace of Richard Russell, and began to look for the sign MADAM TINA. It once stood in front of a house trailer that had been decommissioned beside the road. Amazingly, it was still there. Crude, hand-lettered elements of the zodiac, barely visible, sustained her advertisement. Morris could not tell if the trailer was abandoned. He had always meant to stop before an important game and have Madam Tina predict the outcome. It would have made a good story. Morris looked again at the trailer. What if she actually knew the future? Suppose it was not a trick? What if there, all the time, jacked up on concrete blocks, lay the answer? The traffic was taking no chances, rushing in both directions. The zodiac went by him in a blur.

Morris did not look for the city-limits sign of Sparta. A generation of students had broken their speed from Atlanta at Doug's Barbecue Shack and considered themselves home. Morris slowed but did not stop. Old Doug would be inside, looking out at the weather, rubbing his palms on his huge thighs, thirsting for a long-unseen face that would turn back the conversation to his own team of 1948.

Crossing the O'Hatchie River, Morris was pleased to find the beginning of the town unchanged. Only coats of paint seemed to have been spread over the tired but grand old houses, many with wide porches wrapped around them, and others whose columns carried the burden of their own importance. All of them were lived in, none of them museums. The square block of the downtown was the same nest of automobiles, and kids jaywalking amid the traffic, their lives unable to wait for the changing of the stop lights.

Morris turned the still-unfamiliar car toward the campus. The street narrowed. A&M was an old university. The small, original campus might have been moved from New England, with trees and shade intact. Morris drifted slowly between the buildings, students crossing before him and after him, unseeing, as if he and the car did not exist in the currents of their lives. It was lucky Sherman had passed the university with insufficient time to do his duty. The modern campus sprawled through the trees in every direction, with ultramodern glass and aluminum invented alongside the quiet brick of older buildings, and yet the sum of it was not without grace. The tower clock chimed the quarter hour.

The entrance to the stadium was guarded by the same great sycamore at the south end zone. The next hill was a steep climb, even for the new car, up to the football practice fields. Morris remembered them as a green oasis from one hundred and twenty years of architectural evolution. Now he saw the fields were smothered by a ten-foot-high concrete-block fence, and he wondered if they were walling Harry Carr in or out.

Morris was sure that Harry and Caroline were still together. So many years of method acting. He could remember her in rare public appearances, never at games, tiny, her skin as fair as a girl's under her soft brown hair, never speaking no matter what honors Harry or his team had won, never being interviewed. He was sure no writer had been inside Harry's house in thirty-two years.

Morris flinched to think of fragile Caroline in Baton Rouge, and Harry drunk, a story he never wrote, a story like Monty's two-iron that had walked with him and Harry ever since. Harry was in his suite at the old Baton Rouge Hotel, telling a filthy story about a priest. Several women began to turn away. Caroline walked up to Harry and, to everyone's amazement, tipped Harry's full glass of Scotch down his trousers. "That's enough, Harry." She might have been a small girl chastizing an older brother. The slap filled the room. Harry looked at his huge hand as if he could not believe it had done it. Caroline lay whimpering on the floor. Morris did not need a cane in those years, and he was as wide as Harry. He pushed his way between the shocked women, but Harry had already picked her up in his arms; he was crying. Harry carried her out of the room as if he would kill the man who touched her. Morris was the only reporter in the suite. He went back to his room and wrote the story and picked up the telephone to call it in to the *Atlanta News*. He put the receiver down and tore the story up. He waited for Harry in the lobby. Harry was the only man he had ever known who could sober up with an act of will. He walked directly to Morris.

"How is she?" Morris asked.

"She's married to a goddamn fool."

Morris stood eye-to-eye with him, the two biggest men in the room, and nodded his agreement.

"Did you write it?" Harry's growl of a voice did not ask for charity.

"I wrote it." Morris waited.

"Good," said Harry. "If they have any guts, they'll run me out of town."

"I tore it up." Morris said it as a fact and not a regret.

Harry stood without speaking.

"I wish there was a way *I* could tear it up," said Harry. "Caroline's gone home. Doc's wife is with her..."

"Let me catch a ride with you to practice," said Morris. And Harry was back in his element.

"Goddamn LSU is gonna kick our sorry asses in the Mississippi River," he said. A&M won the game the next night, 42-7.

Morris eased the speed of the rental car and wondered if Doc had gotten fatter. Now he could see the silver tops of helmets on the higher practice field, and punted balls rose in the air, higher even than the tops of the trees outside the fence. He did not stop. Harry was beyond reach when he was at a game or at practice. He answered questions in non-sentences, most of them blasphemous. Morris heard a whistle like a knife in the air and the rolling thunder of leather against leather. The thin, silver line of reserves would be doing Monday battle. Harry never kept a big squad. Those players who did not draw enemy blood on Saturday rarely chose to give their own for long during the week. Morris would see Harry tonight. He wondered what Harry would say. How he would look. If age had gutted out a yard against him.

Chapter Three

Exposed pipes ran from the dead radiator in his room. Two floor-to-ceiling windows were warped at odd angles. The bathtub, its antique porcelain chipped to the iron, stood on four legs like a white beast. The floor slanted downward from east to west. The glass in the windows was smoky with age. It was a wonderful, old, wooden hotel. "It's a standing bonfire," Morris said to the air under the high ceiling. He looked at his watch. It was seven P.M. Some of the Sparta Quarterback Club members would already be gathering at the hotel. Two drinks, and all four hundred of them could whip Bear Bryant with one hand tied behind them. A number of them had played at A&M, many were alumni, some went to other schools, even Georgia Tech, and they ragged one another mercilessly. Plenty of them made their money in the street without benefit of higher education, but on Monday nights in the fall all of them were the same: ten dollars for dinner, one dollar for a drink, and who could laugh the loudest at the guest coach's lowest joke. Tonight was the night they had been waiting for: to hear their own Harry Carr, who despised them all for being in the room in their arrogance and their drunkenness as if they had invented his own victories.

Morris felt a need for a walk in the air before the bullshit and cigaret smoke filled the banquet hall.

The old black man worried the elevator into place, nudging it with his stick control as if it were an early airplane. Morris stepped out into the lobby, his cane sounding on the bare wooden floor. A dust-laden chandelier hung from the thirty-foot-high ceiling. Morris walked onto the wooden front porch. Lights were already on in the street against the gathering dark.

An old man was hustling the afternoon Atlanta newspaper in front of the hotel, calling out the wrestling results. God, it's the same old man, thought Morris. It was funny hearing him again after so many years. Not even in the old days when Morris wrote for the Atlanta paper did they give wrestling more than a one-column, fourteen-point headline and two paragraphs. Unless we did a feature on the White Savage, remembered Morris. The promoter had brought the Savage up to the sports department in trace chains, snarling, with a pack of Chesterfield cigarets in his shirt pocket, which you could see under his overalls when he bent over to sit down. The Savage became a favorite, and lasted six months on the Atlanta card. He was killed in a freak automobile accident at Hobson's Crossing and was buried by his widow in the National Cemetery in Marietta in his chains. Morris had covered the funeral. The old man's system with the wrestling results still worked. He was selling all of his papers. Morris watched him closely. He looked as if he would evaporate with the next effort of his voice.

Morris picked his way along the fractured sidewalk just in front of the hotel. Untended parking meters stood in a row of neglect, their violation flags fixed in their windows. The glow of a streetlight reflected in the raised hood of a dragon of an automobile. Morris was sure that it was a Packard. Its black hood was as long as a subcompact.

Gotta be an eight-cylinder, thought Morris, leaning on his cane. His only uncle had driven such a Packard all the years of the War.

A tall, angular man dropped the rag around the dipstick he was holding. "Goddamn!"

His voice wasn't southern, thought Morris; he couldn't place it. The man retrieved the rag from the bowels of the engine. His curly hair was as black as old oil and seemed to be screwed into his scalp. His body was all angles in his brown suit, his arms half as long as the hood, ending in wide hands.

"Nineteen thirty-seven?" asked Morris, wanting to run his hand over the high front fenders and the encased spare tires riding in their wheel wells.

"Thirty-eight." The man's voice was a deep base. Still, Morris could not place his accent.

"Jesus. Who restored it?" Morris touched the high, louvered radiator grill.

"I did most of it." The man returned the dipstick and carefully closed the enormous hood, looking at the car as if it had just materialized on its great tires.

"John Morris." He switched his cane over and offered his own huge right hand.

The man looked at the old rag he was holding. He shook hands reluctantly, as if he might be touched for a loan.

"Russell Myers." He said his own name as if posing a question.

"Where did you get it?" asked Morris. He was sure the Packard was worth forty thousand dollars as it sat.

"California. It's not mine. It belongs to the boss." There was no inflection in his voice. He might have said the word *government* instead of *boss*. He did not offer his boss's name.

Sure, California, thought Morris; it was an elusive accent. "Nice job," he said. "Glad I don't have to buy the gas for it."

The tall, wide man only nodded his head. His dark eyes were round dots in his long face.

Morris suddenly remembered that A&M's new president was from California; he was sure of it. Stanford, he thought. Morris couldn't come up with his name. "Is your man the new President?" he asked.

Myers looked at him as if Morris were accusing him. "He's not so new. Been here all summer and fall."

"How does he get along with Harry Carr?"

Myers' mouth turned raggedly up at one end in a lethal smile. "What I hear about Harry Carr, he doesn't get along with anybody, except the law—" He caught himself. "Look, you ask them. I just keep this Packard on the road." He turned his back and opened the car door.

Harry doesn't get along with the law, thought Morris; he *is* the law. He turned back toward the hotel. There were already clusters of men in the lobby. He went inside and got back on the one antique elevator which was already crowded. The old operator jerked them to a stop a good three inches above the eighth floor. Morris balanced himself and stepped down into the wide banquet room. Two bars were thick with business. Morris worked his way toward the one at the back. The faces in the crowd were older and heavier, but many of them were familiar to him. One or two of the men looked up at him as if

13

they knew him but weren't sure. They did not stop whatever it was they were saying to find out.

The bartender had put out a mason jar which was filling with dimes and quarters and a few dollar bills. Morris was sure the bills were his own, planted as a false show of generosity. He ordered a vodka and tonic and put in two quarters.

Morris felt a hand on his back. It was Frank Caplin.

"Careful. You're drinking like a journalist."

Morris could not stand Caplin's hand on his back. "Hello, Frank," he said without any false enthusiasm.

"What brings you from the big city? You here to do the "Harry Carr, Boy-Barbarian' bit?" Caplin was reaching for peanuts in a bowl and throwing them in his mouth. Even the dim light did not flatter his profile. He looked all of his fifty-five years. His hair, combed forward over his narrow head, emphasized his baldness. He seemed to have grown taller and bonier. There was still a fixed look of dispassion in his eyes. Morris could remember how they had all feared him on the *Atlanta News* twenty-five years ago. He was unknown outside the South. He did not have the gift of language to make the national magazines. But his sports column was the best read and most feared in Georgia.

Morris ignored his question. "Big crowd. Harry's still Harry."

Caplin drank with no comfort. He poured it reluctantly, like medicine. "Yeah. It doesn't say much for this generation's coaches."

They couldn't beat Harry. Not even whiskey could beat him, and Caplin couldn't bear it, thought Morris. One thing you could say for Harry, he never bowed down to Caplin. Frank looked at his watch. "God, I hate these drunken football clubs. They never change. But be glad you missed all the money-hungry pro athletes in Atlanta. And the unwashed bastards who follow *them*. Of course, you have to deal with the lace-shirt golf set. They're the most spoiled-rotten bunch of all." Caplin, who had paralysis of the arm when it came to picking up a check, and never wrote or spoke a word without a fee, looked again at his watch and drank up to the ice. He was working on a column, and he had to find "somebody."

As Caplin left, Morris was careful to keep his glass in one hand and his cane in the other. He did not have to shake hands.

"How's your buddy?"

14

Morris knew the voice before he turned his head. A thick hand palmed an empty glass over his shoulder to the bartender. Harry Carr was the only man in the room big enough to do it.

"Some buddy," said Morris, putting down his own glass and turning to shake hands.

Harry was old.

Sure, he had to be. But it was a shock to Morris. The last eight years had left Harry an old man. His skin hung loose on his face and over his still-huge frame and made a turkey neck at his throat. His clothes swallowed his wide bones. His hair was still thick but faded a lifeless gray, as if it had been dusted with a chalk eraser.

Harry was old. But his black eyes had not changed. The way he held himself apart from all of them had not changed. The power of him you could not explain was still in the air. He cupped a cigaret in the palm of his hand as if a wind were blowing through the room. He ducked his head toward his hand, dragging breath into his lungs, and talked through the smoke as if it were speaking. "Margaret said you were coming tomorrow. Didn't think you would get mixed up in this—" Harry swung his empty hand at the noise. He ignored a man trying to pay for his drink.

Margaret Stewart had been Harry's secretary all thirty-two years he had been a head coach. God, if she had kept a record of all she knew. "I wouldn't miss it," Morris said of the roomful of unanswered words, clattering of glasses, and heels scarring the ruined wooden floor. "They still believe." Morris saluted with his drink the men who seemed to grow older in their suits in the room.

"Those bastards." Harry laughed in his throat. His deep voice had dropped another octave with age and drink. "They don't believe in anything . . . but whiskey . . . only that, if you *win*." He had his own glass back and drank half the Scotch without lowering it. "They're too old for anything else. Me, too." He laughed in his throat again and poured back the rest of the Scotch. He handed the glass to the bartender without looking at him, keeping his big hand in the air for the refill. Men at the table scrambled among each other to pay for his drinks. Somebody left the bartender a five-dollar tip.

"How's *New York*?" Harry said the two words as if they were contagious. Harry never used anybody's name. He talked

15

around names, as though he would place too much importance on the people if he actually said them. He dragged away at the last of his cigaret and lit another from it.

"Oh, you're still big in New York," said Morris. "I heard your name on the radio Sunday. They said you coached at *Georgia Tech*." Morris laughed.

"Those bastards. All they want to talk about is that candyass quarterback." Harry drank.

"Is Trapwell all that good?"

"Oh yeah," said Harry. "He's a 'pretty boy.' But he's a truck. For a quarterback. A goddamn truck. When he turns the corner and puts it upfield, those pissant defensive halfbacks *look* for somebody to block 'em."

"He's no coward," said Morris. Harry would fight anybody who said a player of his was afraid. No matter what Harry said about him.

"Naw. He's dumb. That's what surprised me. He looks smart. Works at school. But the sum'bitch is dumb. I'm gettin' old. I shoulda known. You can't push 'em when they're dumb. They'll sit down on you like a mule. He's pretty. He *looks* smart, that's what fooled me. And him worried about his goddamn nose. You can push a smart one, like I pushed Mahaffey. I pushed his ass all the way to the National Football League, and he's a girl."

Harry pulled at the Scotch. "I'm old. I used to know how to run off the peckerwoods. Now I'm runnin' off the goddamn talent. Trapwell will be back. You wasted a trip from *New York*. You watch. He'll play against Tennessee. Those bastards up there in Knoxville are laughin' at me. Wait'll they see Trapwell's big ass turnin' upfield. They'll be huntin' holes in that artificial turf to hide in."

Harry finished off the Scotch. "He's a local kid. Too proud to go home. Daddy's not worth a damn. I threw the kid's footlocker out a second-story window the day after the game. You shoulda seen it hit the glass and bust on the ground. Scared hell outa the whole dormitory. But he'll come back. And we'll get right for Tennessee."

Harry quit watching the room and looked at Morris, his black eyes squinting through his own smoke. "When are you talkin' to him?"

"Doc's passing the word for me. I hope he'll see me."

"Yeah, Doc," said Harry. "Always knows everything after it's too late. Tell the dumb kid to come to my office. Tell him to forget what he hears on the television and see me. I'll find him anyway if he dudn't. You're comin' over for lunch?"

"I'll be there. If you're buying."

When Harry laughed, his skin tightened on his face, and he almost looked young again. Morris watched him go through the crowd, slapping one man, ignoring another. He was the same old Harry. If he liked you, he told you everything. He put all the pressure on you for what you would print. The bartender must have seen how long he had been with Harry and gave him a double tumbler of vodka. Morris put another two quarters in the dish.

"You carpetbaggers droppin' all the big tips, spoilin' the help." Doc Jonas Haywood's accent lay as heavy as the smoke in the room. He had grown fatter and, if possible, shorter, as though gravity were bouncing him on the floor. Morris was surprised that he was not old. Twenty years ago he must have been a kid out of medical school. He was not sober, either, the way he squinted through the rimless glasses and wobbled in his own low orbit.

"You down here to *do* us rednecks?" said Doc. It was not a friendly question.

Morris remembered the way Doc talked out of the right side of his mouth when he was upset with Harry or with something he himself had written. Morris ignored the question. He put a hand across Jonas' shoulder. "It's good to see you, Doc." He meant it.

Doc untwisted his mouth and took a drink and offered his right hand, smiling.

"The Old Man's about to coach forever," said Morris, bending down to shake hands. "What have you got him on?"

"Scotch and cigarets," said Doc. "He can stand anything but rest and decent food."

"He's still married?"

"Oh yes."

"Caroline. Does she still come out of hiding once a year? At the banquet?"

"No. She's not well. Never leaves the house."

"But puts up with Harry."

Doc nodded.

"And Harry's still Harry."

"The AP ain't gettin' into all that?" Doc lowered his glass.

"No. Just curious."

"Well." Doc was drinking again. "Nothin's changed. The sum'bitch might as well be twenty. I'm gonna start takin' those pills he lives on."

"Why do he and Caroline keep up the front? Nobody keeps score on divorces anymore."

"It's no front. She's . . . hell, forget it. Get drunk. Get laid. What do you think whiskey's for?" He looked Morris up and down. "You haven't gone to fat. But what the hell is this?" He tapped the cane.

"I use it to vault over low buildings," said Morris. "Actually, it's something I picked up on America's highways fifteen years ago." Doc had missed Harry's Sugar-Bowl trip eight years ago with a disease of his own, and he and Morris had not seen each other in two decades. "Seriously. How is his health?" Morris turned his head toward Harry.

"Between us?"

Morris nodded. Doc had been his best news source in the years he covered A&M. He had been careful not to break his confidence.

"Not good." Doc rocked his hand in the air.

"Why doesn't he quit?"

"Quit? Unbeaten? Why dudn't he shoot hisself?"

"What about the kid who did quit? Trapwell?" asked Morris. "Harry says he'll be back."

"Maybe," said Doc. "It ain't that simple. The boy says he'll talk to you. Here in the hotel. In the morning. Early. We better get a seat." The crowd was moving toward the tables. "Be damn," said Doc. "There's the new president: Theodore Murdock Walker. He oughta know better than to be here."

Doc pointed out a tall, ugly man, nearly bald, in a suit and vest. He had a long, bony face with a ruined complexion. He carried his pocked chin high, wearing his ugliness like a weapon. He moved between the men without speaking.

"I met his chauffeur outside the hotel," said Morris. "I didn't get the idea the good President is bosom buddies with Harry."

"The good president doesn't have a choice," said Doc. "But it ain't the same. Harry's gone too far. His drinking. Women, still. That word Trapwell called him on national

TV . . . *barbarian*. The President's a Stanford man. No place for him here tonight . . . with these drunks, and you know Harry. He's liable to say anything." Doc sweated behind his glasses. He started to say something and didn't. "We better get our seats. I'll talk to you later."

The noise seemed to come back into the room in one rush. Morris found a seat near the front. Harry Carr bent forward at the head table, sending a cloud of smoke from behind his cupped hand. Now he was drinking. When they made the great front runners, they made Harry first. As long as he won, they would all have to like it. Even the new University President would have to like it. Frank Caplin had had to like it for thirty years. But Harry would have to keep winning. They didn't pay ten dollars for a ticket to see him lose. It's not the ten dollars, thought Morris. The alumni don't know what it is they come to see. All they know is, it's not defeat they want. Harry had one sinking spell, four years ago. Two straight teams had broken even. Morris knew many had called him a drunk. They said he was ruthless. They said he was old. They said he was finished. Then he won the national championship for the sixth time. Now he was again unbeaten. They said he was *tough*. It was the only way to be. They wrote newspaper columns about it. Some players quit. As long as Harry was winning, those players were known as quitters.

Morris went back for one more drink. As long as he had something in his glass, he didn't have to eat the food or listen to the captain of the Quarterback Club.

Someone was being paged over the loudspeaker. A funny name. Peacock. Atwater Peacock. The crowd laughed as if it had been a dirty joke. No one got up to leave.

The room was quieter. A very old man was standing to introduce Harry. My God, Bill Sams has to be dead, thought Morris. Sams had been the best end on the 1925 A&M team that did not lose a game. His white, wavy hair was parted just right of center, as in an old photograph. Morris could already hear his elaborate manner of expression. He had gotten it as a boy in Rome, Georgia, from his grandfather who had been Attorney General of the United States. The year Sams graduated from college he talked himself into a job with the first radio station in Atlanta. His southernisms from the 1928 Rose Bowl were a success. He was even imitated. He moved to New York. It was three years before he missed his first assignment, chasing some Broadway dolly. Three years after that, the network fired him.

Morris liked him. He liked to hear Sams tell of the considerable feats of 1925. Harry hired him in the 1950's to broadcast ten minutes of halftime color, and paid him the top rate. He also flew Sams on the team plane, and put him up in hotels, and picked up his bills. Morris had been sure he was long dead.

Sams put both arms over the rostrum and said carefully, in his alcohol-ruined voice, "There is a generation whose teeth are as swords, and their jaw teeth as knives to devour the poor from off the earth. But tonight we come rich with victory."

Morris could hear they were also rich in proverbs.

The room was quiet. No one knew whether to cheer the sentences which sounded nervously biblical.

Sams poured himself an elaborate drink of water. He began again, quietly: "Four years ago, there were those who put us down. They said the 'Old Guard' was too long in the field. They counselled against the honest bleakness of our uniform. They said the instruments of victory had passed us by. They said the block and the tackle were anachronisms in a new game. And even today . . . we hear the warmed-over cynicism of the meek who would tear the world down to fit themselves"—he waited until the exact moment—"They conspire with the cowardly and call us *barbarian*!"

Chairs were thrown over backward, fists beat on tables, the air was primitive with a common indignation. Morris was startled to see that he himself was standing.

Sams dismissed his notes into his pocket. "I give you," he said into the last of the noise, "a man who, in the Valhalla of the gods, will stand with Mars himself. I give you the first coach of football in America: Harry Carr!"

Morris could not believe that any of them had ever been against him. Harry raised a knotted fist. His hair fell loosely over his forehead and shone dust-white and vigorous above the animal momentum in his face that was dark and wet and without age at that distance.

He put his fist down and looked directly ahead. He did not make a gesture until the room was quiet. Nothing is so absent as the vanished noise of a crowd, thought Morris.

Then Harry said, "How many times in thirty-two years we come here to drink good whiskey to a good team?" Some of the noise rolled back into the room. They scraped their chairs around so they could see him better. "'Course, we wasted some prime stuff on a couple of teams playin' grab-ass instead of football." He had a childlike way of cupping his hand over his mouth when he was amused.

A middle-aged speedback on Harry's first Cotton Bowl team could not lift his head to swallow another drink. Morris remembered his name was Fulton.

Then Harry was saying, with no emphasis, "Saturday, we were a great football team." He waited them out. He cupped his hand over his mouth. "We're liable to be tough again next week if the whiskey dudn't run out—" He drank straight Scotch out of his glass.

"Gib'm hell, Harry!"

"They already got the deed to it," said Harry.

All the noise rolled back into the room. He looked directly at the new President at the head table and took another drink.

"No way we can get out of it," Harry said. "We got to go up to Tennessee, Saturday." He waited. "There's a place. Harry Mehre, God rest him, spelled it K-N-O-C-K-S, KNOCKSville. They don't care up there how high you're rated. They'll hit you between the eyes, and see if you can pee a drop."

"They ain't nothin', Harry! General Neyland's dead!" It was not a friendly voice that shouted it.

"I know you, bastard!" hollered Harry. "You put ten dollars on Alabama, Saturday. I hope you put a thousand on Tennessee *this* Saturday." It was like the noise had never left the room. Then it was quiet again.

"I didn't come here to tell you we're gonna bury 'em in Knoxville," said Harry. They were quiet. They didn't want to hear any pessimism. Morris almost missed Harry's words. He was listening to his voice. It sounded of cement-damp November days. "I didn't come here either—" He cupped his hand over his mouth. "—to change the score last Saturday against Ole Bear." They were waiting for him to say it. They were hungry for it.

"It ain't like we beat 'the little sisters of the poor,'" said Harry. "You cain't out-po'-mouth Bear, and you cain't outscore him. How you supposed to beat him?"

Harry took another deep drink. The whole room drank, as if practicing some black liturgy.

Harry cupped his hand over his mouth. "I hadn't seen so many people knocked down and stepped on in so long, I forgot how bare-ass-nasty a team of mine could be in the broad daylight."

They hit the tables with their hands and arms and lifted their glasses. The old speedback, Fulton, jerked up in some alcoholic realization and shouted an obscenity.

The crowd hollered the word Fulton said. Then they were chanting it.

President Walker rose from his chair, the pockmarks sinking deeper into the ash white of his face. His voice, without a microphone, hardly carried across the suddenly still room. "I think, Harry, it's late; it's time we all went home."

Harry waited. The room waited. Harry drained his glass. When he spoke he did not turn his head to look at Walker; he spoke as if the pale, angular, ugly man had already disappeared from the room. "You put your bony ass back in that chair," said Harry.

The crowd stood and screamed: "Bony ass!"

Harry waited them out. Walker stood trembling, but he did not cross his arms or put his hands in his pockets.

"I know that Rolls-Royce," said Harry, "and that chimpanzee you got to drive it." The crowd was with him, but listening. "I know that house, that big house you live in. You couldn't wipe the ass of the man who built it and gave it to the college. And that job you got, that big money, you make: if you wanna keep it, you sit that bony ass down and shut up." Then they were quiet.

"Harry, your'ah lucky sonofabitch!"

Thank God, thought Morris. It was the same hostile voice that had needled Harry before. The crowd stood again to search him out. The President carefully turned from the head table and moved toward the back of the room.

"It dudn't take any hands to be a sonofabitch," spat Harry in the direction of the voice. "They're born every day with four feet." Morris could now see it was Trapwell's father—a physical parody of his old self—who had shouted at Harry. A pushing match was going on at a far table. "Let him alone," said Harry. "There's nothin' I'd rather see comin' than a man-made, double-breasted sonofabitch." God. They couldn't get enough of that. They were chanting the words *son-of-a-bitch*.

"What I want to know is how a single-breasted bastard like HIM could raised up a candyass, titty-pullin' quarterback an' expect me to suit him up and beat Bear Bryant. Shit! It took four to carry him on the field and two to carry him off." They loved that even better.

Morris lost sight of Trapwell, Sr. He was crazy to shout at Harry in here. Or drunk. Or both.

Harry waited. He seemed to turn his wrath on the whole room. "There's only one thing you sons-a-bitches want." He waited again. "You want to *win*." He almost whispered the word *win*, as if it were an obscene act. "I don't care what they write in the newspapers. I don't care what they say on the television. I don't give a damn who goes home with his head between his ass and blood up his nose. I don't give a *goddamn* if we play the last four games with no quarterback and a direct snap from center. There's one thing you sons-a-bitches will know. We'll have ten sons-a-bitches *coached* by a son-of-a-bitch!"

Even if he meant to continue, it was impossible. Theypoured out of their chairs. They didn't bring glasses. They raided the bar and drank out of bottles. They jacked Harry up on their shoulders in uneven spasms and passed him up a bottle. They passed up bottles on each side, and he was riding in lurches around the tables with two bottles by the necks, drinking out of both fists. They stopped to see what knot of them could shout the loudest obscenity. The old speedback, Fulton, could not get up. He was crying. They picked him up, but he could not say anything. The face of the new President was like something behind a locked door while the old Klan rode by up to Stone Mountain. When they fell with Harry at the back of the room, Morris watched the President slide around to the elevator. He did not stop to speak to anyone. It was another thirty minutes before someone brought Harry's coat and put it across his back. They were still reaching into the elevator, a vineyard of forearms and elbows, to shake both his hands, spilling their whiskey, when the doors jerked closed and he was gone.

Morris stood in the carnage of drunks and spilled furniture in the noise-blasted room that seemed empty without Harry in it.

Chapter Four

Morris held his ground in front of the elevator. When it came up empty, he was the first one inside. Others pushed against him and forced words and smoke around him. The old man sent the elevator unevenly downward in its shaft. Morris did not try to get off on his floor. It would have been impossible. And even an empty room would not have offered enough relief. He had to get out of the hotel and stand by himself in the street. The elevator finally settled, as with exhaustion, in the lobby. Morris waited until the others were out. He limped forward, his left knee swollen with fatigue.

The old man outside had sold his papers, or taken them home. Clusters of men talked on the porch. But the street was thankfully empty. The first week of November was in the air. Morris breathed deeply. He picked his way in the near-dark on the sidewalk broken by the roots of the old, heavy trees. The black Packard was gone. He did not walk toward the still-lighted center of town, but circled behind the hotel. The silence was as steady and welcome as the cool night air. There was only the soft tapping of his cane.

The reflected lights of the town were behind him. The street and the sidewalk were dark. The wind was up, making the only night sound. Automobiles emptied the hotel, now two blocks behind him. The traffic thinned. Morris stopped as often as he walked. Harry was old. But he had not changed. Suddenly, Morris wanted a cigaret. He had not smoked in years. Not since Sullivan harassed him into quitting. How did Harry get away with not changing? The town. It was small. So long as he could win, he was safe here. Morris could smell cigaret smoke on his jacket. If Harry ever began to lose, they would tear him to pieces.

Morris felt something, as if the dark were shifting, and then he heard it. The noise of an automobile, accelerating blindly toward him. He twisted his cane, exposed in the air, as the car rushed past without lights, making a loud shadow in the night. Morris tried to see after it; there was a small, dark movement at the wheel, and it was gone. "Yeah, kid. Big time. You'll make one digit in the traffic roundup." His words disappeared in the night. All he could hear was the wind.

Morris took the last step onto the porch of the hotel. He was a long way from New York, and he was beat. At least he had walked off the noise and the booze. It was nearly midnight. The old man was asleep in the elevator. Morris touched him, and he pulled the doors shut before he opened his eyes. Morris stepped out on the fourth floor. The elevator doors closed behind him.

Harry. Morris couldn't get him out of his mind. He turned the heavy key in the door.

What the hell? He was sure he'd left a light on in his room. Sullivan, he thought. All the way from Colorado in one day. Not possible. Sullivan couldn't have her hair done in one day. He flipped on the light, which burned only a faded lamp beside the empty bed. There was an early black-and-white television to tempt him with a late movie. He was in luck. Alan Ladd. There never had been an Alan Ladd movie he didn't like and couldn't sleep through. Luckier yet: a war movie. Something on a ship. With binoculars around his neck.

Morris smiled. "Harry. You're a late movie." A soak in the tub would help. He could listen to Ladd win the war through the open door. He switched on the light. Sounds of heavy guns came behind him into the bathroom. Bent forward into the tub, from his knees, was a man. A big man in a blue polo shirt. He must have severed an artery. The side of the tub was slashed with blood. It pooled on the scarred tile, not yet coagulated. Red handprints were smeared on the sides and the bottom of the tub. An ugly knife, as big as a deer knife, lay between his open hands, bloody. The man was young: blond hair, hanging limp. No color in his face. The room was sour with vomit. He had thrown up on the floor and in the tub. The bathroom floor was littered with twisted papers and dollar bills and cards. Now

25

Morris could see his billfold lying ripped of its contents, and the pockets of his trousers turned inside out. His profile—even drained of color, there was no question. It was the kid Trapwell.

Morris felt for a heartbeat. There was none. The body was not yet cold. "Jesus Christ." He was careful not to touch anything as he backed out of the room, leaving the light on.

Morris took a drink from the bottle in his suitcase. He took it neat, not wanting to touch a glass in the bathroom or even go in there.

The big guns boomed again on the ship. Morris looked up in surprise. Alan Ladd was still fighting the war on television.

It was too late to call Sullivan and tell her to stay in Colorado. He took another drink out of the bottle. He couldn't shake the image of the boy's blond hair hanging motionless over his face.

Chapter Five

Three raps on the door. Morris opened it. He didn't see the uniform at first, just the blond hair swept back from the high forehead. A sergeant was standing beside her.

"Sergeant Redding," he said in the high voice Morris remembered from the telephone. "And this is Lieutenant Blake." The Sergeant didn't say it as an apology. He said it as if every lieutenant were a tall, model-thin blonde. The Sergeant was the same height as the Lieutenant, but he seemed to be several inches shorter beside her thinness. Her eyes were blue and wide set, and gave her a familiar look of being perpetually startled. She couldn't be over thirty, thought Morris. Then he knew exactly who she was.

"You're 'Fessor Blake's daughter," he said. "I'm John Morris. Associated Press."

Her eyes were even wider with recognition. Morris took the Lieutenant's thin, cold hand into his own large one. He remembered her as a child chasing after 'Fessor on the practice field, and eight years ago at the Sugar Bowl in New Orleans, as a grown young lady. 'Fessor had been A&M's faculty chairman of athletics as long as Harry had been Head Coach. They never agreed on anything. 'Fessor was the only man on campus who could tell Harry no to his face, and frequently did. Morris remembered how Harry would cuss him but never removed him from his chairmanship.

"How's 'Fessor?" asked Morris, her hand still in his.

"He died last spring."

All those years seemed suddenly to be lost. Morris released her hand. "I'm sorry." The death in his own room washed over him. "Come on inside, Sharon." He used her name before he realized he remembered it.

Then he was shaking hands with the short, heavy Sergeant Redding, who was carrying a leather grip.

Morris led the way inside. The room was quiet except for their shoes on the wooden floor. He had turned off the television.

"The body's . . . in the bathroom?" said the Lieutenant. Her voice was low and even, but there was a moment's hesitation.

"In there," said Morris. He followed the two of them to the door.

The Lieutenant leaned inside, and then disappeared into the room. The Sergeant followed her. Morris did not watch. The Lieutenant reappeared with both hands gripping her shoulder bag. She offered no comment on the body. "Could you tell me again, Mister Morris, how you found him?" Her voice had taken on a thin veneer of officialdom. The Sergeant stood with his back to the bathroom door. He had left his grip inside.

Morris showed her his Associated Press identification, but not in a hostile way. He began recreating the entire weekend, beginning in New York. "I thought only reporters did that," he interrupted himself.

"What?" She was puzzled.

"Took notes without looking at the note pad."

"Oh, it's just a habit," she said.

"And a good one. You can remember the expression of the guilty party."

"What are you guilty of, Mister Morris?" She had an un-
expectedly full smile.

"Of being tired and a little bit sick." Morris finished telling
how he found the boy. Leaving out only Alan Ladd.

There was another knock on the door. Morris opened it.
Doc Haywood squinted, plump and tieless, through his rimless
glasses. He looked as if he had thrown his clothes on in the
dark after Morris had called. Behind him was another pudgy,
middle-aged man who had to be the coroner. Doc introduced
them. The coroner's name was Floyd Harris. He disappeared
into the bathroom with Doc and the Sergeant behind him.

"The boy's so..." The Lieutenant searched for an exact
word "...young."

"*Was* young," said Morris. The boy was the same now as
if he had never lived.

"You didn't expect to see him—" She looked at her notes.

"Until morning. The kid told Doc he would see me
here...early. He didn't give an exact time. Just 'early.'"

"Who else knew you were in town?" Now she kept her eyes
on her notebook, as if she was embarrassed to look up.

"Harry. His secretary. You know Margaret Stewart?"

She nodded yes. Now she was looking up, but not at him.

"I didn't call Eddie Martin. The Sports Information Director. He can breathe in, but he has to check with Harry to breathe
out. The hotel knew. And Doc, of course. Half the town was
at the banquet tonight. The bar opened at six-thirty. By ten the
crowd couldn't recognize each other. Much less me."

"What... were you going to write?" She looked directly at
him. Her eyes were not apologetic.

"I don't know. For sure," said Morris. "There was the trouble, of course, between the kid Trapwell and Harry." I didn't
care about the kid, he thought. I wanted to know what had
happened to Harry. How he still won. Why he still cared. How
he could survive, the last honest outlaw in a phony, public-
relations world.

"We'll have to go over this entire room." She looked around
as if it were a suite. "We're just a small-town department. It
will take us quite a while."

"I'll get another room," said Morris. "I couldn't sleep in
here anyhow."

"Jesus," said Doc from the bathroom. The coroner appeared

behind him, rubbing his free hand over his bald head as if testing its temperature. He yawned twice, and seemed too sleepy to speak.

Now the room was filling up. A photographer came and disappeared into the bathroom. Two ambulance drivers, youngsters, brought in their own chairs. They were used to waiting. They dealt a continuing game of gin rummy. The one with a beard was down ten dollars to the other one. The hotel manager phoned and then came up. He was at least seventy-five. He looked as old and frail as the hotel. He was too nervous to stay in the room, and went back down to the lobby, and came back up again. All he could do was give Morris the keys to another room. He was a tired, polite old man who finally wobbled off to bed.

Doc came out of the bathroom and lifted Morris' bottle and took a drink neat.

"What do you think?" asked Morris.

"I *know*," said Doc. "Somebody killed the boy with a knife."

"It must have been a giant. Big as the kid was."

"My twelve-year-old daughter could have done it. Sick as he was."

The two ambulance drivers paid them no attention. They dealt the cards as if they were waiting in an empty room.

"Sick on whiskey?"

"Cheap bourbon," said Doc. "I've thrown up enough of it to know it. Don't need any laboratory analysis. Seen you drunk, Morris. In the old days. Never saw you sick."

"He couldn't have killed himself?"

"Naw. Not likely. He would have felt too bad to kill hisself. All he coulda thought about was not throwin' up his stomach lining. Besides—"

"Besides what?"

"He was . . . What's the word? . . . fass . . . you know, neat as a old lady—"

"Fastidious."

"Yeah, that's it. Always clean. His locker coulda passed muster at Parris Island. Harry hated it, always wants to see dirt and blood on everything. You know Harry. The kid wadn't that way. He never woulda killed hisself in a mess like that."

"Even drunk?" said Morris.

"In my opinion. And sump'in else. I never saw Trapwell

take a drink. Not even a beer at Jake's, and he could get 'em free after a game."

The Lieutenant emerged again from the bathroom. She looked steady enough. "Okay boys," she said. "He's yours."

The ambulance team picked up the cards in mid-hand as if they had rehearsed it a hundred times. "That's eleven twenty-five you're down," said the one without the beard. He began unfolding a body bag while the beard picked up the collapsible stretcher. They disappeared into the bathroom. The medical examiner came out, still rubbing his bald head with his bare hand. He was not yawning anymore. He nodded at the Lieutenant and left the room without speaking.

The ambulance boys were fast, but it was a job, jockeying the stretcher out of the bathroom. The short, fat sergeant followed them, offering advice in his falsetto voice. In the dim light, the kid was huge in the bag.

"Is that all, Lieutenant?" the Sergeant asked.

She nodded. "We'll finish in the morning."

Morris thought of the old man on duty in the elevator. They would have to prop the body erect to get it inside. It would wake the old man up. Morris braced himself upright with his cane. His left knee had stiffened. His heavy shoulders were all fatigue. At least he hadn't unpacked his suitcase, except for the bottle on the table.

The Lieutenant was looking at the bottle.

"It's Scotch," said Morris. It was nearly full.

"Could you spare a drink?"

"Sure."

"If you don't need a glass," said Doc. "And no ice."

The Lieutenant held the bottle at arm's length. She drank, gritting her teeth. Then turned to Doc. "Can you come by the station tomorrow and read my report? See if I left anything out? If you haven't heard, Chief Harper's in the hospital with a heart attack. I need all the help I can get."

The invitation was small-town protocol and a polite dismissal, thought Morris. He remembered Chief Harper, a thin, morose man, as another of Harry's lackeys.

"The whole town's coming apart," said Doc. "I'll come by, but don't quote me to Harris. He'll think I'm runnin' for county coroner. I'm havin' enough trouble tryin' to keep Harry from tearin' the arms and legs off my football team."

The Lieutenant sat down. They were alone.

"Doc said it was bourbon that made him sick," said Morris.

"One thing we have an inexhaustible supply of in this town . . . is Doc's opinion."

Morris caught himself as he swallowed wrong, and coughed a Scotch taste in his throat.

"Doc doesn't change. Harry hasn't changed. Doesn't anything change in this town?" he asked.

"No. Not much. Not in the thirty years I've lived here."

"One thing has changed. No one ever killed a football player before. Trapwell's billfold was ripped and scattered all over the floor, his pockets were inside out. What was the killer looking for?" asked Morris.

"I don't know. It obviously wasn't money. He left the few dollars. When we find a kid dead today . . . whether it's murder or suicide or accidental death, even if it's a traffic accident, we first ask, 'What drug was he into?' It's a helluva indictment of our time, but we've learned to ask the question, because most of the time that's where the answer lies."

"I thought this kid was Mister Clean," said Morris.

"I think he was," said the Lieutenant. "But I won't accept it until I see the lab reports. Even if he wasn't a user, whoever killed him might have been. I know I sound paranoid about drugs. Show me a police officer today who isn't. Old cops tell me there used to be a time when husbands simply killed their wives, and vice versa."

"Whatever the killer was looking for had to be as small as a piece of paper," said Morris, "if Trapwell could have carried it in his billfold. Maybe it was an address, or a telephone number."

She nodded yes. "Perhaps it was something he was going to show you."

"That's possible. I can't imagine what. Doc only said that he seemed anxious to meet with me." Morris looked at her as if he suddenly remembered who she was. "How did you get to be a cop?"

"'Fessor taught pathology." She smiled. "I don't think I ever called him 'Dad' in my life. He wanted me to be an M.D. But I couldn't see it. I always wanted to be a cop." She paused. "You get to wear a uniform." She was teasing him. Then she put down her glass and looked at him seriously. "I remember you. Especially when 'Fessor took me to practice. He used to read me your stories in the *Atlanta News*. Then we saw you at the Sugar Bowl. How many years ago?"

"Eight. But it all seems like another lifetime."

"'Fessor loved football better than pathology. He could even put up with Harry Carr." She said the name with a strange emphasis.

"You're not a fan of Harry's?"

"When you are a girl in this town, you know you are grown when Harry makes a pass."

Morris shook his head. "You have to hand it to him for hanging in there."

"It's only worse if he doesn't make a pass." She used the same good smile. "*Morris*, they call you by your last name, don't they?"

"And other things."

"You were a help, I know, to the police in Atlanta last year. During the golf murders."

"I'm not sure you could call it *help*. But I was there. It was a very sad U.S. Open."

"This town is going to be on its ear tomorrow . . . this morning. With the Chief in the hospital, I'll need all the help I can get."

"Then you're sure Trapwell didn't kill himself."

"I can't speak for the Medical Examiner. And we'll have to finish our lab work. But I think Doc's right. There was only one set of prints on the knife. Bloody ones. At the top of the blade and the bottom of the handle. Set the way you would *pull* a knife out of your own stomach. Not stab it in." She bent slightly forward, as if with sympathy pains.

"And why would he pull it out at all, if he were trying to kill himself? Unless the pain was so bad. Or he changed his mind." It was not a happy thought. "Something else bothered me," said Morris.

Her wideset eyes were alert.

"How would he carry a knife that big? He didn't have a scabbard. Cool as it is, he wasn't wearing a coat."

"You're right," she said. "You can't walk into a hotel carrying a twelve-inch, unsheathed knife, even if you mean to kill only yourself. The hotel was running over with people. The manager says there were four hundred and forty-seven reservations at the banquet."

"I believe it," said Morris. "It began breaking up about eleven-twenty. When Harry left. I went down in the elevator about five minutes later. I took a slow walk for several blocks, behind the hotel. Got back just before twelve. I just remembered—"

"What?" She leaned forward.

"A car passed me. I thought it was a kid. Probably was. No headlights. Going like hell."

"You couldn't see what make it was?"

"I couldn't see anything. Anyway. When I got back, the lobby was empty. I didn't go in the bar. The kid by then was already dead. He was still warm when I touched him."

"I doubt he had been dead for half an hour when you found him. We'll know more tomorrow." She waited. "You will still be doing your story on Harry Carr?" She did not look at him.

"It's a different story now," said Morris. "How well do you know Harry?"

She turned through her notes. "I don't think anybody in this town *knows* Harry Carr."

"What can I write about Trapwell's death? I'll have to call the bureau."

"Say I *think* he was murdered." Her voice was low but firm.

"I don't want to put you on a limb."

"No. You saw him. But emphasize *think*. We'll know more after the autopsy. Morris, you're a professional interviewer. Will you share what you learn when you talk with the players, or with Harry, or anyone near the team?"

"Sure. But you can forget Harry. He might kill someone in the stands or on the bench. Harry would never kill a starter."

She laughed as unguardedly as she had smiled, surprising him.

"I'll tell you anything I see or hear. But you're the pro. I'm just a word jockey. Listen, I've got to move down to the second floor and call the Atlanta bureau. You better go through my bag before I move it. I want you to, for my own protection."

"Sergeant Redding already has." She didn't pretend to smile.

"I thought this was supposed to be a 'small town department'!"

"We only search our friends," she said.

"Someone is calling the boy's family? And Harry?"

"Doc. Only Trapwell's father is alive. I'm afraid he's an alcoholic. Harry..." She paused. "I'll call Harry. He'll be sick."

"I heard the boy's father at the banquet. He was in rough shape."

"He'll have a reason to be tomorrow." She stood up. She had good legs. It was lucky the good legs reminded him of Sullivan.

Chapter Six

The kid took dictation as if it were a new religion and he chiseling the last commandment.

"You said eleven fifty-five?" he triple-checked.

"Yep," said Morris. *Yep* didn't sound right for a new religion.

"*Four hundred and forty-seven* reservations?"

"You got it." Morris propped the telephone on the pillow.

"Lieutenant *Marion Blake?*"

"*Sharon*. S-h-a-r-o-n," spelled Morris, his eyes shut. "A dame."

"A woman?" The boy sounded like a disbeliever.

"You know, the girl-type lieutenant."

"I didn't catch it."

"But we both will if we don't get this on the wire sometime before the funeral," said Morris. It was already too late for the morning papers, except on the west coast.

"When's the funeral? I don't have anything about the funeral."

"Good night and thanks," said Morris. He hung up. "*I don't have anything about good night*," he mimicked. Yeah, Morris, he thought, you never were a nervous kid, were you? He went to sleep in his clothes.

The deep carpet outside the athletic department was a web of umbilical cords leading into a rough circle of unlit floodlamps. Morris recognized two network cameramen. Neither of them had shaved. He also recognized the AP man from Atlanta; Morris couldn't think of his name. He didn't know the others, all of them jockeying for position in the small room. Morris stood until Margaret Stewart saw him. Her hair was now entirely gray, but cut youthfully short. She was very much in charge. The timid sports information director, Martin, sat in a corner, hoping no one would ask him a question. Margaret put both arms around Morris as if he were back from the war. He was pleased that she was taller than he remembered.

"Don't you know you are not supposed to grow any taller?"

"I'm shrinking, actually. I just keep raising my heels." Her voice might have been taped twenty years ago. She lost her smile. "Morris, isn't this awful? That poor boy. Harry's beside himself. He's got to make a statement. He can't imagine what happened."

"Nobody can," said Morris.

"He said for you to wait."

Morris nodded.

She made herself smile. "Where's your girl . . . What's her name . . . Sullivan?"

"She would love the word 'girl.' In Colorado, I think. She still talks about the Sugar Bowl trip."

"As I remember, I made a fool of myself."

"It's a misdemeanor in New Orleans not to." Margaret had once been more than Harry's secretary, but that was a long time ago, even before New Orleans. She looked older when she wasn't smiling.

"He didn't . . . kill himself? Harry is sick, thinking he might have."

Morris shook his head. "It doesn't look that way."

"Whatever happened, it's terrible."

Harry came through the double doors, opening them both, as if he could not enter a narrower space. He stepped ruthlessly over the black electrical cords until he dominated the room.

White lights fired on individually, as if searching for an

escaped prisoner. Harry looked terrible. As though he hadn't slept at all. He squinted against the lights, deepening his wrinkles and waited. The cameras hummed in the room. He began without a signal, his throat a deep rasp:

"It's a terrible thing, a young man dyin'. A fine young man, Harvey Trapwell. Our hearts go out to his family, here in Sparta." Harry looked directly into the lights. "You can get old, and you've seen everything. But a young man dyin'. It hurts. You all know Harvey Trapwell *fell out* with me. He was probably right. I'm dumb as always, just older, too. But I still counted him on the team. I still think he woulda played. And it wouldn't have made any difference if he hadn't. He was a class young man. I don't know what happened to him. We're all sick about it, here at A&M. That's all I can say."

The room was a cross fire of questions, but Harry turned and walked back through the double doors, closing both of them behind him.

Words collided in the air. Someone tripped over a cord, pulling down one of the hot lights.

"Fool!"

The man wasn't hurt.

They couldn't get the light up. It was singeing the carpet.

"Cut it off, idiot!"

All of the lights were now off.

Reporters struggled for telephones. Margaret had held a line open for the AP. The Atlanta reporter was dialing the bureau. Morris remembered his name: Jack Pruitt. He had been in Atlanta for years.

UPI was steamed with Margaret.

"You have to ask," she said without malice.

The room began to empty.

Pruitt did not take long with his call. He was a pro, a slight man with bad teeth and a hesitation in his speech.

"I'm going . . . down to the police station. The . . . Lieutenant is making a statement. I'm at . . . the Holiday Inn, room . . . two-sixteen . . . if you need me."

Morris nodded. "I'll take you up on that. I'm seeing Harry. I'll file anything new he has to say."

The cigaret shook in Harry Carr's hand. He cupped it in his palm and bent over to inhale. He turned in the chair without relief. The desk was as big and abused as Harry, with ashes scattered between uneven piles of papers. Morris knew the papers held telephone messages Harry would never return. On the wall were photographs of his six national championship teams, the players standing in even lines of anonymity. And it was still there, the postwar photograph of Walter Deihl. Leather helmet, low on his head; ugly, high-topped shoes; dark, ill-fitting jersey; standing unposed, his own Sicilian darkness captive and unbeatable. The other walls were empty.

"You found him," said Harry, his voice beyond all involvement. He fumbled the cigaret in his mouth.

"I found him. He didn't look much worse than you do."

"Doc called me this morning. Goddamn Doc."

The way Harry said it, Doc Haywood might have killed Trapwell over the telephone. Harry was not hung over. He was exhausted. He must not have slept at all, thought Morris. It would be awkward. Lieutenant Blake would have to know where he spent the night.

"They shoulda killed his sorry daddy instead . . . needed killin' twenty years." Harry hid his concern behind a long drag of smoke. "You don't think he killed himself?"

"No. Not that way. Doc says he was too drunk to pick up the knife."

Harry flinched at the work *knife*. Tension seemed to shake him out of his fatigue. "Any reason he was in your room?" It wasn't like him to ask a question. Ever. Of anybody.

"No. Not last night. He was supposed to see me this morning. He'd been drinking. He was a sick kid last night. No doubt about that."

"Funny. He never drank. Mighta helped him to get hisself drunk and his ass whipped. Mighta taught him the difference between a game and a war."

"I thought teaching that was your specialty." Morris put his weight on his cane, emphasizing his contempt.

Harry stamped out his cigaret and lit another with an uncertain flame, spitting flecks of tobacco off his tongue. "I shoulda known something. I've had his kind before. They can make it. But it ain't easy." It was the nearest Harry could ever get to an apology. Morris was not sure what he meant.

Harry coughed a deep, rattling cough, then sucked down more smoke, as if to spite his own lungs.

Morris was sure he saw fear in his eyes. Of what?

"I don't understand any of it," said Morris. "Why was he in my room? Who knew he was there? Who knew I *wasn't* there? Was it somebody at the banquet? Or a teammate? Or a kid jealous over a girl? It doesn't make sense."

"He was dumb. I told you that. He got hisself into sump'in nasty. Sump'in nastier than he could handle." He sounded like the old Harry. But the cigaret trembled in his hand.

"For the record. When did you see him last?"

"Yesterday. About eight A.M. I told you. I threw his foot-locker through a second-story window to get his attention. That'll give you all sump'in to write about."

Morris continued taking notes. Harry ignored it.

"He woulda come back. I'd bet a week's pay. Where could he go? Not home. His daddy's nothin'."

Somehow, to Harry, that squared it. That Trapwell had nowhere to go. Harry was probably right. He would have come back. Harry ran off the *dogs*. He called them worse than that. He was never ashamed to go after any great athlete who quit. If you practiced and played for Harry Carr, sooner or later you knew it wasn't worth it. But if you could play the game he taught, you always came back when you quit. Why was it? wondered Morris. If you could grasp it, you could know how Harry won for thirty-two years, from the Notre Dame box to the T formation, from skinny-legged white guards to black receivers who could outrun daylight.

"For the record, were there any other problems between you and Trapwell? Other than his broken nose?"

"For the record, *no*," said Harry, but his eyes were combative. "I told you. He was no coward. Even if he was 'pretty.' He wasn't smart. That hurt him as a player. But it would take a helluva man to jump him, knife or no knife, if he wadn't sick."

"Who was close to him?" asked Morris. "Did he have a permanent girl friend?"

Harry looked past him. "Not that I knew about."

Harry always knew. He hated for a player to get married. Not many of his players did, and if they did, Harry made sure their wives despised him.

"Who did he room with?"

"The end, Mitchell." Harry squinted through the smoke.

"There's a football player. Tough, if he is bright. And another dumb-ass roommate, Crawford. The linebacker. But he ain't too dumb to break you in two."

High praise from Harry. Mitchell was not the big talent. He was the Captain, the iron guts of the team. Harry never appointed meaningless weekly captains. The seniors voted for one kid, before the season. There had never been a captain for Harry Carr who wouldn't die in his cleats for him. And all of them would kill you in your own shoes. Harry thought plenty of Trapwell to room him with Mitchell.

"Do you mind if I talk to his roommates?"

"No. Lieutenant Blake already has. Or is. A woman cop, what'll they think of next? 'Fessor's daughter. You know her. The Chief's had a heart attack. He wouldn't know a killer if he was strapped in the electric chair. He does know the football team comes first in this town." Harry fell into another coughing spell that bent him forward in his chair.

Morris remembered the Chief, a tall, thin man. Played on Harry's first team with Walter Deihl. He was superstitious; wore the same hat to every game.

"I hated to hear 'Fessor's dead," said Morris. "His daughter, the Lieutenant, seems to know her job."

"Like her old man," said Harry. "He shoulda been dean of the medical school. Kept turning it down to plain teach. Never missed a scrimmage. Came in once and told me my language on the field was 'a disgrace.' Can you goddamn believe that? I told him he was right. But I told him they only fired me if the *team* was a disgrace. We never agreed on a damn thing. Lucky he had only one vote as faculty chairman of athletics. I got what I wanted, but I didn't get his vote twice. I wouldn't let him resign, either. I liked the old sonofabitch."

Morris looked at Harry. It was a small confession. But it was strange to hear him say he liked any man. "I came down to write a series of pieces about you and all your teams. Especially this one. And of course, about Trapwell, too. I didn't come to write a murder story. But that's what we have. It's not a football story until the police find out what happened to Trapwell. I'm staying until they do."

Harry came up out of his chair. "This ain't no big town. They'll find whoever did it. It's a damn shame. Nothin' like it happened before in thirty-two years, three thousand players.

But I didn't kill him. My team didn't kill him. We're gonna bury our dead and get ready for Tennessee. Up in Knoxville, they don't care who's dead. They don't care why. They want *us*. We're gonna be ready. And you can write it."

"I'll write it," said Morris, leaning on his cane. "But I wouldn't go to the bank yet on who did or didn't kill Harvey Trapwell." Morris started toward the door.

Harry coughed and grumbled in his throat.

"Did you write the kid any kind of formal note he might have had on him? Or know of any message he was carrying that might have worried him?"

Harry only shook his head.

"I don't think you made any points with the new President last night," said Morris. "I can see Caplin's next column. And you won't like what I'll have to write."

"Walker and Caplin deserve each other," said Harry, drawing on a new cigaret and coughing into his hand. "This town has been making a ass out of itself on Monday nights over fucking football for thirty years. You're welcome to stop it if you can."

Morris turned to see him lower himself into his chair like an old man. Harry knew damn well he wouldn't write plenty of what he had said. Not with the kid dead.

Morris looked back once more from the door. Harry was deep into the papers on his desk. He looked up through the smoke: "Something you can put on that wire service of yours: anybody kills one of my players *better be ready to kill me, too*." Harry's ruined voice seemed to threaten the air with the words.

Chapter Seven

The cameramen were gone. But reporters still waited in the athletic department. Harry would have to see them. They were a hungry bunch, and they couldn't live long on a cold statement.

"What are you filing, Morris?"

"Not much."

"What the hell's Harry doing?"

"Smoking too much. And worrying."

"Does he have any idea what drugs the kid was into?" The last question was Frank Caplin's. Morris had not seen him when Harry made his statement. But Caplin had never been one to take his notes with the masses.

"*Into*," said Morris. "Do you know something the police don't know?"

"I hear rumors there are drugs going around this team."

"Maybe you had better come back as a medical examiner," said Morris, turning his back.

"Is Harry calling off practice?"

Morris recognized the local *Sparta Times* sports editor. He'd had the job forever. His paper also took the Associated Press. "No. Harry said he was sick about the kid. But that he didn't kill him. And his team didn't. He said Tennessee didn't care who was dead. Tennessee was waiting for them in Knoxville. Harry said his team will be ready. He said to write it." They'll love reading it in Tennessee, thought Morris. They'll stick it on the wall and swear what they'll do Saturday. Until they look across the field and see Harry. Then they'll try to swallow. None of the eighty thousand in the stadium will remember that Harvey Trapwell was ever alive.

"Is Harry requiring the body to be at practice?" It was Caplin again. Even when you agreed with Caplin, he made you want to throw up on your own opinion. Morris ignored him to lean over Margaret Stewart's desk.

"How is he?" she asked.

"More worried than he'll say. Can you dial the Georgian Hotel for me?" She didn't have to look up the number. She handed him the receiver.

"This is John Morris. Room four-oh-nine. Do I have a message?"

The operator rang the front desk.

"Let me see," said a voice, not young. "Yes, Mister Morris. You do. An envelope."

"Who left it?"

"Sir, it seems to be from..." He was quoting. "...The Colorado School of Mines. Yes."

"Would you please open it and read it to me?"

There was a wait. "I'm afraid there is nothing to read, sir." The voice was puzzled.

"You mean it's empty?"

"No, sir."

"Well, what's in it, then?"

"A rock, sir."

"A rock?"

"Yes, sir."

"What kind of rock?"

There was another wait. "I can't exactly say. It's a small, round rock."

"Do you think it's female?"

A pause. "Excuse me, sir?"

"Would you ring my room, please."

"I'll get the operator." Another pause. "Operator, would you please ring Room four-oh-nine. And thank you, sir."

"Thank *you*," said Morris. The call had become an exercise in politeness. There was no answer in 409.

Morris handed the receiver back to Margaret. "Tell Harry he still owes me a lunch."

"You're not leaving?" Margaret seemed to have shrunk in her chair with fatigue.

"I'll be around."

Morris moved toward the door. He could see Caplin waiting

for him, his narrow head fixed in his direction, dividing the room with its coldness.

"Something's finally happened in this town Harry can't cover up." Caplin did not try to disguise the pleasure in his voice.

"You think Harry knows who killed the kid?" Morris made it more an accusation than a question.

"I wouldn't be surprised. Harry's lost whatever vague sense of responsibility he ever had. That scene last night with the President was a disgrace." Caplin smiled.

"How did *you* get along with Trapwell?" Morris smiled.

"I'm for anybody who can't play for Harry Carr."

"The only thing tougher... has been to play against him." Morris swung his left leg forward and moved toward the door.

Caplin's voice cut ahead of him. "I understand Trapwell had a drug problem. And he was not the only one on the team."

Morris pushed the door open. Caplin was well hated for quoting the sentence "I understand" as a true source. "I'm a journalist," said Morris. "When it comes to drugs, I only understand lab reports." He let the door close after him. Caplin could get away with whatever he wrote. How could a team defend itself? Or Harry? Harry didn't have to. As long as he won. Morris stopped and looked back at the Athletic Center. But not even Harry could survive murder, if it came close enough.

Lieutenant Sharon Blake stopped on the cracked sidewalk and studied the Athletic Center as if she had never seen it. She looked good in blue. Every cop should look so good, thought Morris. But she was bracing her hands against her shoulder bag. She saw him. She smiled, but kept her hands tight against her bag.

"Is it all right to tell a lieutenant she looks unlawfully attractive?"

She laughed that surprisingly unguarded laugh. Her left hand let go of the bag.

"Harry will be glad to see you. He'd rather meet a firing squad than those writers. Do you carry your gun in your bag?"

She actually blushed. Then patted the bag. "You'd be surprised what I can hit with it."

"I never want to find out. Harry's expecting you. He knows the Chief is sick." She held the bag again with both hands.

"Harry was remembering your father. He told me how much he liked him."

"I don't think they ever agreed on one single thing. He came to 'Fessor's funeral," she said, looking past him, her mind perhaps back among the gravestones. "He even made a donation to the medical school in his name."

"That's Harry."

She looked up as if she had just remembered why she was here. "Was Harry close to Trapwell? Did he know him well?"

"Harry insists he was 'not smart.' He didn't say much else. But Harry knows *everything* about his best players. When they breathe in and out. Especially his quarterbacks. Harry's not the type to be *buddies*. He likes the proven slave-master relationship."

"Who were Trapwell's friends?"

"I'm not sure. Harry 'didn't know' if he had a girl friend. Looking at him, even dead, you could believe he had his own sorority. I'm going by the hotel. Then I'll try to catch his roommates. Have you questioned them yet?"

She nodded yes. "I didn't learn much."

"What does your coroner say? Or should I ask?"

"No. It's all right. The boy had enough alcohol in him to be terribly sick. There was no trace of any other drug. We're waiting on other tests. No needle marks. He had bruises. What you might expect of a football player."

"Did he kill himself?"

"No. It would have been impossible. But there were no other prints on the handle of the knife." She looked at the building as if it held an answer. "Morris. He was pitifully drunk and sick. It was murder. It was brutal."

"Can I write that?"

She nodded yes.

"We can meet later this afternoon and compare notes."

"Yes. Call me at the station. I'll leave a message if I'm going to be out."

Morris touched her on the shoulder. "Be tough with Harry. Like your old man. Make him tell you what he knew about the kid." That may not be so easy, thought Morris; Harry in his time has ducked a hundred thousand questions.

She walked toward the front steps, both hands tight on her

bag. She had great legs. The legs reminded Morris again of Sullivan.

"John Morris." The voice was deepest Alabama. "One thing a man never gets too old to do: watch a good-lookin' pair of legs."

It was Johnny Moore. His crew cut was dead white, but stiff as a salute. He couldn't weigh a pound more than the day he kicked Tennessee into the mud in Tuscaloosa forty-one years ago. He'd been with Harry from the first year he became a head coach, and still ran the offense.

"Good Lord." Morris shook hands, feeling his own 219 pounds swell up around him. "Do you play, Johnny? Or coach?" He was sixty years old, but in the Deep South he would always be Johnny.

"I may play quarterback Saturday. A terrible thing, Morris. He was a nice kid, a helluva athlete. Is Harry makin' sense?"

"Halfway," said Morris. "What can anybody say? Did it shock you?"

"Yeah." Johnny ran his palm over his crew cut, whch sprang back to attention. "He was no troublemaker. He just needed to grow up. Harry kept pushin' him. But Harry's pushed plenty of 'em to the top."

"Harry seems tired. I hear his health is not the best."

"Doc talks too much. Harry will outlive us all. I keep fit, jumpin' when he hollers. You writin' this mess up?"

"I came down to do a series on Harry. I was going to talk to Trapwell, of course. But you know what happened. In my own bathroom. Now it's another kind of story."

"I hope they keep the electricity up for whoever did it." Johnny never raised the level of his voice, even when he was on the practice field. He and Harry were a team, Mr. Quiet and Mr. Loud. But no one was mentally tougher than Johnny Moore.

"I'll buy you a beer."

"Can't. Got to look at film." Johnny offered his iron grip. He would never say anything he wouldn't tell Harry to his face. But he was his own man, in his own way. "They'll catch him, Morris. Nowhere to hide in this town. Then we can get back to what we know best: football."

Morris watched him climb the steps to the athletic department. He had the same rolling, pigeon-toed gait that had made him famous. Johnny might be wrong. Morris leaned on his cane. Too much had happened. It might never be the same here again for Harry, or Johnny, or football.

Chapter Eight

Morris held out his hand for his envelope and his rock. He offered no explanation. The old man behind the front desk was even older than the hotel manager, who was nowhere in sight. There were no young men working in the lobby. The bellboys were old. The elevator operator was too old to stay awake. Even the paperboy who would soon be calling out the wrestling results near the front porch was ancient; you expected the news in his papers to be from out of the archives. It was as if time had circled the old, wooden hotel and aged the very air. The old man handed over the envelope without speaking.

"Tell me, can you get a sandwich in the bar?" asked Morris.

"Yes, sir." It was the same polite voice Morris knew from the telephone.

"Do they serve a chicken salad sandwich?"

"I believe they do, sir." The old man's eyes were carefully impersonal.

"Thank you," said Morris. Their politeness seemed to fit the old hotel, the wooden floor under them, warped, tilted down to the west, as if toward a gentler age.

Morris stopped in the doorway to the bar. He filled it up with his bulk, making the dim room even dimmer. Now he could see the bartender. It was astonishing: he was very young. Morris had a sense of being in the wrong place. His eyes adjusted to the dark. Someone was sitting in the far corner. He walked over. Her head was tilted back, watching him.

"I don't care what the bartender says, you don't look like the Wicked Witch of the West to me."

"Bartender!" Her voice was always lower than he remembered. "I would like a Scotch and a companion."

How could you be lonesome for a voice? thought Morris. He held up the envelope with the rock. "Is this what happens to failed lovers in Colorado?"

"He objected to my nose." She had one hand on his cane. She pulled herself out of her chair and put both arms around him. She was amazingly strong, to be so slim. He bent down to touch her hair with his face.

"What am I going to do with you, Morris?"

"Give me half of your chicken salad sandwich."

"All those poor golfers in Atlanta. Now a body in your bathroom. I think it's Georgia. I think it always has been Georgia. I don't think it was Sherman's fault at all." She was still holding him.

"Nothing like a vacation."

"Why can't you get a quiet assignment? Like the Middle East?"

"If I have to be a rock, can I be a kidney stone? I need revenge on an old editor."

"Was he the boy you came to write about?" She could not will the anxiety out of her voice.

"The quarterback," said Morris.

"What happened?"

"Somebody killed him."

"I'm sure it's Georgia." She held herself at arm's length. "It could never happen in Colorado. No one has ever killed a quarterback in the history of Colorado. Who did it?" She squeezed his wide wrists with her slim fingers.

"Someone who was afraid."

"Of what?"

"Of his talking with me. I think."

"Why?"

"I don't know. I could be wrong. The boy was drunk. He wasn't used to drinking. He could have started a brawl. Or owed money. Or picked up the wrong girl. But even while I'm saying these things, none of them makes sense."

"What kind of boy was he?"

"Big. Sinfully good-looking. A serious student. But Harry

47

says he was not smart. Harry kicks himself for not realizing it sooner. And for pushing him too hard. Says he was fooled because of Trapwell's looks. And his work in class. Harry says he was a *dumbass*, if you will excuse the expression."

"Harry gets to the point. Drunk. Knifed. It's not the brightest way to get yourself killed." She leaned against him again. "Listen to me, drinking my second midday Scotch." She looked up at him. "Was it terrible?"

"I'm like Harry. I'm too old. I've been gone from my first job—the police beat—too long. He was splattered all over the bathroom."

She buried her head in his chest.

"I don't understand why he came to my room *last night*. Why he didn't wait until morning. We had an appointment. He must have had something with him the killer wanted. Or was afraid of. Something written, maybe. His pockets were turned inside out, and his billfold was shredded open, the few dollars left on the floor."

"Maybe Trapwell was afraid of what he knew," said Sullivan. "Maybe that's why he was drinking."

"Sullivan. I think we better put you on the case."

"If you don't kiss me, Morris, I'm flying back to the Rocky Mountains."

She was nothing to lift. It was not only her voice that he had missed.

"Now can I have half of your chicken salad sandwich?"

She took his cane away and limped outrageously to her chair. He sat, needing a drink. "How did you get here so quickly?"

"The Greek. Monty's old partner. He happened to call. Said he was flying east. He dropped me here in his jet. Next thing, I'll be flying off to the Cannes Film Festival."

"You can't trust those Greeks. I was pulling for the Trojans."

She laughed. "Alex is seventy-seven years old."

"Age has nothing to do with Greeks."

"You're right." She laughed, holding him off with his cane.

Morris had not seen Alex in years. He was grateful to him for making Monty Sullivan rich, for selling him downtown Denver before anybody knew it was there. Before he was killed. God, how they had missed Monty. For years. But Julia had achieved peace. And she could afford to come and go. How do you know if you've found peace, or if you're just bored, thought Morris; Well, I'll know soon enough when the old expense account stops and the phone quits ringing from New York.

"I know what you're thinking," she said.

"Oh, you do? And what are *you* thinking?"

"How can a woman know only two men? And both of them the best and the damndest."

He touched her hair. "That means I get my half of your chicken salad sandwich."

She rattled his cane on his chair. "I can't believe it. Only an hour ago I had my own Greek."

Morris held up an arm until the bartender saw him. "Could I have a vodka and tonic, please." The bartender, still amazingly young in the old room, nodded to his work.

"What do you do now?" asked Sullivan, handing over the half of her sandwich with a bite out of it.

"File a brief interview with Harry. He didn't say much that I can print. Just enough to infuriate the whole state of Tennessee. Harry said Tennessee didn't care who was dead . . . that he and his team would be ready Saturday."

"That's the other thing I love about Harry," said Sullivan. "He's a humanitarian."

"Then I'm interviewing Trapwell's two roommates. One's the captain of the team. The other's the 'enforcer.'"

"The *what*?"

"Enforcer. As Harry would phrase it, when he hits you, you can't pee for a week."

"Wonderful. I didn't know Harry was a linguist."

"Maybe I'll see the team manager. Managers know everything. Then I'm supposed to compare notes with the Lieutenant. A Lieutenant Blake."

"Oh, a lieutenant. Is he cute?"

"The Lieutenant is cute all right."

"Will you introduce us?"

"I can't wait to introduce you."

The bartender was standing awkwardly with his drink. Morris had not seen him. He apologized. He lifted his glass. "To you."

Sullivan lifted her own. "To you."

"Careful with that nose. Don't drown in your glass."

She was smiling again.

"Morris?"

He was looking at her eyes. You couldn't tell they were blue in the dim light.

"What's going to happen to us?"

"You know what the man said: The good die young . . . I guess that leaves us out. We'll have to finish the course."

"Do you think it's possible we will ever live on the same side of the Mississippi River?" She kept the fun in her voice but not in her eyes.

Morris lay both large forearms on the small table, shrinking it between them. "I think it's possible." He reached inside his coat pocket and pulled out an envelope and dropped it between them. Even in the light he could see the Associated Press' New York address. Julia couldn't. Not without her glasses. She sat back in her chair as if afraid to touch the envelope.

His own wide hand pushed the letter into Sullivan's lap.

She bent forward over her glass as if the envelope were a foot high. Finally, she lifted it with both hands back onto the table.

Morris opened her purse on the chair between them. He took out her glasses and put them on her. The lenses were round and huge. She looked very young behind them and knew it. But her smile was dying in her face. Then she pulled the small, once-folded memo from the envelope and read it at once, like diving into cold water.

YOU WANT OUT, YOU'RE OUT. DUMMY.

Coleman had signed it. Just his first name:

GERRY.

She did not drink again from her glass.

"Morris." The lenses magnified the blue until you could see it in her eyes, even in the dim light. "No," she said.

"What's it like, west of the Mississippi?"

"You can't just quit." Her hands were lost on top of the table.

"Retire. Not quit. Twenty-four years is enough of anything."

"You're too young." She almost smiled. "*I'm* too young."

"I want to be kept."

"The truth, Morris."

"I want to see you, and—"

"Am I that selfish?" Sullivan was no crybaby. But the lenses swelled the blinking of her eyes.

"You? You couldn't spell it. Of course—" He cracked his lips. "—you can't spell anything. Listen. I want to write what I want to write, for a change. I'm no Papa Hemingway. But I know what's news. I'd like to chase it in another way . . . with a rich widow."

She was folding the memo carefully back in the envelope. He took it and put it back in his coat pocket.

"Promise me you'll think about it," she said.

"I did."

"Some more."

"Are you backing out on me?"

She put her hands under his.

"I have to get back to work," he said. "I'll pick you up later. Say . . . four. I want to introduce you to the Lieutenant."

Morris grinned and couldn't wait to see Sullivan measure the Lieutenant's legs with her eyes.

Chapter Nine

The lobby of the athletic dormitory was imitation Roman, with statues of athletes around a fountain that didn't work. Harry had grown a new sense of humor, or a fat-cat alumnus had made a gift he couldn't refuse. More likely the latter.

Morris walked around the room, expecting to come on a slot machine. There was a large, awkward, impressionistic painting of a starving athlete on one wall and, oddly out of place, photographs of six national championship football teams. Harry had kept one hand in the décor, thought Morris.

The boy at the desk was no athlete. He was thin as hope, and had his head in both hands over a textbook.

"Excuse me," said Morris.

The kid took his head out of his book reluctantly.

"I have an appointment to see Jack Mitchell. In his room."

"Sorry. Nobody goes up to the rooms. Only relatives."

"I have permission. He's expecting me."

The boy was shaking his head.

Morris picked up the telephone receiver on the desk and handed it toward him. "Call Harry Carr. Tell him you are talking with John Morris of the Associated Press. Or ring Jack Mitchell and tell him I'm coming up." Morris laid the receiver on top of the open book.

The kid looked down as if it were going to explode. "It's against the rules—" But he was dialing the room. Morris could read the numbers, 3-2-5.

"Jack, you expecting somebody?"

Morris was already walking toward the stairwell. It was just like Harry to put up with a little Roman-decadent show in the lobby, but no elevator. Climbing was good for the humility, not to mention the leg muscles.

Morris swung his left leg up the last step and balanced himself with his cane. A month ago he would have been puffing. The swimming had helped. His weight was down from 225. He didn't have to knock. The door was open.

Morris stood half a head above the young man inside, who was looking up at him with two sea-blue eyes, nearly green, under dark brows; a straight line of black hair grew directly back from his forehead. He lifted a bare arm wrapped in muscle, but with a curiously small hand.

"Mister Morris." His voice was as level as his hairline. "Jack Mitchell."

His hand disappeared inside Morris' own.

"Thanks for getting me past the gestapo at the desk." The boy did not smile. Morris looked around the double, corner room. It was all business. No nudes. No net hanging from the ceiling full of beer cans. Three desks: one bare, two stacked evenly with papers. Three oversized beds, one stripped. A cork board with notes neatly pinned across it. A calander, without Cheryl Tiegs. Instead, two photographs of carefully beautiful girls, smiling, as if they auditioned with the furniture.

"You're here about Trapwell." It was not a question.

"Yes."

"That was his corner." Mitchell led the way across the large room. He was nearly as thick in his shirt as he was wide. Not the physique you would imagine for a big-time college end. "The police took what was left of his personal gear, even his books."

"A lady lieutenant?"

"Yes. And a couple of others. They went through our things, too."

"Your roommate is—"

"Frank Crawford. The 'Hulk.'" He smiled in spite of himself. "He's eating an early lunch. He'll have the late one in another hour." Again a smile moved the formal lines of his face.

"What kind of football player was Trapwell?"

"Talented."

"Was he a coward?"

"No." Mitchell's strong face held at attention. "He was young. A sophomore, still only eighteen. His nose was broken in two places. We had the game won. But Harry loves to see the blood fly."

"I take it the rent here is high," said Morris.

There was the fraction of a smile. "Most of the kid's stuff went through the window there. Sunday morning." The glass had been replaced. "Harry helped him check out of the dormitory. He was coming back for his other clothes and books."

"Do you think he would have come back on the team?"

"Yes." Mitchell was polite enough. He cut his answers short of a "sir." God, Harry always had one like him. Couldn't hurt him with a train, thought Morris.

"Did you like him?"

Mitchell didn't answer. Then he sat down on the stripped bed. He took his time, as if he had never considered the question. "Normally, the captain shares this double room with one teammate. Harry asked me—us—to take the kid in. He was only seventeen then. A helluva talent. But a kid. His family background was not the best." He hesitated. "His daddy is a drunk. He worked hard in school. He was studying premed, the same as me. It didn't come easy to him. But he got it. Harry knew from the first he could run the team. I knew it

when he got up after the Hulk blind-sided him in practice."
Mitchell looked out the window that had been replaced. He
looked back at Morris. "I respected him."

"You couldn't talk to Harry, Sunday?"

"You've seen him mad?"

Morris nodded.

"That footlocker sounded like a bomb hitting the window."
The fraction of a smile again. "Sunday afternoon, Harry wanted
him back . . . goddammit."

Mitchell meant the goddammit. Morris watched him pull
his temper under control. "Do you blame Harry?"

"For what happened to Trapwell? No. I don't see any con-
nection. Only . . . if he'd been here studying . . . they couldn't
have killed him."

"Did he have girl trouble? Money trouble? Drugs? Gambling?"

"There are ninety-five football players in school," said
Mitchell. "Ninety-five of them have girl trouble. Especially
those who are married. Ninety-three have money trouble. Two
have rich daddies. God knows why they play football for room
and board." He bit off the bitterness in his voice. "Drugs?
Not and play quarterback. Gambling? No. You flip for a Coke
here, and Harry will have you on a Trailways bus home before
it hits the table."

"Were you surprised that Trapwell was drunk when he was
killed?"

"I don't believe it."

"If you had seen him, you might. There's also a lab report."

"I still don't believe it. Trapwell hated the smell of whiskey.
He hated what it did to his old man."

Morris did not argue. "Did the police take away a photograph of his girl?" He indicated the two other pictures in the
room.

"No. He threw it out. Or did something with it. I haven't
seen it since . . . I don't know when."

Morris rubbed the top of his cane. "A local girl?"

"I believe so. She went to high school with him. I never
actually met her. Her name was Patty . . . Patty . . . something."

"What did she look like?"

"Small, I think, from the photograph of the two of them.
Of course, he was big as a door. Nearly as big as the Hulk.

Yes! Jennings. Patty Jennings. Her father's on the faculty. Something in English."

"How did they break up?"

"I don't know. Just one day the photograph wasn't there anymore."

"Was he upset?"

Mitchell looked out the window at the campus. You could see down onto the practice fields. "Funny. I never asked him about it. Harry was killing us in September. 'Getting us ready,' he calls it. I'm sure the photograph disappeared in September. Early in September." Mitchell seemed to be trying to remember something.

"Where did Trapwell go when Harry threw him out?"

"To the PKA house. He wasn't a member of any fraternity. But he had a friend there. Teller. Paul Teller. A premed student. Teller was paid by the athletic department as a tutor. They studied together. Sometimes here in the study room. Why would anybody kill Harvey?" asked Mitchell.

It was the first time Morris had heard anyone call Trapwell by his given name.

"I don't know. The more I find out about him, the more amazed I am he's dead."

The boy hesitated. He looked again out of the window. "How can you ever really know anybody?"

It seemed too pat a question. Morris did not speak, and the silence bothered Mitchell. For the first time, he looked uncomfortable.

Morris put a hand on the bare desk and shifted some of his weight against it. "I'm missing something: Harvey Trapwell. Who was he?" He waved his cane. "I know. He was a live-in quarterback, Rhodes scholar, Eagle Scout, never had a drink in his life—No wonder they killed him. Who could stand to be around him?" Morris looked up at the shock on Mitchell's face. "A few minutes ago, why did you say 'They'...'*They* killed him'?"

"Me?" Mitchell stood up without his composure. "I didn't realize I did. It was just...a figure of speech."

"Yeah," said Morris. He softened his voice. "When you don't see Trapwell in this room, Jack, what do you miss?"

Mitchell sat back down on the bed. "I don't know. He was...quiet."

Quiet. It was the first description Morris could *feel*. Could any way relate to the dead boy kneeling in his bathroom.

"Did he have many friends? Did he have *any* friends besides Paul Teller?"

" . . . No." Mitchell's answer came reluctantly.

"You mean he had *no* friends?" Morris watched the blue in his eyes. "You mean no one *ever* called him?"

Now Mitchell blinked his eyes. "Since you mentioned it. He did get an odd call or two."

Morris squeezed his cane. "What do you mean *odd*?"

"I mean, just a voice. Didn't leave a name or a number. I only answered once or twice when the kid wasn't in. He was always either here studying or in the library studying."

"Was it the same voice each time?"

"I don't know . . . I'd say yes. I couldn't be sure."

"A man's voice?"

"Yes. Not Teller's. Didn't sound like a kid's voice, but I could be wrong about that."

"When did he last call?"

"I really don't know. This fall, I'm sure. Maybe . . . in August when Trapwell moved in. I don't know."

"Why did you say the call was odd? Just because he didn't leave a name? Or the voice itself?"

Mitchell seemed confused. "I'm not . . . I guess it was odd for Harvey to get a call at all. And then a voice just saying, 'Is Harvey there?' Then 'thank you,' and that was it. Once he was in, and all Harvey said . . ." Mitchell's voice accelerated as if he were hearing the conversation again. " . . . All Harvey said was 'Yes, Yes, Yes, okay.' Even the Hulk laughed at him, said, 'Goddamn, rookie, Can't you say no?'" Mitchell seemed amazed to remember.

"Could you describe the voice? You said it didn't sound like a kid."

Mitchell shook his head. "No. Not a low voice. But . . . deliberate . . . I mean low-key."

"A southern voice?"

"Yes. I mean, I don't remember it being different. Probably just someone who wanted to borrow his notes. He took careful notes."

"Did anyone call here for Trapwell *after* he was kicked out?"

56

". . . No." Mitchell put his large hands in his pockets.

"Something bothering you?" Morris watched his sea-blue eyes.

"It's probably nothing. I noticed . . . today."

Morris waited.

"Some things in my desk drawers seemed . . . out of place. I keep it neat. I have to. I have a lot of homework. Nothing missing."

"Did you tell the police?"

"No. I just noticed. Just a few papers slid out of place."

"Maybe your other roommate—"

"No. We have an absolute agreement. We never open each other's desks. I asked the Hulk. He just shook his head. He doesn't know about his own desk. God couldn't find anything in that mess."

"Who has a key to this room?" asked Morris.

"No one but us. And the maids. The coaches make inspections. Harry doesn't allow any outsiders in this dorm."

The door swung open against the wall. "Might as well not eat. Liver! Barely could choke down a second helpin'."

He was not so tall. It was just that he was massive. Morris could not believe the layers of muscles that rolled through his shirt that was too thin for November, even in Sparta. The boy stopped in the door, looking at him as if he came without permission from an unknown race of people. Morris did not speak.

"It's all right," said Mitchell. "This is Mister John Morris. He's a writer with Associated Press."

"No shit," said the Hulk. He didn't offer to shake hands. "Damn quarterbacks get all the ink when they're alive. Then they get it when you kill 'em . . . Once." He slit his mouth in a smile and rattled the bridge holding his top front teeth.

The Hulk was a beauty. Morris wondered how he would be if you stirred him up. "I understand Trapwell took anything you linebackers had to offer." A heavy roll of flesh moved across Crawford's forehead. His chest breathed in without seeming to breathe out. His arms grew in their sleeves. Then he seemed to be over it. You wouldn't want to turn out the lights and take him on, thought Morris. "Did Trapwell have any problems?" he asked.

"What're you talkin' 'bout, *problems*?" Crawford didn't like the word. "You tryin' to stir up sump'in? We got enough problems with a dead quarterback."

"Somebody has more."·

"Like who?"

"Like whoever killed him."

The Hulk didn't like that, childish as it was. He looked down at Mitchell and stood there awkwardly, with nowhere to put his massive arms.

Morris tried another tone. "Was he a good roommate?"

Crawford looked again at Mitchell. Then back at Morris. He breathed out as well as in. "Yeah. He was okay. Always in the books. Never said much."

The Quiet American, thought Morris. He would like to catch Crawford alone, when he couldn't look toward Mitchell every time he wanted to rattle his teeth.

"Do you remember taking any phone calls for Trapwell?"

The Hulk caught Mitchell's eye. Then shrugged his huge shoulders. "That kid Teller called him." It seemed a physical pain for him to remember.

"Anybody else? Anybody leave their name?"

"No. Nobody I remember."

"Anything missing this past weekend from your desk?" asked Morris.

"No." He was shaking his great head as if the questions were a test of concentration.

"Anyway, thank you," said Morris. Mitchell nodded. The Hulk, watching Mitchell, nodded slowly. Neither boy offered to shake hands as he left.

The kid was knee-deep in a sea of jockey straps and socks. He kicked his way out of them and closed the wire door to the equipment bin behind him.

"You the head manager?" asked Morris.

The boy blinked behind his steel-rimmed glasses. "Yes. Henry Young." He held out a thin but strong arm.

"I'm John Morris. With the Associated Press. Down to do a story on Harry. But it looks like the news now is all Trapwell. Where did he dress?"

"Does Coach Carr know you're here?" The boy's voice was tentative.

"I just talked with Harry." Implying Harry knows I'm here, thought Morris.

"Coach is paranoid about who comes in the dressing rooms." The boy closed the lock on the equipment bin.

"Is practice on for this afternoon?" asked Morris.

"Sure. Coach said the team played on national television the weekend Kennedy was killed. And he voted for Kennedy. He said most of the pros cancelled out. He said 'long as we got eleven on a side, we practice.'" It was not a bad imitation of Harry. Better even than Doc's. The boy looked at him apologetically. "You know Coach, he hated it about Trapwell. I saw him crying—" He looked down as if he'd said something he shouldn't have.

"I know Harry. I've known him for twenty years. Where did you say Trapwell dressed?"

"This way." The boy took long strides with his thin legs. He turned down a double row of lockers without doors. He stopped. "The third one, here."

"Mind if I look inside?"

"No. I've got to collect his equipment. I've been putting it off." He began lifting out the wide, quarterback-thin shoulder pads and the battered, once-silver helmet. "Harvey always liked the silver helmet and the game pants. He got excited for the games. He hated practice. But you know how practice is here."

"Harry hasn't mellowed?" said Morris. There was a thin pile of papers in the top of the locker.

The boy blinked behind his glasses. "You coming to practice today?"

"Not today. Tomorrow."

"You'll see."

The manager had both pairs of big shoes under his arms, and was almost buried under the helmet and pads. "I'll be back," he said.

Morris picked up the loose sheets of paper. Three of them were old practice schedules. The torn bottom sheet was not typed. On it were three or four words in hurried block letters. Morris folded the torn sheet into his coat pocket.

Henry Young was back, empty-handed.

"How well did you know Trapwell?" asked Morris.

"Oh." The boy shrugged his light shoulders.

"Was he honest?"

"Definitely. He never picked off even a towel. He took care of the football he threw in the summer. Used to clean the mud off his own practice shoes. Didn't bitch, as much as he hated practice. Being manager would be a snap with ninety-five like Harvey." He was biting his bottom lip.

"Did anything seem to be . . . bothering him?"

"Yes."

Morris squeezed the top of his cane. "Any ideas?"

Henry shook his head. "Not really. He never said a lot. He used to joke with me about how skinny I was. Said he was going to have Harry suit me up and make me block the Hulk. He hated the Hulk." The boy looked up. "I mean everybody hates to practice against him. Crawford doesn't have mercy on anybody. Coach loves him. Anyway, Harvey hardly said a word all last week. I thought maybe he was worried about Alabama. How good they were. That wasn't it, I don't think. Not the way he played." The boy ran out of words.

"He didn't say anything . . ."

"Not really." Henry turned his head. "He did say something funny. Sometimes he said funny things to me. He was grabbing a cube of ice, Friday. Before practice. He said, 'Stop the world, I wanna get off.' Funny, the way he looked at me when he said it."

Morris was sure he had imitated Trapwell's voice to a nuance, and it made him shiver. "It was probably nothing," said Young. "Just something fun to say. I think it was the title of a song. It's just that what happened to him made me think of it."

"Was Harry wrong to throw him off the team?"

"No." He said it clearly. "Coach knows if you're hurt bad. When he sends you in, you go in. If you play here."

Morris changed the subject. "What about his girl?"

"I met her once. After a game his freshman year. He got to play some with the varsity as a freshman. He had more talent than anybody I've ever seen here. I don't remember her name. She was small. I think they split."

"Any reason?"

"No. Not that I know of. He used to have a snapshot of her in his locker. It hasn't been there this year." Young looked in the locker. He turned over each piece of paper, back and front. The boy looked puzzled, but didn't say anything.

Morris was afraid the manager might somehow miss the single torn sheet in his own pocket. It would have fit easily into Trapwell's billfold. Whoever killed him might have been looking for it. The thought closed Morris' eyes.

"Did Harvey drink?" asked Morris.

"No. Never." The boy blinked.

"Was he ever short of money?"

"Sure. He didn't get any from home. He worked in the summer. But that money usually ran out before spring. The NCAA won't let an athlete work during the school year. And they've taken away the fifteen dollars a month spending-money from the scholarship. It's ridiculous. But that's the NCAA. Our black players can't afford to buy toothpaste. I don't blame Coach for—" He looked wide-eyed at what he almost said.

For slipping them a few bucks, thought Morris. "I don't either," he said. He could remember the NCAA offices in Kansas, where they lived like oil-rich sheiks and could be just as arrogant.

"Has anyone been around looking for Trapwell's locker?"

"No."

"Not even the police?"

The boy shook his head.

Our Lieutenant missed a beat, thought Morris.

The silence bothered the manager. He began to talk.

"Harvey got by. He didn't go out much. Usually alone. Most of the time he studied. He was in premed. And that's tough. I know. I was a pharmacy major." He emphasized *was*.

"If you remember anything else Trapwell said or did that triggers something, call me," said Morris. "I'm at the Georgian Hotel. I'll be around all week." Morris paused. "I wish I could have seen him play."

"He could play," said Young, standing on his thin legs.

Outside the Athletic Center, Morris unfolded the note. Printed, actually in a scrawl, right to the edge of the torn page was: CHECK THE TIME. And under it: OBERON.

Who, or what, was Oberon? he wondered.

Morris let the steering wheel slip through his hands. He was still an hour early for his meeting with the Lieutenant. On impulse he swung the car toward the old Science and Literature Building where 'Fessor once had his office on the first floor.

The Dean's secretary could not have been more polite. She was a heavyset woman with short curly hair and a gift of patience. "Just wait here, and I'll speak to him. I think we can fit you into his schedule." She rang the Dean on the intercom, then disappeared into his office.

Morris stood rather than sat. There was a thin Sparta phone book and a heavy Atlanta phone book on the secretary's desk. Morris turned to the *o*'s in both books. No Oberons. The Dean's name was Edward Marshall. Morris had never met him. In minutes the secretary was waving him inside.

Dean Marshall came around his desk to shake hands. He was startlingly young, with blond hair worn over the tops of his ears.

"Yes, Mister Morris." He had a firm grip. "How can I help you?"

"Can I see Harvey Trapwell's records?"

The Dean lifted a brown file on his desk. "I'm afraid you can't. I've gotten his file together for the police. But the privacy act doesn't allow us to release so much as a student's grades to his own parents. Figure that one out."

"Can you tell me a few things about him?"

"I think so, if we keep them general enough."

"How was his standing in school?"

"He was a good student. In the top ten percent of his class. I think I can tell you that his class performance exceeded his entrance tests. Which indicates good work habits. But I would ask you not to write that. I'm not sure I should have said it."

"Was he having scheduling problems? Or were there any other reasons for your office to contact him? Did your office contact him this fall, on the telephone?"

Marshall turned through the file. "I see he was pre-registered for the winter quarter. He had signed up for two labs that he couldn't make this fall because of football practice. No problems. His winter schedule was already in the computer. I only wish all our students had his record. His death is a true tragedy." Marshall buzzed his secretary. "Is there a record of anyone from this office calling Harvey Trapwell this fall?" He put his hand over the receiver. Then spoke into the phone. "No. Thank you." He shook his blond head. "We haven't called him."

"What about his academic counselor, could I speak to him?" asked Morris.

"Certainly. His name is Brewer. Doctor Marvin Brewer, in the history department. His office is on the fourth floor of this building on the north wing. I just spoke with him this morning. I'll have my secretary call him and tell him to expect you."

Morris stopped at the door. "By the way, is there any mention in his files of Oberon? That's O-b-e-r-o-n . . . for any reason? Or does the word have any meaning for you?"

Marshall was again shaking his head. "I've read the file twice. I'm sure I would remember such a name. It has no meaning for me."

Morris thanked him and left him standing by his desk holding the plain brown file.

The elevator was not working, and Morris was slightly out of breath by the time he got to the fourth floor. Office number 423 was wedged in the corner of the hallway. The door was open. A wide, heavy man with a full beard was sitting behind a desk spilling over with papers. He was wearing round, wire glasses and blinked his eyes as if Morris were shining a light in them.

"Doctor Brewer?"

He stood, nodding his identity. He was even softer and fatter than he had looked sitting down.

"I'm John Morris. Associated Press. I think the Dean called."

Brewer blinked his eyes even faster. "Yes, he did. I'm not sure I understand how I can help you." His voice was tight with nervousness.

"How well did you know Harvey Trapwell?" asked Morris.

"I . . . Let me see. To be exact, he was only in my office twice." He lifted a manila folder from the mass of papers on his desk. "Yes, twice. The last time was in September. He wanted to reschedule two chemistry labs for the winter quarter." Brewer seemed to gain confidence from his records.

"You haven't heard from him since?" Morris watched his eyes blinking again.

He shook his head. "I didn't think of him until . . . the newspapers . . ."

"Did you arrange for his tutor?"

"No. The athletic department did that." Brewer looked at his records. "The young man Paul Teller was doing a good job. Trapwell's class record was excellent." He said the words as if he had rehearsed them.

"How were you selected as his counselor?"

Brewer lifted his heavy shoulders. "Just the luck of the draw. I'm assigned a few new freshmen each fall. I wish all of them . . ."

"Yes?"

"All of them were as conscientious about their work as Harvey Trapwell was."

"Isn't it odd that the Dean's office would assign you to a premed student? Your being in the history department?"

"No. The first two years, all student courses are very similar. And if a student develops special academic problems, we get him special help."

"You haven't telephoned Trapwell this fall, in his room?"

"No." He was shaking his large head and beard. He took off his glasses and cleaned them with his handkerchief.

"I do thank you," said Morris, turning for the door, then pausing. "Let me ask, does the word *Oberon* mean anything to you?"

Dr. Brewer put his hand on his desk and lowered himself into his chair. Several papers slid off into his lap. He shook his head again, blinking his eyes as if against the light. "No. No, it doesn't." He opened his mouth as if to ask a question, but did not.

"Nothing at all?" asked Morris. "Well, thank you again." He did not look forward to walking down the four flights of stairs.

Chapter Ten

The police station was a two-story Victorian house with a wide porch and a wooden turret. It had been restored, painted a virtuous white, and given to the city of Sparta by one of its oldest families. Morris learned all of this from the telephone operator, who said it as if she were reciting it.

He stood in front of the house amazed, expecting to see Agatha Christie coming down the steps.

The front door opened, and Lieutenant Blake waved to him. He might have been coming over for Sunday dinner.

He climbed the wooden steps, holding onto the carved bannister.

"How do you like our station?" Smiling, she looked young, even without sleep.

"You must be getting a better class criminal."

"Not so you would notice." Her smile faded. Her hand was cold. "Have you learned anything?"

"This and that," said Morris. "No true confessions. You?"

She shook her head. "Routine answers."

"How was Harry?"

"Impossible. He answered all my questions. But didn't say anything."

"Did he ask you out?"

She looked past him at the street. "Come on inside."

"Just a minute," said Morris. "A friend from Colorado is joining us."

"A writer?"

"Never writes anything. Can't spell 'Colorado.'" The rental car wavered in the traffic in front of the house and then pulled, awkwardly, into a parking space. "Can't drive, either," said Morris.

Sullivan stood, memorizing the house, as if the two of them were not standing in the door. She came easily up the steps without touching the bannister.

"Julia Sullivan . . . Lieutenant Sharon Blake."

"You're from Colorado," said the Lieutenant.

Sullivan openly measured her legs. "No wonder all the men in Sparta are under arrest."

"I never can remember where it is on the map, but I hear it's a beautiful state."

"If they give you a key to the city, Morris, it better not fit the jail."

"Let's go inside," said Morris, maneuvering himself between the two of them.

Sullivan ducked under his arm and took one of the Lieutenant's hands between both of her own. "I love your police station. *And* your uniform."

"We have coffee inside. You can tell me where you got your shoes."

The door closed behind them, leaving Morris standing on the porch.

"Sorry, old man," said Sullivan, sticking her head out.

Morris followed their conversation inside like a stranger.

"Notice the wallpaper. It's original, but God, it's gloomy."

"Just right for a jail," said Sullivan.

Both of them giggled.

The coffee smelled amazingly fresh. He poured a cup and drank it without interrupting them.

"Say something, Morris. We need to get on with this investigation. Sharon knows an antique show on the South Carolina line that's only slightly outrageous."

Morris looked over his cup, shaking his head. "The killer . . . hasn't got a chance."

The two of them put their cups down at the word *killer*.

"Do you read the sports columnist Frank Caplin?" asked Morris.

The Lieutenant made a face. "'Fessor always disliked him. Even more than he disagreed with Harry."

"Like father, like daughter?"

"I don't know much about sports. He writes so so. He's cynical. He thinks a lot of his own opinion."

"You know everything there is to know about Caplin," said Morris. "He stopped me this morning. I'm sure he's going to write that Trapwell had a drug problem. That the team still does."

The Lieutenant forgot her coffee. "What did Harry say?"

"Caplin stopped me after I saw Harry. When Harry reads it, he'll have a tizzy with a crocheted tail. I saw Trapwell's roommate Jack Mitchell."

"Yes. I also talked with him."

"He denies the drug use, of course. Insists that no demon booze ever passed Trapwell's lips...There is the awkward problem that he died drunk...What about the lab report?"

The Lieutenant shook her head. "No trace of drugs. He was soaking in alcohol."

"Doc would have to know it if he had been into drugs." That doesn't mean he would tell the truth about it, thought Morris. "If this team has been playing stoned, you would hate to meet 'em sober. Just for the record, you might call Harry for a quote. Caplin's column will stir up a lot of noise."

She nodded.

"One thing. The roommate Mitchell did say that Trapwell had gotten a couple of odd telephone calls. Odd in that he seemed to have no friends other than Teller."

"Man or woman?" asked the Lieutenant.

"Man. Mitchell said it 'didn't sound like a kid.' But he couldn't be sure. He described the voice as low-key, deliberate, and southern. Nothing 'different' about it. He left no name or number for Trapwell to call. The one time Mitchell answered the phone that Trapwell was in, Trapwell simply said, 'Yes, Yes, Yes, Okay.' And hung up. That's about it. I did ask Harry if there were any unhappy gamblers in town."

"What did he say?" asked Sullivan as if it were her investigation.

"He said I had an appointment tonight in Samarra."

"That sounds like—"

"O'hara," said the Lieutenant.

"Harry said, no way the game was influenced. By anybody. Harry said he'd had his head buried in every play. And he'd seen the film twice. Of course, Adolph Rupp once said they couldn't touch his basketball boys 'with a ten-foot pole.' He was right. They used money." Morris drank the last of his coffee. "The hell with what Rupp once said. I wouldn't bet a dime against Harry's opinion of the way his team played. Besides, they won a game they were supposed to lose."

Morris looked across at the Lieutenant. Suddenly, he knew he was not going to mention that someone had been through the captain's desk, or the sheet of paper he himself had taken from Trapwell's locker. It might mean nothing. It might be a major story. He would have to weigh his own obligations to the Lieutenant, and to the AP. The hasty scrawl CHECK THE TIME had been printed with a pencil, apparently against a rough surface, the way the pencil had bounced. Morris did not understand the odd way it was signed: *Oberon*. The Dean's office was no help. His academic counselor admitted he had only met Trapwell twice. *Oberon* meant nothing to any of them. Maybe the message meant a schedule of football meetings. That made no sense. The coaches dressed down the hall. They didn't have to telephone a message. He'd ask Harry. Then Morris wanted another go at the manager Henry Young. Find out if he took the note, and if he did, when and from whom. If Young wouldn't help, or couldn't, he would turn the note over to the Lieutenant.

"What are you thinking?" asked Sullivan.

"How far it is to Samarra," said Morris.

"It's—" The Lieutenant checked her watch. "—seven hours until tomorrow. And we don't know much." Again she smiled her surprising smile.

"You haven't said what you learned from Harry. Or the players. What did Doc say about your report on Trapwell?" asked Morris.

"He corrected my grammar."

"Doc's a grammarian? What did he do, rephrase it in plantation Southern?"

"He thought it was complete enough, medically. He was a little picky about the autopsy report, the description of the knife wounds. He and the coroner have a thing. I try to stay out of it."

"How drunk was he?"

"Terribly. He hadn't eaten since lunch. He must have drunk nearly a fifth of bourbon. If he wasn't used to it, no wonder he was sick. There was almost enough alcohol in him to be toxic."

"He didn't throw up *after* he was stabbed?"

"Doc agrees with the coroner. He was sick before. There was no blood in what he threw up." She put her coffee aside. "It's not a very pretty report."

"No sign of any drug abuse?"

"No. Doc says we can forget it. He was a perfect physical specimen."

"I've only seen his photograph in the afternoon paper," said Sullivan. "It was a double sin to kill him."

"You went through all of his things?" Morris asked.

"Yes."

"Any correspondence? Phone numbers?"

"Mostly classwork: lecture notes, football notes. He was a very thorough note-taker. But not one letter, from anybody."

"Not even his girl friend?"

"No. He grew up with a girl here in Sparta. I don't yet have her last name."

"Jennings. Patty Jennings," said Morris.

"Have you talked with her?" The Lieutenant's eyes were blue with surprise.

"No. His roommate Mitchell remembered it, finally. I also asked a local telephone operator for directions to the police station. She gave me a lecture on the city history. And the murder. She said it was murder. She knew Trapwell. Her daughter and Patty Jennings are friends. Patty is now a freshman at A&M. Lives in the freshman dormitory."

"That's as far as you go," said Sullivan. "You could catch pneumonia, all those girls with their hair dryers blowing. It's clearly a job for the police."

"Sullivan. I'm going to give you to the Hulk. I believe you could tame him."

"I love him already. Who is he?"

"Trapwell's other roommate. You wouldn't believe him, Julia. He's big as a gorilla cage."

The Lieutenant held her pencil in her mouth and stretched her hands far apart.

"What are you measuring?" Sullivan asked wickedly.

"You'd love it, the way he rattled his false front teeth," said

Morris. "But if we could get back to the crime in question. Sharon, did you pry anything out of the roommates?"

"Just his daily routine. Mostly it was football and books. In that order. He was a loner. Not many close friends, if any. There was a boy he studied with . . ."

"Paul Teller."

"Yes. I missed him this morning at the PKA house. Trapwell spent Sunday night there. Morris, why did Harry throw him out of the dorm? He won the silly game."

"Honor," said Morris. "Honor among brutes. You play for Harry, you play bloody, with the snot slinging."

"Ooooh." Sullivan made a face.

"Sorry about that. Trapwell broke the code. Came out of the game."

"That's the silliest thing I ever heard."

"Yeah. But it's worked for thirty-two years."

"Maybe you could look up Teller while I talk to the girl Jennings," said the Lieutenant.

"Sullivan, you can help me if I can trust you on fraternity row."

"Didn't Oscar Wilde say, 'I can resist everything except temptation'? Or maybe it was Billy Graham."

"One thing," said the Lieutenant. "Trapwell hadn't been sleeping well. He was up walking the room late Friday night. Mitchell said it could have been pre-game jitters. But he'd never done it before. The other roommate, Crawford, didn't hear him. Says he 'dies at night.' Says he 'wouldn't hear a safe fall.'"

"Had any other players noticed any change in him?" asked Morris.

"Yes. His substitute at quarterback. He said Trapwell had lost ten pounds since the first game. Harry makes them weigh in every day and write their weights on a chart. I looked it up. His weight began dropping two weeks ago. It wasn't his health. The coroner swears. And Doc."

Morris almost quoted the manager, who said something was worrying Trapwell. He didn't. Maybe she had questioned him, maybe not. Maybe it was the manager's imagination. The manager was his best hope for a news lead. "Harry couldn't add anything to what you found out?"

"He finally made a speech. You heard it first. 'The team

lives.' And all that. I think he's afraid. I'm not sure of what. I know he was shocked when the boy was killed. Now the dumb incident in the dorm is really bothering him."

"Harry said all that?"

"He didn't say any of it." She drank her coffee.

He wouldn't have to, thought Morris; if you were bright and you knew him well enough. "Sullivan. Behave on fraternity row, and I will buy you two the finest dinner in Sparta, Georgia."

"I've got my own Greek, remember. What do I need with the alphabet?"

"Call me," said the Lieutenant. "I'll be here at the station."

"Thanks for the coffee," said Sullivan. She took the Lieutenant's arm. "You're doing a good job. You've already gotten more help out of Morris than the Associated Press ever did."

"On second thought, we could have a chili dog and onion rings at the Varsity," said Morris.

Outside the station, the wind blew cold and damp. Morris wondered if the young PKA Teller would use the word "quiet" again to describe the corpse of Harvey Trapwell.

Chapter Eleven

Ivy insinuated itself up the imitation-Tudor house, giving it a look of near-authenticity until the music jumped through the open front door. A short, muscled young man in dungarees went in search of Paul Teller, leaving them captives of the rock band bounding off the walls and making it impossible for the scattering of PKA brothers and few girls in the huge front room to do more than nod to each other. It seemed to be enough.

The boy coming toward them might have been a young Errol Flynn, without the wickedness in his eyes. His soft blue-

and-brown sweater and gray tailored slacks seemed to deny the noise in the room.

"If I faint, catch me," said Sullivan between the beats of the music.

Morris couldn't hear what the boy said. His handshake was solid. He motioned for them to follow him. They went through a long dining room set for supper and into a well-lit hall, and then into a dark, comfortable room that seemed to be a library. No one was inside. Teller closed the door behind them. Morris could still hear the thump of the music, like an engine buried in the bowels of the house.

"This is Julia Sullivan. I'm John Morris with the Associated Press."

"I got the message that you were coming." He wore his voice as carefully as his clothes. He indicated they should all sit down.

"Harvey Trapwell was a friend of yours. And a pupil," said Morris.

"Yes. The athletic department hires me to tutor certain athletes. It pays the rent here." He looked around the room. He folded his arms to find something to do with his hands. "Harvey was more than a student. He was a good friend. He was killed in your hotel room. Why?"

Morris shook his head. "I don't know."

"I mean, why was he there last night?"

"I have no idea. I had an appointment to see him at the hotel this morning. To talk football."

"He loved it and he hated it."

"What do you mean?" asked Morris.

"God knows he was good at it. He always had been. I played against him in high school in Augusta. You couldn't stop him."

"Why did he need a tutor?"

"Football. It's a full-time job. The night meetings took so much of his study time. He wanted to practice medicine in Atlanta. He would have been good at it. But he needed the football scholarship. He had a good mind, but not a facile one. He had to work at it, but what he learned, he learned well. His background in chemistry was weak, and it gave him the most trouble." Some of the careful stiffness had gone out of the boy's voice.

"He came here when Harry Carr threw him out of the dormitory?"

"Yes. He called. Carr had just left his room. He said he needed a place to stay for the night. I told him to come on over."

"He was upset?" said Morris.

"He was furious. He brought over what was left of his footlocker. That ass Carr threw it through the window of his room. If you can believe that."

"I can believe it," said Morris. He almost smiled in spite of himself.

"Harvey said he was through with football. That he would get a part-time job. He had enough money to finish the quarter. We were going to find him a room."

"How furious was he?" asked Morris.

"He couldn't sit down—or stand up—for long. He even took a drink."

"That was unusual?"

"I never saw him drink before. He picked up a cheap bottle of bourbon from somebody in the house. He barely splashed a little water in it, and he finally drank himself to sleep."

"Did anybody call him?"

"Yes. By noon Sunday, Carr was calling from Atlanta. He does a TV show there after each game. It's a disgrace to the university. Harvey wouldn't speak to him. I was busy with lab work until mid-afternoon. I saw Harvey one last time. About four o'clock. He came by to change clothes. He put on a tie and coat. He was still drinking. I tried to talk him into having dinner with me. He had to go. He didn't say where. He was very nervous. He hardly sat down. He took a shower and changed clothes. He seemed even more nervous than before. 'Nervous' isn't exactly the word. Maybe it was nervous excitement."

"What, specifically, did he say?"

"He said he had solved his money problem. I assumed he had found a job. I don't know how, in that condition."

"You didn't ask him how?"

"Sure I asked. But he wouldn't answer me. He said he'd tell me later. But he would have no trouble finding a job. Sober. I could have gotten him one in the lab. They need help."

"He didn't stay here Sunday night, after all?"

"No. When he left, he said, 'Don't wait up for me. I'll be late.' He was gone." Teller paused. Morris did not break the silence. "He was a great athlete. He was mentally and physically tough. But he was a gentle person. He would have been an outstanding doctor." The boy kept remarkable control of his voice.

"Did Trapwell have any other close friends?" asked Morris.

Teller shifted his weight in his chair. "Not that I know of. He was the most private person I ever met. And he only had time for football and books. I never knew him to go to a movie."

"Someone called his room. Two or three times. Not you. His roommate knows your voice. The caller was a man. He didn't leave a number. You couldn't guess who it might have been?"

Teller again shifted his weight. "No. Unless it was another premed student. Most of us hang together. Help each other with assignments. But we aren't all necessarily friends."

"Did you get the feeling any time this weekend, that someone might have gone through your room? Anything missing?" asked Morris.

Teller hesitated. "Why do you ask that?"

Morris waited.

"I . . . I can't say. I thought my sweaters were out of place. I'm particular about my clothes. Nothing's missing I know of. This place can be hectic. People borrow your things without asking. No matter how you complain."

"Before Saturday. Was anything bothering Trapwell? Did you notice he had lost weight?"

"He was thinner. Maybe quieter. He was having a rough go in chemistry. But he was getting it. He did tell me he was having trouble sleeping. I think he had come to hate football. More than he loved it on Saturday. This Carr is inhuman. The team was unbeaten, and there was a lot of pressure." Teller's face was tight with anger.

"Did he hate Harry Carr?" Sullivan's voice seemed to fit the quiet shadows in the room.

The boy waited. "No. He didn't. I don't know why not. He hated all the wasted time and effort. He was a nervous wreck Sunday. He told me what happened in the game. His nose was broken and still bleeding. It had to be painful . . ."

Morris could still hear the music thumping in the walls.

"Do you have any idea where he spent Sunday night? Was he walking when he left here?"

"No." Teller fingered the crease in his trousers. "I don't know where he spent the night. He doesn't have a car. Neither do I. He could have borrowed one of the brother's. I doubt it. I would have heard."

Morris looked straight into his gray eyes. "Did Trapwell have a drug problem?"

Teller laughed, a true, easy laugh. "No. He wouldn't take Novocain when he had a tooth drilled. He was . . . he was the sort of person you would like to be . . ." He shook his head. "I don't mean he couldn't drive you up the wall asking a hundred useless questions about a simple chemical process."

"One other thing," said Morris. "How close was he to Patty Jennings?"

"Patty? They went to high school together. She's a . . . simple girl. She was always more serious about him than he was about her. They more or less broke up this fall. He liked her. Like a sister."

"How awful. For Patty," said Sullivan.

Morris stood up. They all stood up. They all shook hands again. "Lieutenant Sharon Blake wants you to call her." Morris gave him the number. "One thing. Does the word 'Oberon' mean anything special to you?"

Teller stepped toward the door. Morris could not see his face. He turned. "No. Sounds like a constellation? It doesn't . . . have any special meaning."

"Was Trapwell having a schedule problem?"

"No. He was already registered for next quarter."

"We do thank you," said Morris. "I'm sorry about Harvey Trapwell. I'm sorry I never got to meet him . . . I hope I meet whoever killed him."

Teller stopped at the door. The music was jumping down the hall.

"What did you think of him, Julia?"

"I know something's bothering you when you call me 'Julia.' My God, he's beautiful. He seemed . . . remote. He's too young to accept death so stoically."

"Why would he lie?"

"About what?"

"Something that couldn't matter, that's so obviously un-true."

"Tell me, or I'll let the air out of your tires," said Sullivan.

"He said he saw Trapwell one last time. About four o'clock Sunday afternoon. That he came by to change clothes. That he put on a *coat and tie*. Later, he said Trapwell never came back."

"Well?"

"Trapwell wasn't wearing a coat and tie when he was killed Monday. He had on a blue polo shirt."

"Morris, you don't make a permanent record of everything I say, do you?" Sullivan reached over and straightened his tie. "You think Trapwell went back to the room Monday and changed clothes?"

"He had to. Or that's not his shirt he was wearing. He didn't go back to the athletic dorm. The clothing stores are open. We can check. But what happened to his coat and tie?"

"Maybe he had a girl friend we don't know about. Maybe her apartment had a few of his clothes in it."

"You might have something there. We'll have the Lieuten-ant check the laundry marks on the shirt. You haven't said what you think of our Lieutenant."

Sullivan raised her chin and looked down at him. "She's a *sweet* girl. Georgia girls make wonderful police officers."

Morris covered her knee with his hand.

"What about me?" she asked.

"What about you?"

"Would I make a good police officer?"

"Sure," said Morris, sliding his hand higher. "But you would make a great criminal."

Sullivan lowered her chin. "Don't you have to read me my rights?"

"You have the right to remain silent." That was as high as his hand would go.

Chapter Twelve

"One more slice of pecan pie, Sullivan, and you're going to have to move to a larger state."

She closed her eyes and held the fork as if it were a baton and she the conductor. Finally, she swallowed. "Ohhh. I think that was a religious experience."

"Maybe we can have a king-sized bed sent up to our room," said Morris.

Sullivan aimed the fork like a javelin. Then she dropped it on her plate. "Listen. Do you know what's going on in this typical-American, southern, sleepy college town?"

"Sure. Nothing's happened in the world in the last five thousand years that hasn't also happened to the seventy-five thousand people who live in Sparta, Georgia. Somebody killed somebody else. If he had done it on Saturday night in a joint on the county line, we wouldn't know it had happened unless we had to buy the casket for the victim. Of course I don't know what's going on. But I came to do a piece on Harry Carr, and how the hell can I do it until somebody finds out who killed Harvey Trapwell? I cover sports. I haven't been *paid* to keep up with murder since I was twenty years old and on the police beat in Atlanta. It was a rotten job. You've seen the exit point of one bullet hole, you've seen all you need to know about the subject. The most boring people kill each other, Sullivan. Usually they live together." He put his big hand on her arm and tried to smile. "Listen, if this thing drags on, we'll see the game in Knoxville; I'll knock out something for ye olde Associated Press; and we'll move along to that vacation they owe me. Okay?"

"Okay." Sullivan lifted her glass of iced tea.

The old man stopped the elevator without so much as asking them with his eyes what floor they were on.

"Every time I open a door in this hotel . . ." warned Morris. He let the door swing inward without finishing the sentence. The room was a wreck. Not one object was left on top of another. The sheets were torn off the bed. The drawers were pulled from the dressers and slung on the floor. The two suitcases had been snatched apart and every piece of clothing in them thrown across the room. Morris' briefcase was zipped open and individual papers spilled and wadded in balls all over the room.

"God *damn*," said Morris.

"I love room service as much as the next person," said Sullivan, "but this is too much."

Morris reluctantly checked the bathroom. Their toilet items were scattered in the sink and tub and broken on the floor.

"I think the rival United Press International has gone too far," said Sullivan. She could not help but giggle at the total chaos of the room.

Morris sifted through his papers. His notes to himself after his interviews were gone. None of them would be intelligible to another human being.

"What do you suppose they were looking for?" asked Sullivan. She was in good spirits. She might have been standing in the littered gallery of a golf tournament.

Oh, I know what they were looking for, thought Morris. The handwritten record of Oberon's telephone call was in his jacket pocket. Who could have realized it was missing from Trapwell's locker? Other than the manager Henry Young? It would be a pleasure to take the goddamn training room apart as their own room had been trashed.

"Not talking?" said Sullivan.

"Not yet," said Morris. He began to pick up their clothes thrown to the four corners of the room. It looked as if nine suitcases had been emptied.

Sullivan's smile suddenly disappeared. "Morris. I'm afraid."

He put one of his heavy arms around her. "It's not a pretty sight. But I'm not a drunk kid, and whoever did it might need all the Boy Scout knife he can carry if he comes back."

"Do you think he'll come back?" Sullivan shivered against him.

"I doubt it. But I don't think he found what he was looking for."

"Shall we call the Lieutenant?" asked Sullivan.

"We'll see her tomorrow. We might as well pick things up. Whoever did it would have been careful not to leave prints." Morris turned his suitcase upright. Under it, shredded in a dozen pieces, was his photograph of Julia Sullivan. He did not try to conceal the pieces, but lifted them in his two hands.

She buried her face in his shoulder. "Morris." Her voice shook against him.

He took his time. "Julia. I don't think this was just a sick joke. I think whoever killed Harvey Trapwell did it. Or he knows who did it. It's not going to get safer here. Let me put you on the plane to Denver, and I promise in thirty days, you and I won't be apart again until you're bored with me." He tried to laugh.

"John Morris. I'm scared. But I'm not going to leave. We'll do what has to be done." Her voice was not shaking anymore.

"We'll call the Lieutenant tonight," suggested Morris.

"No. You were right the first time. We'll see her tomorrow. We promised her dinner. Somebody wants you out of this town," said Sullivan. "He doesn't know you, Morris. He made a terrible mistake."

Chapter Thirteen

The boy guarding the gate to the practice field was a weight lifter. He had to be. His white T-shirt was stretched to ruin. He wore a brace on the knee that had ended his football. Now he was keeping the gate for his scholarship, and lifting weights.

Harry would like the psychology of it: "You oughta see the animal he has, just to keep the practice gate." Morris identified himself. The boy checked his name off on a clipboard he was holding.

"What's the schedule today?"

"It's gonna be rough all over." The boy said it with all the arrogance of knowing he wouldn't get any closer to the action than inside his white T-shirt.

"Is *he* with you?" the boy asked.

Morris looked at his own feet as if someone were standing under him. Then turned to see a tall, angular man waiting surprisingly close behind him. His face was more than familiar. Then Morris remembered his name. "I know him, and I know his Packard."

"Myers," the man identified himself. "Russell Myers."

The antique Packard wasn't there to distract him, and Morris got a more revealing look at the man. Myers was as wide and tall as he remembered. He even had a tall face. His wiry hair was still black, though he had to be over fifty. But something was wrong with him. His high cheekbones pressed through his drawn skin. He was pale, even for November. His tight, round eyes blinked against the weak sun. He was too thin. He looked like a man who had recovered from a nasty illness.

Myers nodded at Morris, but did not offer to shake hands.

"I don't have a Myers," said the boy, looking at his clipboard, spreading his huge legs as if the absence of a typed name were a breach of national security.

"They called," said Myers, no inflection in his voice.

"They who?"

"The administrative office."

"Ain't but one office out here. And that's up on that tower." The boy's head turned up toward an iron, erector-set tower in the middle of the practice fields. "No name here—" He hit the clipboard. "—no luck." He spread his legs wider. He avoided Myers' eyes as if he had seen him before, thought Morris.

Myers stood easily, not so much as shifting his weight. "I believe Mister Myers works for the President," said Morris.

Myers acknowledged it only with his eyes.

The boy wavered. He looked down the list again. "I don't have a Myers. I'll have to check with the head manager."

"Mister Myers and I will wait inside," said Morris, poling

his way through the gate with his cane. The boy turned, giving ground, looking behind him as if for help.

Morris stepped onto the grass that practice had killed to its roots. Myers paused beside him and lit a cigaret.

"You follow football?" asked Morris.

"I've seen it played here and there." Myers offered nothing in his voice.

"They don't actually *play* it here," said Morris. "What did Earl Blaik say? 'Football is the nearest thing to war you can have without killing somebody.' Blaik never beat Harry Carr."

Myers had a wolf grin behind his cigaret.

"I won't ask you what the President thinks about Harry?" Morris looked up at the figure high on the tower.

"No secret about that. He knows it doesn't make a shit in this town what he thinks about Harry."

For the first time, Myers' voice was not a monotone. Morris thought he might laugh. He dragged on his cigaret instead.

"You like Georgia?" asked Morris.

"It ain't California."

"What about Doctor Walker?" Morris decided to lift Myers out of his easy stance. "Does he have any thoughts as to who might have killed the kid? Does he blame Harry for anything?"

Myers squinted at him with his small black eyes. "What are you, a reporter or something?"

"Yes. Associated Press."

Myers took a step away from him, then stood without moving. "You want to quote somebody, you talk to him. Not to me." He seemed to be trying to recall exactly what he might have said.

"Good advice," said Morris. "I'll take it." He hadn't talked with Dr. Theodore Walker. He would do it. Though presidents always answered questions in press releases. Morris lifted his cane in a peace gesture.

Myers did not respond, but moved away up the embankment toward the next practice field.

Morris followed awkwardly up the slope in the same general direction.

Three of the practice fields were natural grass, their crowns by November scarred beyond repair. The uppermost field was artificial turf. Harry despised it. How could you bleed mud and guts on a clean, imitation field? He only used it in self-defense, when the next game was to be played on it.

A Harry Carr practice varied each day, but had not lessened in intensity, Morris was certain, in thirty-two years. Other coaches imitated his methods, especially his former players and assistants, but they never duplicated his success. He understood practice as a physical science, broken into minutes and reaction drills, to separate the quick from the dead, all continuously accelerated in pace and intensity until the players were unable to stand or breathe. Assistant coaches, like Parris Island drill instructors, swarmed among the groups, screaming for instant reaction to the trap, the draw, the pitch. Ten minutes later a whistle blew, and separate waves fled to exhaustion under punted balls, damned to hell if they violated coverage lanes. All the time, the offense was divided between skill players—receiving and throwing and softly cradling the ball, timing their steps like music—and the hitters, rehearsing violence one against the other. Players wore colors commensurate with their status. They sprinted from group to group like brightly plumaged birds making community nests. At some time in the ninety minutes, whistles brought them together, colors against colors, and team offenses and defenses were executed according to a rigid game plan. Harry, fearful of injuries, rehearsed his plans only under simulated conditions once the season had begun. Unless his team lost. Then he might risk anything.

Harry knew all the systems. He invented as many as he stole. He knew when to abandon them. That was the secret the other coaches couldn't imitate. That, and deciding—not even deciding—*knowing* which twenty-two of the ninety-five players were winners and at what positions. It was frightening to see Harry stomp a practice schedule into the grass and rip the starting jersey off a three-letter senior and sling it at an unmarked freshman. His "Old Boys," who played under him and coached under him, were in great demand by universities as head coaches. Some won, but only in their own image. Others perfected all his weaknesses: his random drunkenness; his paradoxical, pious religion; his appetite for girls; his string of bad investments until powerful cronies made him rich in spite of himself; terrible, filthy stories when he told them; a raging temper; blind loyalty; his reflex defense of any of his players, past or present, no matter how mean and unworthy their lives;

contempt for all authority; a need for glory; and obsession with winning games of football to the exclusion of life and thought. As head coaches, all of his Old Boys put together had won only *two* games against him in forty. Both flukes. How could they imitate an unexplainable boyishness; a hidden, true generosity in an old man uncorrupted by his own sins, who *knew* how to win, whose players would volunteer their lives for one grunt of approval? Maybe it was some kind of new, unteachable religion, thought Morris.

A stringy kid in steel-rimmed glasses, with a football under each arm, raced past Morris. "Hey, YOU!"

Morris was surprised to hear so thin a face make such a shout. It was the head manager, Henry Young. He was yelling at Myers. He ran right up to him. "The Man says you'll have to leave." He didn't bother to explain who the Man was.

Myers looked down on the kid as if he would drive him from between the two footballs with his fists. The kid didn't back up. Myers turned and walked carefully toward the gate without speaking.

Morris looked up at the tower.

Harry stood on top, motionless, a battery-operated megaphone hanging from one hand. He held it up and said something, an electronic blip of a sound that the defensive players under him all seemed to understand without looking up. Morris only caught the word *hands*. Now two of the assistants were raging, "Get those *hands up*! Get 'em in his eyes!" The defensive fronts were rushing the passer, each wave waiting its turn on one knee. The artificial turf—identical to what they would play on at Tennessee—was hot, even in the cool November sun. The players were sweating through their jerseys.

Morris only recognized the Captain, Mitchell, in the starting offensive that broke from the huddle. A wide receiver came hurtling toward Mitchell, flat-out, head down, arms driving, feet reaching for the sideline, aluminum and rubber and leather pads no longer cumbersome but fluid under the faded silver jersey that was bright with motion until it all stopped itself upon a predetermined but unmarked triangle of turf; all the time, five yards across the line of scrimmage, as if mirrored, was his defensive opposite. Down the scrimmage line, knees cleared the turf; heads raised; two lines of eyes avoided engagement. The tailback and the fullback burst motionless with undeclared speed, one behind the other. The defensive secondary bent forward, hands pressing against the invisible air. The quarterback straddled the center, his arms down, his hands cupped below and above to receive the ball, his mouth creating an urgency of words and numbers as his head turned impassively from left to right to left. The snap came silent as smoke from a far-off gun. There was an instant of parallel delay, and then a diagram of noise and motion and collision. Bodies recoiled in the air as if lifted by their own inhuman grunts, only to disengage in mock combat. Upraised arms converged on the tall, thin quarterback who released the ball, spinning it in the air like glory, *through* the hands of the wide-open tight end, Mitchell.

There was an electronic "goddamn" that Morris did not miss. Harry had seen enough. He slung the megaphone from the tower, smashing it against the turf, scattering batteries among the players. He worked his long legs down the tower steps, grumbling to himself.

"Oh shit," said one of the players, rolling his eyes.

Harry might have been a young man. Ferocity firmed the sagging wrinkles in his face. He tore away his black-and-silver baseball cap and put his teeth against the intricate, old-fashioned, three-piece noseguard on the helmet of his captain.

"Mitchell!" He choked out the name. "Are you in there, Mitchell?"

"Yes, sir."

"You're not hurt in there?"

"No sir."

"Do you think I'm a barbarian, Mitchell?"

"No, sir."

"By God, I am!"

"Yes, sir."

"And you're the tip-toein'est, ass'grabbin'est, iron-handedest, titty-pullin'est sonuvabitch supposed to be a player I ever coached. The whole goddamn field is runnin' over with candyassed, Ivy League losers. You wear lace pants, Mitchell?"

"No, sir."

"They all do. That's why Tennessee is gonna stomp our nuts out. If we got any. And because our fatheaded captain can't leave on a count of two and catch a football thrown up his ass. They love you in this league, Mitchell. They know you don't have a gut in your body."

"Yes, sir."

Mitchell was Harry's favorite. Ninety-four athletes held their breath. If Harry would say that to *Mitchell*, what would he say to them?

Harry grabbed a fistful of worn jersey. His voice was suddenly dead level. "You're the best we got, Mitchell. I need eleven-on-a-side who'll go to Knoxville."

Mitchell tore his helmet off by the noseguard and slung it against the bottom of the tower. "We'll play their ass bareheaded."

Players were turning and slamming their helmets against the tower that rang with an iron echo. The air was savage with voices.

"Aw'right," said Harry. "Aw'right." Harry raised his hands and arms, lifting the curses out of their mouths. The mob became boys again, standing awkwardly without their helmets. "Show me," Harry said. He started up the tower, not looking down.

The sun was finally down behind the concrete wall. The players were running wind sprints. All you could see after they had run fifty yards were their silver helmets; actually, you could only see the silver, which seemed to stand out above the helmets.

Doc Haywood stopped and spat tobacco over his folded arms. Morris had forgotten his "smokeless" tobacco habit at practice. "You gotta be goddamn young to play this game for nothin'."

"What about ignorant?" said Morris.

"Nobody's that ignorant. You gotta be young. Never coulda been a Napoleon without them wide-eyed, eighteen-year-olds. None of 'em think they can die till you hit 'em between the eyes with a thirty-ought-six. What's happenin' about Trapwell?"

"I was going to ask you."

"A lot of nothin'. Got hisself stuck to death, drunk. No doubt about that."

"Did you read Caplin's column this morning?"

"He's a beauty, Caplin." Doc spit again. "Trapwell didn't have a drug habit. Even the nitwit coroner of this county could see that. Oughta make that asshole Caplin cut the boy back open and prove the drug damage." Doc shifted his chew. "We got our share of hypochondriacs. But the people on this team needin' a drug have gotta hole hit in 'em somewhere. It's easy to have one if you play for Harry."

"Who's the new trainer?" asked Morris. "What does he think about what happened?"

"Andy Walker." Doc pointed out a tall, slump-shouldered man of about thirty-five who had a pained expression on his face. "He can't chew gum and wrap ankles at the same time. You hadn't met him?"

Morris shook his head.

"He's been here 'bout five years. Knows his sports medicine. Scared shitless of Harry, that's his problem. He'd play a amputee if Harry said send him in."

"Call him over," said Morris.

Haywood waved the trainer over to them. He introduced Morris. The trainer kept looking back to see what Harry was doing on his tower.

"Morris read Frank Caplin's column," said Doc. "Wants to know who we got on the team on heroin."

The trainer tumbled his words through a mouthful of teeth. "That fool. I called a lawyer. I may . . . I may sue him."

"Save your money. Harry's gonna kill him," said Doc.

"Trapwell didn't use hard drugs?" asked Morris.

"I don't give hard drugs. Only the doctor." The trainer opened his mouth, showing his teeth. "Harvey Trapwell wouldn't take aspirin."

"Other players aren't so particular?" said Morris.

"Never without Doc's consent. Only when there's no danger of an injury being made worse." He might have been a tape recording.

Harry said something into his megaphone, and the trainer took off at a jog.

Morris shook his head. "Does Harry keep him for a house pet?"

"He's the best I ever saw with a sprain. Fixes anything that hurts that dudn't matter. Leaves the knees to me, the sonofabitch. The truth is, he's workin' on his Ph.D., if you can believe that. Probably wind up teachin' at Yale. The ballplayers are nothin' to him but cuts and knots. Just knows their numbers, can't remember their names. Leaves more than he ought to to the managers."

"And to you," said Morris.

"And to me," said Doc.

"Can you prove Caplin's wrong about what he wrote?" asked Morris.

"How can you prove what ninety-five kids do with their-selves for twenty-four hours a day? Hell no, I can't prove that nobody on the team's got a drug habit. But not many teams full of junkies rank Number One in the nation. You hadn't found out anything yourself?" Doc kept folding and unfolding his arms.

"Not much. Trapwell must have been a serious young man. The Lieutenant talked to his high-school girl friend. It was a tame sort of romance. He called it off this fall. You hear anything about it?"

"No," said Doc. "The only conversations the kid and I ever had were medical. He always wanted to know *why* I was doin' this or that. I told him to save it for medical school. I think he just got hisself into somethin' nasty. Fell in with somebody he had no business knowin'."

"You may be right," said Morris. "The state attorney general's boys are in town. I just talked with Lieutenant Blake. She's glad to get any help she can. Have the state boys talked with you?" Morris watched him fold his arms again.

"Yeah." Doc spat. "Won't get much help from those dum-mies. They all play the three-team *parley cards*. And lose their tails. Wanted to know if it's *safe* to give Tennessee an' seb'en, and us without a quarterback in Knoxville. State inspectors, my ass. Those boys couldn't catch syphilis."

"Doc."

"Yeah."

"Somebody trashed my room last night. I think I know what he was looking for: a note I found in Trapwell's locker. From 'Oberon.' Does that name mean anything to you?"

"Oberon? Never heard of it. What did the note say?" Doc sounded worried.

"I'm turning it over to the police. After I talk to your boy manager Henry Young. Doc, don't hold out on me if you know anything."

"No," said Doc, spitting over his folded arms. "I gotta look at who's wounded. Listen." He stepped nearer. "I do wanta talk some more. See me before you leave."

Morris nodded. Something was making Doc fold and unfold his arms.

The players were now walking, dragging themselves toward the one exit in the concrete-block fence. Morris spotted the manager Young dispatching his assistants in three directions.

"Count the fuckin' footballs again . . . we're still missin' one." His voice was lost on a figure disappearing in the now-real dark.

"Henry." Morris limped close enough for the manager to recognize him. The two hours of standing had swollen his knee.

"Oh. I can't talk. I'm in a panic, have to get this equipment under the shed. It may rain."

Morris matched strides with him toward the prone figures of blocking dummies like casualties in a land war. "One question. Did you take this note for Harvey Trapwell?" Morris shined the pencil light he carried with his apartment keys.

Young was reading before he could stop himself. The loopy printing was distinctive, even though it had been done against a rough surface.

"Well . . . yes . . . I think I did. Were'd you get it?" His voice was tight in his throat.

"In Trapwell's locker."

"Why didn't you ask me then?" Now he was angry, slinging a heavy dummy over one shoulder.

"I wanted to study it. What does it mean: 'Check the time'? Who is Oberon? Was it a local call?"

"I don't know."

"Was it a woman or a man?"

"A . . . *woman* . . . I think. I got to get to work."

"You *think*."

"I'm not sure. It's been a week, or two weeks. I don't know what it meant. I just copied it down."

Morris put his large hand on the manager's thin shoulder. "This is no pop quiz. It's *murder*. You better think who made that call, a man or a woman, what week it was, what day it was, what hour it was! You'll have to answer those questions to the police."

"Police? I haven't done anything. I can't help what I don't remember . . ."

Morris could feel the boy's lean muscles quivering under his own hand. "Do you remember tearing up my hotel room last night? What were you looking for? Did you find it in Mitchell's desk? Or Paul Teller's room?"

"No. Listen . . ." Young's voice faltered. "I don't know anything about that. You leave me alone. I have to go." He was trotting in the dark with the heavy dummy loaded over his shoulder.

Morris could hardly breathe. He shifted his weight on the scarred wooden bench. The low concrete ceiling seemed to press the steam back down, hard into his lungs.

Harry Carr sat obscenely naked with no towel wrapped around him. His thick gray hair was heavy with sweat that ran down his face and off onto the floor. He did not ask if it was too hot. Or if Morris had had enough. He sat there powerfully in the steam, leaning over, running with water, his heavy arms resting on his legs, like some patient animal in a rain forest.

Morris breathed easier. The damp heat felt more comfortable.

"Don't tell Doc I was in here," said Harry.

Morris lifted his head.

"He'd raise hell. What does he know? I feel better in here." He shook the water in his hair free. "The police find out anything?"

"I expect you could tell me," said Morris. Harry didn't respond. "Nothing important—that I know. Despite what Caplin wrote, the boy didn't have a drug habit."

"That shit Caplin." Harry flipped the water off his thick hands and arms.

"I don't think Trapwell had a desperate girl problem."

"No." Harry shook his head.

"He didn't drink, but he was drunk. It doesn't make sense. Did he have any *schedule* problem, or *time* problem that you know about?"

"I don't fool with schedule problems. Long as they make practice and the meetings. I only hear about classes if they don't go. No problem with Trapwell. He went."

Morris described the note and how he found it in Trapwell's locker. "Does the name *Oberon* mean anything to you?"

Harry groped with his hands, as if for a cigaret. "Never heard of it. The boy's dead. It might not be the worst thing in the world if *why* was buried with him."

"What do you mean?"

"I'm just an old sum'bitch who's seen too much trouble." His voice aged in the wet air.

Morris couldn't understand why Harry was changing his tune. Yesterday, whoever killed Trapwell had better be prepared "to kill him, too."

"Somebody tore my hotel room apart last night. They may have been looking for the note."

"Nobody hurt?" Harry stared through the sweat.

"No. Nothing taken. Just whatever peace of mind I had left. You missing anything?"

Harry looked away, shaking the sweat out of his thick hair, then shifted gears. "Didn't practice make you want to vomit? Tennessee'll kill everybody who's left alive. We can bury the whole team."

"I think you're right," said Morris.

Harry sat up in the steam with both fists clenched. "What the hell do you mean?"

The first thing Morris had ever learned about Harry: no matter what he said, or how obscenely he said it, never agree with him how sorry his team looked. Or be ready to whip him. Morris laughed. "I'll give you Tennessee and seven."

Harry laughed with him.

Doc didn't seem to be in the Athletic Center, but he could be anywhere. It was huge, with five dressing rooms, a weight room, handball courts. Morris gave up and stepped outside. Clouds had lowered the night. He could smell rain in the air. The wind was cold enough for December.

Morris heard him spit. "Doc?"

"Yeah."

"What are you, hiding from your patients?"

"You might say. I'm tryin' to keep this team alive, and Harry's tryin' to kill it. Where you parked?"

"In the back."

"I'll walk you to your car."

It was darker in the parking lot. Morris felt his way with his cane. The car was where he had left it.

"Let's get in." Doc spat out what was left of his tobacco.

Morris worked his stiff left knee under the steering wheel and rubbed it with both hands. "You confess?"

"I what? Very funny. I gotta problem."

Morris waited him out.

"You lose a few bottles of this and that. Break a few. Leave 'em on the plane. Give somebody a ampule of Demerol and forget to put it on your log. Goddamn the Drug Enforcement Agency. They don't know this team's like treatin' a combat battalion. Somebody's always hurtin'. I keep my supplies in my bag. Damn bag weighs too much to carry around; I put it down. It's over yonder by the tower, an' I'm somewhere else. It's supposed to stay locked up if I ain't holdin' it. That's bullshit. How can I keep it locked up on game day? Or any day? Especially on the road?"

Morris watched him talking out of the right side of his mouth, and folding and unfolding his arms over his round stomach, all the time squinting through his rimless glasses in the dim light.

"My drug log this year ain't the most complete thing ever put down. Or *any* year." Doc rolled down the window and spat the last fragments of his tobacco. "I wouldn't bet my life I can account for every two-cc ampule of Demerol I've shot into somebody in the last twelve months."

Morris did not help him by speaking.

"Broke a thirty-cc *vial* of Demerol Saturday. Damn if I know how. You can't hardly break one. Somebody stepped on the glass before I knew it was broke. Sump'in else. That bothers me more." Doc spat out of habit. "Damn sealed bottle of morphine sulphate tablets. Used a couple of tablets last week. Hadda dislocated elbow. One of them hurts like a barbed-wire enema. Tablets did *nuthin'*. Got the boy to the hospital. His heart rate was up. Pupils dilated. Dryness of the mouth. Didn't make sense. Looked at the tablets, one-one-hundred-fiftieth-grain tablets. Somebody had emptied out about half of 'em and put in plain atropine sulphate, which is no painkiller. And resealed it. Checked another bottle. Same thing. I had 'em since summer. Coulda been switched anytime."

"You tell anybody?"

"Harry."

"What did he say?"

"Said keep up with my damn bag. He's right. Harry's always right. Makes you wanna throw up."

"Could it be this team does have a drug problem?" asked Morris.

"Naw. It couldn't. Somebody might get turned on here and there. I'm sure one or two do. They'd have to be blind and dead for none of 'em to get mixed up in sump'in at this university. But a team of junkies? No way."

"Somebody used it, or sold it."

"Or both. Probably sold it. Small-time operation, what little was stole. But it could pay a bill or two. Buy a few kicks."

"Buy enough to kill Trapwell for? Do you think he was selling drugs?"

"I can't believe it," said Doc. "But live today, and you can learn to believe anything. Anyway, the damn state investigators have been hasslin' me about drugs I can't account for. Now the police will be. I'd hate to see it in the paper. You see the Lieutenant. She trusts you. Don't let her use me as a scapegoat in a cheap headline."

"Yeah." Now Morris knew why Doc was folding and unfolding his arms all afternoon. Caplin would love it. "Doc." He put the keys in the ignition. "The lieutenant's looking for a murderer. Not a scapegoat. I'll only write what you told me if the time comes I have to."

Doc opened the door and got out, spitting again in the dark.

"Tell me this," said Morris. "Is Harry on hard drugs?"

"What kinda question is that? You know he's on medicine. I prescribe it. That's a dumb-ass question." Doc slammed the door.

Morris rolled down the window. "Murder is a dumb-ass game. I'll see you, Doc."

Morris drove all the way to town before he remembered his pocket tape recorder. He was sure he had left it in Harry's dressing room, just off the steam room. Morris only used the recorder to make notes to himself after an interview. There were some things on the tape that would embarrass him. He would rather Harry not hear a few of the questions he had raised to himself: "Did Trapwell come to his hotel room to tell him Harry was on drugs? Or that Doc was selling them? God knows Harry didn't need money, or did he? Did someone ask Trapwell to shave points? Was someone blackmailing him? Did Trapwell see something, or hear something, that got him killed? What? Did the manager Henry Young know who was involved?"

Morris circled back in the dark toward the Athletic Center. The cross-campus traffic was heavy; the going was slow. Morris stopped in front of the Center. Lights were on inside, but the building seemed abandoned. The front door was not locked. Now, if he could find the room. The building was almost as complicated as the Pentagon.

Morris stopped at a sign: "Room 601. Private." He was sure that was it. There was no light under the door. But he thought he heard something, a sound, inside. He tried the door. It was not locked. Morris pushed it open. The sound, the rhythm of it, was unmistakable. The words were not words at all, they were breaths, "Oh my god," then they were breaths again. Morris saw the blue police skirt on the floor in the one slice of light before he closed the door. The sounds had not stopped.

Goddamn, Harry, thought Morris, it's indecent that somebody killed your quarterback and not you.

Chapter Fourteen

"*I can't eat* another bite . . ." Sullivan reached over with a fork and speared a fried potato off his plate. ". . . Maybe one more."

Morris put his chin on both hands. "I love to watch you eat."

She drank a swallow of iced tea. Then lifted the last morsel of stuffed flounder on her fork.

"You could play a lady Tom Jones."

"My bosoms are too small." She held her breath and laughed.

"They are just right."

She was buttering the last roll.

"My God, where do you put it?"

She grinned through a streak of butter.

"How much do you weigh?"

"I always weigh a hundred and twelve."

"That means you weighed ninety-three pounds when this meal started."

"I don't think I can eat the pecan pie."

"What pecan pie?"

"The one I was thinking about ordering."

Morris ordered the pecan pie.

She waited with both hands carefully in her lap.

"You look like you're starving."

She smiled, the trace of butter shining on her lips.

"You look like you haven't eaten in a month."

She turned both palms up, innocently.

"My mother would have loved the way you clean your plate."

She looked directly at him.

"She would have loved you, period."

She reached across the table and touched his arm.

"Tell me again what your mother was like."

"She was tall. Kinda skinny. Couldn't you guess?"

She laughed.

"Skinny, but strong as hell. And tough. She ran the concessions at Grant Park Zoo. We didn't have the expression then, but nobody ever ripped her off. If you didn't have any money, she could be a soft touch for an icey. I wish I could lose a pound for every day I spent at the zoo. I never got tired of it. My favorites were the elephants. One of the elephants is still there. He has a broken tail. He looks exactly the same as when I used to hang on his fence. He watched me, last summer. Do you think he remembered me?"

"Sure. Elephants never forget a friend." She touched him again.

"The thing I liked most was when she read to me."

"What did she read?"

"*Treasure Island* was my favorite. And *The Last of the Mohicans*. Her feet hurt. But she was never too pooped to read. She would read lying down."

"So you became a writer."

"Reporter."

"You never overwrite, even a sentence."

"Oh, yes I do. They fix it in New York. The computer fixes everything."

"Morris. Are you really going to leave the Associated Press?"

"No . . . I already left. I gave them notice through December."

"Are you scared?"

"Sure. How am I going to keep you in pecan pie?"

The pie came.

"The old AP never paid a lot," he said, "but there was always the expense account. You could live on that."

"You'll be busy. You wait. Everybody will want to use what you write. Because they can believe it."

"I hope that's true."

"You're doing it because you want to. Not because of me."

"What if it were?"

She put down her fork.

"I'm teasing you," he said. "I've had it. I've enjoyed it, but I've had it. I want to see what I can write that someone else will print. I have some ideas. As Travis Walker once said, if he lost his golf swing, he could always 'dig ditch.'"

She was smiling again. She had a big fork of pecan pie in her mouth, giving her smile a whopsided look.

"You should make commercials. The way you look eating . . . It's like a religion . . . except a lot more fun."

She drank the last of her iced tea. And patted her flat stomach as if it were an old friend.

"Now tell me what you've been hiding in your jacket pocket."

Morris was startled. His hand reached inside his jacket to touch the folded paper. He pulled it out and handed it across the table. "I found it in Harvey Trapwell's locker."

Sullivan unfolded it carefully and spread it on the table as if it were a map. She read the scrawled capital letters aloud: "CHECK THE TIME. OBERON." She read the words to herself several times. Her tongue found the smudge of butter on her lips.

"Whoever wrote it was left-handed," she said.

"How do you know?" Morris leaned to her.

"See . . . how the letters slant backwards." She wrapped her left hand and wrist around the top of the paper and imitated drawing the words from above, from left to right. "We're a disadvantaged group. Us left-handers. We learn to write in right-handed desks." She made a fake muscle with her left arm. "Most modern elementary schools have left-handed desks."

"I know who wrote it. Who *says* he wrote it," said Morris. "I don't know if he's left-handed. Or if he's lying. I'll find out tomorrow. He's the manager of the football team. Henry Young."

"What does the note mean?"

"I don't know. It was in Trapwell's locker yesterday. It could have been there a week, or since September, for all I know. Young says he took the message on the telephone. He *doesn't remember* if it was last week or if it was two weeks ago. *Doesn't remember* if it was a man or a woman who called. Said he *thought* it was a woman. Again, he doesn't have any idea who Oberon is. He says. He's all innocence. And awfully nervous."

"Has the Lieutenant seen it?"

"I was going to give it to her tonight if she had shown." Morris drank from his own tea. Maybe he should have read the note to her in Harry's dressing room. "Maybe she'll be over for breakfast."

"Who says you'll be up for breakfast?" Sullivan tossed her napkin in his lap.

"I'll tell her not to come early."

She rolled her eyes.

"You're not only expensive. You're impossible."

"What does the word mean? Oberon." She cocked her head as if she could hear the definition.

"I have no idea."

" 'Check the time.' What 'time' could it mean?"

Morris shook his head. "The Dean's office hasn't any idea. Or his academic counselor. All his classes were set. Even for next quarter. It didn't seem to mean a football-related time. I talked to Harry and Doc. I haven't talked with Trapwell's former girl friend. We'll do that. And to Teller at the PKA house. We'll ask his roommates, and anybody else close to him. But first I think the Lieutenant and I need to question the kid Young."

"I'll go to the library and research *Oberon*."

"You can't."

She looked up from the note.

"They don't allow food in the library."

She pantomimed tearing up the note.

"Speaking of Doc."

"Were we?" she asked.

"He's worried. He has a right to be. You read what Caplin said in his column. That Trapwell had a drug problem. That the team has one. It's not true. Trapwell was Mister Clean. But Doc is worried. He told me tonight he has been missing certain narcotics this fall. Here and there. Somebody switched pills in his bag. Doc says it's a small-time theft. But it could be important to one person if he sold it, or if he used it. No way could it be a team-wide problem. He *says*."

"Does the Lieutenant know?"

Morris shook his head.

"You two are going to have a long breakfast. I'm glad I'm sleeping in."

The waiter brought the check.

"I better pay now," said Morris. "She may ask to look at tomorrow's menu."

The waiter smiled and took his credit card.

"Let's have a nightcap in the bar," said Sullivan.

"Wonderful. I thought you were going to say, in the kitchen."

Chapter Fifteen

The young bartender held the telephone receiver on end, as if it were a Scotch on the rocks, and said across the bar, "Mister Morris!"

Morris reached across as though he had been waiting for the call. "Morris here."

"This is Sharon—Lieutenant Blake." She was trying to control the panic in her voice. "Someone's been killed."

Morris pushed himself erect at the bar. "Who? Where?"

Sullivan stood, as if she could help.

"I don't know who. A night janitor just called the station. He was terrified. He found a body. In the Athletic Center. In one of the training rooms. Can you meet me there in ten minutes?"

"Yes." Morris lifted his cane from the next stool. "Is it a man or a woman?"

"I don't know." She was calmer. "The station says the janitor was spooked. He left the building and called from an all-night Quick Mart."

"I'll see you at the Center," said Morris, hanging up.

"Who was it?" asked Sullivan.

"The Lieutenant. Someone's been killed at the Athletic Center. She doesn't know who." Morris finished his drink in one swallow. "I'll be back with all the grisly details."

A squad car was pulling up in front of the building.

The Lieutenant stepped out. She held her shoulder bag with both hands. Then seemed to make up her mind and walked over to Morris' open window.

"Can I get in?" she asked.

Morris opened the door. She sat looking straight ahead. "I saw you open the door, Morris. So you know how it is with Harry and me. Maybe you think I should resign." Her voice was almost natural.

"I think you are the acting chief of police of this town. And a good one. We better see who's dead inside."

"A minute won't make a difference."

"Listen, I'm sorry. I left my tape recorder in the building."

"You think I'm a fool." She was looking at him.

Morris smiled. "At least I know two reasons why Harry came to 'Fessor's funeral." There was no malice in his voice.

"My father would kill me." She held onto her shoulder bag. "Look. I'm...I'm not a quitter."

"What if it all leads back to Harry? If he killed the boy himself?" Morris' voice still was without malice. Maybe it's Harry who's dead inside, he thought.

"He couldn't." She was shaking her head. "You know Harry." She opened her own door. "Morris."

"Yes."

"Thanks." She closed the door and took the steps two at a time.

Too bad 'Fessor's not alive, thought Morris.

Sergeant Redding waited at the front door with the janitor. "All right. Lead the way," he said as if he were imitating his own soprano voice.

The old man took one step inside. "I got to?"

"It's a big place. It might take us an hour to find him."

"He be in the main training room."

"You lead us to the door. You don't have to go in the room."

"Lord, no." The old man started forward reluctantly.

The rooms were dark. Only the long hallways, like tunnels, were lighted.

"You were working alone?" asked the Lieutenant.

The janitor was glad of an excuse to stop. "Yessum. The others come in at eight."

She nodded him forward. Finally he stopped outside the room Morris remembered as a long training room. The lights were on. The old man didn't move. The Sergeant stepped inside with the Lieutenant behind him.

Morris saw the legs in the air before either of them. The head and body were down in the metal whirlpool. Morris limped across the slick floor to look in the still water. He could see the short, dark hair floating away from the skull. The body was small. Morris was certain who it was.

The heels of the Lieutenant and the Sergeant sounded behind him.

Sergeant Redding reached in the water. "He's ice cold." His voice was as high as a girl's.

"I hate to leave him like that," said the Lieutenant. She made herself look in the water.

The janitor moaned incoherently in the door.

It was the manager, all right, Henry Young. Morris struck the tile floor with his cane.

The Sergeant's hand went to his gun.

"Why did you do that, Morris?" Lieutenant Blake slipped and almost fell on the wet floor.

"I'm sure I helped kill him."

"You what?"

"His name is Henry Young. He was the head manager of the football team. I don't know who killed him. But I might have prevented it."

"What do you mean?"

Morris handed her the folded note from his jacket. "I found this in Trapwell's locker. Yesterday. I haven't been able to make any sense of it. Or to find out who Oberon is. Or what it means." Morris gave her time to read the message twice. "Henry Young took it on the telephone. Or he admitted to me he did, late this afternoon. He denied remembering when he took it. He *guessed* last week, or the week before. He didn't know who called, he *said*. He *didn't remember* if it was a man or a woman who called. He *guessed* a woman. I told him he would have to refresh his memory with the police. He was plenty nervous about it."

"'CHECK THE TIME. OBERON,'" quoted the Lieutenant. "Have you asked anyone what it might mean?"

"Yes. I saw Trapwell's dean, a Doctor Marshall. And his academic counselor, a Doctor Brewer. The word *Oberon* meant nothing to them. Or to Trapwell's tutor and friend, Paul Teller — he *said*. Teller was an uneasy interview. I hadn't found the note when I talked to Trapwell's roommates." Morris slowed his voice for emphasis. "I did mention the note itself and *where I found it* to Doc. And to Harry."

"What did they say?"

"Nothing that helped. They never heard of Oberon. Harry did say something funny. He said it might be better if we never found out why Trapwell was killed. It didn't sound like Harry at all."

The Lieutenant was shaking her head. "The note might be nothing. It might be anything. Why didn't you give it to me?"

"I don't know. Maybe it was some kind of dumb, grandstand play. I thought I'd talk to the manager again. I did, today after practice. I was going to tell you tonight . . . but that's no excuse," he added.

She didn't speak.

"I thought we could talk about it in the morning. Give Henry Young time to work on his memory. Somebody worked on it for him." Morris listened to his own flat voice as if someone else were speaking.

She was biting her lip.

"Look, I had two days to show it to you. I asked all over about Oberon. If he's a person, he would know I found his message. I blew it."

Lieutenant Blake looked directly at him. "Without you, Morris, we wouldn't know there was a note. Turn in your martyr's merit badge. Let's get on with what we have to do."

Now the Sergeant was directing the lab team from the station. His thin, high voice was out of place in the training room. The coroner was there. And a photographer.

"How long has he been dead?" asked the Lieutenant.

Floyd Harris, the coroner, squeezed his bald head with his free hand. "Three or four hours, probably. I'll know later."

"Drowned?"

"I would think. But not guess."

"It took a *man* to stuff him in there," said Morris. "He was skinny, but I saw him run with a heavy blocking dummy over one shoulder."

Harris squatted beside the body. "He put up a struggle. Two of his teeth were broken off. Probably on the metal rim of the whirlpool. They were in the water. With his glasses. His fingers seem to be shattered."

There are gorillas on Harry's team who could drown King Kong, thought Morris. He could not imagine a player, even the Hulk, killing either of the two kids.

Morris guided the Lieutenant aside. "Can we talk?"

"I'll take a break in half an hour. I'll be questioning coaches, players, others."

"There's a coffee shop down the hill, opposite the stadium. I'll wait for you. I have to call the bureau's man here in Sparta. We won't release anything until you notify his parents. You do think the two murders are related."

"I will assume they are until we learn differently."

"Do you want me to release the message from Oberon?"

She began biting the fingernail on her left thumb. He hadn't noticed her do that. "No. Please don't. Not yet. Not until we have a chance to pursue it quietly."

"Not until you say."

Morris rang Room 216 at the Holiday Inn. Finally, Jack Pruitt answered.

"Sorry. Morris here."

"What's . . . happened?"

Morris could almost see the hesitation in his speech. "Better get on the horn to Atlanta. Harry's head manager, a kid named Henry Young, was killed tonight. Drowned in a whirlpool in the training room."

"I . . . have a pencil."

Morris gave him the details. "Lieutenant Blake said she will assume the two murders are related until she learns differently. Just before I left her, they reached the boy's parents. In Savannah. You can go with the story."

"I'll call in a . . . bulletin," said Pruitt.

Morris finished his second cup of coffee before the Lieutenant joined him. She sat down without speaking.

"Any surprises?" asked Morris.

"Young's locker had been searched, his books and clothes scattered everywhere. No way to know what might be missing. We're talking to the other managers, the trainer, and to Doc."

"So. Someone killed him on purpose. Or did he walk in on something?"

"No way to know. Obviously, he knew too much. Maybe he threatened the wrong person."

"I wouldn't be surprised." Morris looked at a menu. Death was such a part of journalism. Even for a sports reporter. Sooner or later, every athlete was an obituary. It never got easier, especially seeing the photographs of them in their youth, uncorrupted by time. And there were those who died young, like Trapwell. Nothing you could write then made any sense at all. Morris was not embarrassed to be hungry. "Can you eat breakfast?"

"I have to. I didn't have much supper." She did not avoid his eyes.

They ordered eggs and bacon.

"You need to know something Doc Haywood told me. Tonight after practice." Morris described the smashed and missing drugs. The swapped pills.

"Doc's sure that's all he can't account for?"

"More or less. The state inspectors are giving Doc trouble about his sloppy bookkeeping."

"Would you have told me if the boy hadn't been killed?"

"Yes. Doc's got his tail in a crack. But it can't be helped."

"I don't look forward to seeing Harry."

"You mean to questioning him. I think he trusted the little manager too much. He was a tough kid. Harry must have liked him for that."

"You don't think Harry could—"

"No. But he's strong enough, despite his health."

"What do you know about his health?"

"What Doc told me. That it's not good. That he lives on cigarets and Scotch."

"Doc—"

"I know, talks a lot."

"I don't try to change Harry . . . but I'll question him within an inch of his life."

They ate without speaking until Morris lowered his cup. "Something you should know about. Happened at practice yesterday."

The Lieutenant looked up.

"A man named Myers, Russell Myers, was chased off the practice field by Young. Young said Harry wanted him out. You know how Harry is about hangers-on at his practices. You might check with Harry to be certain Young was following his orders."

"Who is this Myers?" She made a note of his name.

"He works for the President. Chauffeurs his antique Packard. Came with him from California. That's all I know about him. He doesn't look healthy to me. I heard him tell the boy guarding the practice gate that Administrative had called in his name to the athletic department. So that he could watch practice. I'm going to see the President. I'll ask him. All of which doesn't mean a damn thing."

"You don't think Mister Myers is Oberon?"

"I don't think he could spell it." Morris laughed.

"You'll come by the station tomorrow?"

"If you like," said Morris. "One thing. I knew Young was lying to me about the note, but I didn't imagine he would be killed for it."

"No." She shook her head. "I don't think he realized how much trouble he was in."

Morris turned the cup in his hands. "Maybe he was in it all the way. Or got in too deep before he knew it."

"Oberon couldn't take a chance on how much Young knew. Or he was a more corrupt young man than we have reason to believe."

Morris drank the last of his coffee. "If the killer was Oberon, what spooked him? Two days after the first murder?"

"Your finding the note?"

"That's what it seems to come back to. And Trapwell had an appointment with me. You better be careful, talking to me."

"Trapwell would have been interviewed by someone else. What happened would have happened."

"Of course I told Doc and Harry about the note. And questioned the Dean, and Trapwell's academic advisor, and Teller...asked them if the word *Oberon* meant anything to them. Am I forgetting anybody?"

"Sullivan."

"Sure. I also told her. She would make a great criminal. Asking five or six people, just mentioning the name *Oberon* to them, I might as well have asked the entire university. And Oberon would know he had called a message to the dressing room. Wouldn't he? If he thought the message still existed, he'd want it back."

She nodded, smoothing her note pad.

"I was going to tell you at dinner: someone ripped our hotel room apart. Scattered every movable thing, looking for something. I think it was Oberon's note, which, luckily, was with me in my coat pocket."

"Did he take anything?"

"No. But he shredded my photograph of Julia."

"You should have called."

"It was late. There was nothing you could have done. Also, the team captain, Mitchell, feels someone broke into his desk. Nothing missing. Teller thought someone had been through his clothes. But nothing taken. I'd bet my ass—if you will excuse the anatomy—it was our boy Henry Young looking for something."

"You may be right. I wonder if he found it?"

Morris tapped the table with his cane. "Let's don't forget the most important person I asked about Oberon: Henry Young himself."

"Yes. And somebody killed him before he answered."

"We better start another round of questions. Now we have two places the killer had to be. At two specific times. But we've only narrowed the suspects to twenty-thousand students, ninety-four teammates, the coaching staff, and anybody in Georgia on drugs or with a thousand dollars bet on a football game."

"Do you really think it's someone we haven't met?"

"No chance," said Morris. "No one ever kills a stranger . . . on purpose."

Morris stepped into yesterday's trousers and pulled a fresh shirt on from the top of the suitcase. Sullivan's head was buried under the pillow. He ran his hand along her back and pulled the covers over her. It was chilly in the room. She could sleep through an Ice Age. He closed the door behind him.

Morris opened the door to his U-Drive-It. Harry would be covered up in media. Most of the reporters and television jockeys hadn't left town, and wouldn't, until Saturday's game in Knoxville. Morris steered toward the main administration building.

He turned into a Visitor's parking place just as the tower clock chimed the half hour. Following him was the great black Packard. It swung into the President's reserved parking place, next to his own Chevrolet that shrank with inadequacy. Myers, tall and wide in a brown jacket, got out of the Packard, stepped on a cigaret, and raised the car's impossible hood.

Morris walked up behind him. "Still want to swap cars?"

Myers hit his head on the hood. "Damn." He recognized Morris. "Fucking carburetor."

"Is *he* inside?" Morris pointed toward the President's reserved-parking sign.

"Unless he walked home. I'm supposed to pick him up in half an hour."

"See you," said Morris. Myers blinked behind a pair of dark glasses. It was nothing unusual for the university President to have a chauffeur or handyman. The old President had had a man who was both: *Bully*, they had called him. A black man. A wonderful bartender. He could also remember every athlete who had ever played for Harry Carr and their nicknames and the worst trouble each of them had ever gotten into and exactly how Harry had kicked their asses. His memory was like an endowment at homecoming games; old players would give him whiskey and pay him ten-dollar bills to tell their sons how wicked they had been. Morris wondered what had happened to Bully. He was also a gardener, and had planted all the climbing roses on the trellis behind the old President's mansion. The man Myers did not look like a gardener. He looked like old trouble.

Morris rode the elevator to the fourth floor. The President's suite took up one end of the floor. Morris identified himself to the secretary. She was not impressed.

"I'm afraid you'll have to make an appointment." She had short, dark hair with a scattering of gray; a strong, not unattractive face with a rather heavy jaw, and the body of an athlete. Her hands were blunt and strong like the rest of her.

"Tell him the Associated Press wants to see him. About last night's murder. On campus."

She did not flinch. "When and if Doctor Walker has a statement to make, he will notify the press." She looked down as if to take up her routine work. She was signing her name. He could read it: Elizabeth Morgan.

"I think you should tell 'when-and-if' Doctor Walker, if he won't be interviewed about the murder of two students at his own university, that I will call the Chairman of the State Board of Regents. And if *he* won't talk, I'll call the Governor. I know he'll talk. He's running for re-election."

She wavered. Then pushed an inter-office button. Morris

heard a word on the speaker. It might have been *who?* She did not look at him, but got up and disappeared between two large double doors, closing them behind her.

Morris remained standing. He had only seen Dr. Theodore Walker once. From a distance, at the drunken Quarterback-Club banquet. It was not a face you would forget. Morris looked around the room; you had to admire his choice of art prints; there was an early Matisse, and copies of his cutouts, after he was old and blind.

The double doors opened inward, and the President stepped out.

"Mister Morris." He offered his hand. His grip was tight. He carried his chin high, daring you with his badly pocked face.

"I wanted to speak with Harry Carr before making a statement. I hope you understand." He didn't lower his chin.

Morris relaxed his grip on his cane. "I really don't need a statement. I'd like to talk. See if I'm missing something I should know about. But *on* the record."

Walker stepped back into his office. He was a big man, graying but trim, with thick shoulders and meaty hands. He moved like a one-time athlete, his weight balanced forward on his feet. His secretary slipped between them without speaking.

"Please hold my calls," said Walker.

The huge length of his office surprised Morris. The man's desk was at least eight feet long. The conference table would seat twelve. It might have been the home office of a steamship company. The old President could have put his furniture in the anteroom.

"What did Harry say when you called him?" Morris sat without being asked. He resisted the urge to massage his left knee.

"He agrees with the police, the *woman lieutenant.*" It was not a happy inflection. "That the two murders are related. He can't imagine how. Neither can I. Not that I knew either boy."

"Did the manager Young have a record of disciplinary trouble?" Morris deliberately looked away from him.

"I don't know. The Dean's office is bringing over his records."

Morris looked at him. The light was not kind to his acne

scars. "Do you approve of college football?" Morris didn't know why he asked; it was hardly an appropriate question.

"I played at Stanford." Walker said it matter-of-factly. "Their first team after the War. It's a difficult sport. Difficult to coach well, difficult to play well. I think it damages as many young men as it helps." He put both his hands in his jacket pockets. "It's a big sport at this school; it's *bigger* than a sport. I knew that before I accepted the job." He turned his skin-damaged smile on Morris. His eyes were large and gray.

"After two murders, how do you protect an entire football squad? Not to mention coaches, managers."

Walker leaned back in his chair. "You can't. You try. We're doing that. All of us, I think, felt the first death—murder— of an outstanding young student-athlete was an awkward mistake. But now. Two deaths seem . . . intentional. Premeditated. We are cooperating with the police every possible way."

"But the team will go to Knoxville," said Morris.

"We're under contract to go to Knoxville. I agree with Harry Carr. We will honor that contract. And that tradition. For that matter, our players are obviously as vulnerable on campus as in a hotel. Maybe more so."

Morris did not miss the trembling hands; the President put them carefully back in the pockets of his jacket.

"What if you didn't agree with Harry Carr?"

Walker stood up behind his desk. "I'm not going to play the 'what if' game with you, Mister Morris."

"Off the record?" Morris found his gray eyes.

"I don't know you."

"You know the AP. We don't print gossip. I like Harry. The best things I like about him are the worst things he's done. Don't ask me why."

Walker sat down. "Harry's an anachronism. He's the last dinosaur."

Morris laughed, tapped his cane on the floor. "I think he might like that."

"God knows he can coach."

"God help the man who replaces him."

Walker shook his head. "That will be a day's work. I won't take it casually if the next coach asks me to 'sit my bony ass down,' if that's what you wanted me to say." The light drilled into the holes in his face. "Harry? Harry does his job better than I do this one. Who can change him? But he can't go on forever."

Morris searched his voice for malice. Without luck. He would have to know the man better to trust what he said.

"Is that all, Mister Morris?"

"You said you hadn't met either boy."

"Not really." He raised his chin higher. "I saw them at games. Twice this fall I visited our locker room after wins. It's an old tradition here. But you know that." Walker stood up, this time in dismissal.

Morris lingered. "I met your man Myers." Now Morris stood. "And I covet your Packard."

"Oh yes. Russell doesn't trust me to drive it myself. He put a lot of time in that car, restoring it."

"Let's see." Morris reopened his pad as if consulting notes to himself on the blank lines. "Myers went to football practice yesterday. Harry had him thrown out. Did you know Myers wanted to see practice?"

"I asked him to go."

Morris looked up in surprise.

"I'd seen one or two of Harry's early fall practices. They were rugged. Even bloody. But not brutal. I just wanted to be sure Harry hadn't . . ." He fumbled for the right expression.

"Gone around the bend," offered Morris.

"I don't think I want to read that in the morning newspaper," said Walker.

"No. Why did you send Myers? Is he an expert on brutality?"

"Russell played some ball in his time."

"What did he think of practice?" asked Morris.

"He was impressed. How tightly it was organized. How much got done. Before they threw him out." Walker smiled. "I only run the university. I don't expect to run Harry Carr's practices."

"What's the story on your man Myers? He doesn't look well."

"It's not a short story. Russell had a bad World War Two. I knew him in school. At Stanford. He dropped out. Had more than his share of troubles. I kept up with him."

"One of his troubles nerves?" asked Morris.

"I think it might have been the first three. But he's been better, more stable, for the last year, since he left the VA hospital and came to work for me. That's why I brought him to Georgia with me. He was doing so well. I'm sure Russell will go back to California when he thinks he's ready to be on his own. Anything else, Mister Morris?"

The way Walker said "Russell," he might have been his brother, thought Morris. "Yes, there is. I found a note two days ago in Trapwell's locker. Just a few cryptic words for him to 'check the time.' It was signed *Oberon*. The manager Henry Young told me yesterday he took the note on the telephone. He was killed several hours later. Do you know the word *Oberon*?"

"I suppose I should be embarrassed to admit it, but I never heard of the word. But the note . . . it doesn't sound like a coincidence. I'm sorry I can't help you."

Morris held onto his cane, avoiding the necessity of a handshake, and walked toward the door.

"Goodbye," said the President, closing the double doors on himself.

Morris stopped outside the main building to watch the squirrels and their quick, Charlie Chaplin takes. The great oaks drizzled leaves in the November wind. The clock chimed the quarter hour. The rain must have blown over to the east, thought Morris. There was a parking ticket on his rented Chevrolet. In the next parking slot was the black Packard. Empty. Myers was nowhere to be seen. Morris looked at his watch. Hadn't he said the President was driving to town in thirty minutes? Morris put the parking ticket under the seat. So, Harry "can't go on forever." Well, he has for thirty years. God knows what's kept him going. Football? Women? Harry made careers of them both. And yet, has he ever found what he's looking for? Who could know? Not even Johnny Moore could know, and if he does, thought Morris, he'll die knowing. The sun was high. It was nearly noon. Maybe Harry had shaken the press. The funeral for Trapwell was at two. And now there was another boy to be buried.

Morris slowed the car in front of the Athletic Center. Then stopped. He called Margaret Stewart from an outside office. She recognized his voice.

"You're looking for Harry?"

"Yes."

"He just finished with the writers and the police. Morris, it's awful. When is it going to stop?"

"Let's hope it has."

"You can catch him if you drive around back. Johnny is taking him home for a nap. Before the funeral. He's dreading the funeral. We all are."

"I know. Thanks."

Morris wheeled the Chevrolet into the back parking lot. Harry was getting in his car. Morris pulled alongside and rolled down his window.

Harry dragged his voice out of his chest like a heavy chain. "I'll tell you, same as I told her. Catch him. Catch him quick. Before I kill him."

Morris leaned out of his window. "Yesterday you didn't want to know who killed Trapwell."

"Yesterday I was stupid."

"*Two* murders changes your mind about something. What?"

"Everything." He threw his half-smoked cigaret on the asphalt. "I was wrong about everything. But nothin' happens in this town I can't run down. So you catch him. Or you won't have to." He leaned his long, heavy body into the front seat and closed the door without waiting for an answer.

Chapter Sixteen

Sullivan sat on her legs in the middle of the bed. Xeroxed pages floated around her as if she were holding paper maneuvers.

"What's this, the H.M.S. *Pinafore*?"

"Morris, where have you been?"

"Disturbing a President in his modest digs Howard Hughes

couldn't afford. And seeing Harry. I'm worried about Harry. What have you got?"

"The answer."

"I'll bite. To what question?"

"Oberon."

"You're serious?"

"Of course I'm serious."

"Tell me."

"In medieval folklore, Oberon was the King of the Fairies."

"You're kidding."

"No. That's oversimplified. The legend is a bit wordy." She indicated the pages. "But that's our boy, King of the Fairies."

Morris repeated the title. "What does it mean?"

Sullivan shook her head.

"Do you think it's a code name for some gay group? Or is that dumb macho prejudice?"

"Probably."

"Do you think some secret society? Or cult? Took Harvey Trapwell as a sacrifice?" asked Morris.

"It's possible. I don't believe it. Maybe I should say, I don't want to believe it. What do you think?"

"I think whoever used the name Oberon was a scholar."

"You're right. Or was close to someone who was. I looked up Trapwell's transcript. I traded on your credentials."

"I'm surprised you're not incarcerated," said Morris.

"He'd taken standard freshman English, three quarters. World history. American history. The rest, science and math. Nothing that would likely have covered fourteenth-century mythology."

"Professors have a way of working in their favorite subjects."

"I talked to his two history profs," said Sullivan.

"Damn if the AP won't hire you to replace me."

"Only one of them even knew the legend of Oberon. He's never taught it."

Morris smiled. "You don't think Trapwell picked it up in the huddle? Or maybe at practice, from the Hulk."

"No. I don't think he read it on the sports page either."

Morris threatened her paper ships with his cane. "How do we find out who left him the message?"

"We look at the people who knew him best. Maybe one of them is a closet historian."

"What did you find out about the other boy, Henry Young?" asked Morris.

"A physical education major. A senior. Barely making it. He was suspended once for cheating when he was a freshman. He 'busted' out of premed. He's been on academic probation as recently as this summer. His grades this fall have been marginal. I'm not supposed to know that. Students have the legal right to fail in the privacy of their own apartments. Oh yes. He was left-handed. I've seen his handwriting, his printing. He definitely took the note from Oberon. I'm surprised our Mister Young could *spell* Oberon, even with someone dictating it on the phone. Morris, why did you say you were worried about Harry?"

"Something's changed him. Something about the second murder. He won't say what. He did say we better catch who did it. Or *we won't have to*."

"You think he's serious?"

"God never made a more serious man than Harry Carr. Yesterday he was ready to forget who killed Trapwell. Now he's ready to play vigilante. Why? It doesn't make sense."

"The second murder changed Harry's mind as to why Trapwell was killed or who killed him," said Sullivan. "Why doesn't he just tell the police?"

"Maybe he's only guessing. But Harry hasn't made his living being wrong, about very much."

"I'm not so sure about that." She twisted her mouth in thought.

"Not you, too. What do you mean?"

"There must have been something in Trapwell's past that Harry wanted buried with him."

Sullivan's skirt rode appealingly above her knees on the bed.

"You better watch it, or we'll both miss lunch," said Morris.

"Is that a promise?"

Sullivan leaned her nose against the stained glass in the round room above the police station. The street was a fantasy of reds, a distortion of toy cars on an Oz-like street.

"Send my bag over, Morris. I always wanted to live inside a turret."

A tall, plain window gave a clear but somehow unsatisfactory view of downtown Sparta. The room itself was empty.

"We haven't decided what to put in here," said Lieutenant Blake.

"Put me," said Sullivan.

"Let's have our coffee on the back porch if it's not too chilly."

"The sun's out." Still Sullivan lingered, obviously hating to leave the tall, round room.

Morris followed them into what had been the kitchen and then onto the porch. Carrying the coffee, he felt as if he were home years ago in Atlanta, visiting his mother's two favorite aunts.

"So, what have you found out about the note?" asked Morris.

"Nothing that helps. Julia's right. Henry Young was left-handed. The note was in his handwriting. I did find the word again: *Oberon*." She offered the cream pitcher.

"Where?" asked Sullivan before Morris could speak.

"Trapwell wrote the word—actually, he drew it, shaded it with a pencil in the margin of his physics notebook. Just the word *Oberon*. Nothing else. He was in the class this quarter. I talked with his physics professor. He couldn't imagine what it meant. We went through all of Trapwell's notebooks. Piles of them. You would think he was a senior instead of a sophomore. I still don't know what *Oberon* means."

"Sullivan's the resident expert on the subject," said Morris.

She pulled the Xeroxed sheets out of her handbag and began quickly to explain the history of Oberon.

"Do we arrest all the historians?" said the Lieutenant.

"Absolutely," said Morris. Then, seriously: "It may be a code word for a group. I'm afraid to say 'for a cult.'"

"That's all we need, a cult murder." The Lieutenant shivered.

"Did you talk with Trapwell's parents?" asked Sullivan.

"His mother's dead. His father all but broke into the station, drunk—pitiful really, if he hadn't been so nasty. He was incoherent. He kept cursing Harry Carr. Saying that he had killed his son. Accusing us of covering it up. He was in no shape to drive home. Two of the men put him to bed. They said the inside of his house was a nightmare. I don't know how the old man will make the funeral this afternoon."

"I saw him Monday night at the banquet. Drunk and nasty," said Morris. "Speaking of Harry, he said today he was wrong about who killed Trapwell. Why has he changed his mind? Who *did* he think killed him?"

"I don't know," said the Lieutenant. "But he's threatening to kill whoever did it. Do you think Harry could do something . . . crazy?"

"I would hate to know he was looking for me. We better take him at his word and get there first. I don't know how you can protect him from himself."

"All we can do is try." The Lieutenant looked in her note pad. "I also questioned the PKA friend, Paul Teller, this afternoon. He told me essentially the same thing he told you."

"What did he say about Oberon? And did you ask him if he knew what Trapwell was wearing when he was killed?"

"About Oberon—our young man Teller frowned, lit a cigaret, and said he didn't know what it meant."

"Do you believe him?"

The Lieutenant swept her blonde hair out of her eyes like a little girl. "I don't know why, but I don't. He also swore Trapwell was wearing a suit when he left his room Sunday. And that he never returned. Teller 'didn't remember' a blue polo shirt. He'd never seen Trapwell wearing one. He *said*. By the way, the shirt had no laundry marks. It was new."

"Speaking of by-the-way," said Morris, "I asked the President if he knew his man Myers had gone to football practice yesterday."

"And . . ."

"He knew. He *asked* Myers to go. To be sure Harry hadn't gone bonkers, and wasn't running a concentration camp. Also, I was right: Myers is not a well man. He's a war casualty, recovering from his latest nervous breakdown."

"That just leaves everybody else in Georgia as a suspect." The Lieutenant made fists of her long fingers. "Including your friend Frank Caplin."

"You're the second person who's slandered me as being a friend of Caplin's." Morris lifted his cane to his lap. "What have you found out?"

"We did a routine check on long-distance telephone calls charged to Trapwell's room. Didn't expect to find a thing. The boy hardly spoke to anybody in Sparta. But he talked with

Frank Caplin the week before he was killed. On Wednesday. They talked for eleven minutes!"

"Caplin must have called him to do a column," said Morris. "Nothing unusual about that."

"If he wrote a column last week on Trapwell, he didn't publish it," said the Lieutenant. "Remember, the call was charged to Trapwell's phone. *He* placed it, not Caplin."

Morris leaned forward, resting his chin on his cane. "I see. Eleven minutes—that would be routine time for an interview. But a long telephone conversation just to chat. Nobody *chats* with Frank Caplin. What the hell could Trapwell have told him?"

"Maybe he had the same conversation with Caplin that he wanted with you," said Sullivan. "Don't ask me what that means."

"Possibly," said Morris. "Have you talked with Caplin?"

"No," said the Lieutenant. "But I intend to. After the funeral."

"I would love to be a spider on the wall when you do," said Morris.

"I'll tell you what he says when you get back from Knoxville."

Morris looked at his watch. "We better go. Graveside services start in thirty minutes."

"Thanks for the home tour and the coffee," said Sullivan after an unusual silence. "Join us later for dinner."

"I'll try," said the Lieutenant. "I'll call you." She collected their cups and saucers and backed inside with the tray in her hands.

Sullivan caught the screen door. "Now, what criminal has a chance against anything as civilized as midday coffee?"

Morris led the way to the car. "You drive," he said. "Are you going with me tomorrow to Knoxville?"

"No. I want to talk to as many of Trapwell's professors and classmates as I can. I'm afraid they won't remember much. The freshman classes are so large, and most of the sophomore classes. I want to visit his high-school teachers."

Morris put his wide hand over her shoulder. "Listen. You be careful. You know a lot. Someone has killed twice. Because of what two people knew."

"I promise, if you won't break my shoulder."

"Sorry." He patted her on the back.

"Morris. I hate funerals."

"I know." He helped her into the Buick.

Chapter Seventeen

The wall running the length of the old cemetery was evil with moss. Sullivan turned the car into the shadows under the huge oaks. Sinking into themselves at the entrance were the first graves, from the eighteenth century.

Cars were abandoned at odd angles along the patchwork of narrow roads; clutches of figures moved slowly under the trees. "We better park here," said Morris.

They sat, reluctant to step out into the quiet.

Sullivan took his arm. "I love cemeteries, but I still hate funerals."

"'He who dies this year is quit for the next.'"

She gripped his arm.

No one who passed them spoke.

When you bury the young, it's always in silence, thought Morris. He could remember the deaths of his great-aunts, and the greetings and soft laughter afterward among old friends, the end of a natural cycle of time. When the young die, there is nothing to be said.

Now the couples and groups became rivulets of people threading between the graves and the old, solitary trees. It was strange to see so many students. They seemed even younger against the iron fences and over-grand monuments abused by time.

Sullivan touched his hand. The tent was pitched over the ground, between headstones. People stopped in a wide circle so that all of them could see. The family had not yet taken their seats in the thin, single line of folding chairs under the green tent.

Sullivan touched his hand again. Morris turned. Behind him, the team was coming through the trees. The players wore their blazers that were now forbidden on road trips by the NCAA in its piety, so that no school might subvert an athlete with so much as a team jacket. Let them regulate death, thought Morris. The coaches walked in front, but you only saw Harry. His long legs moving without effort; the great bulk of him in the crumpled suit; his eyes not turning left or right; the weight of his presence dominating even the trees. Behind him the players moved with awkward strides, hurrying and slowing, boldly out of place in their silver blazers.

Morris could not see the hearse through the now-standing flood of people. But coming into the clearing were the pallbearers, all athletes, in their knight-like jackets, the casket riding between them weightlessly. The roommates, Mitchell and Crawford, moved at the front of the casket as if at the bow of a ship, gliding without effort toward the tent, which filled in the wind as if under sail. All of the players were huge and strong as life. The seriousness of their faces left them even younger and without guilt.

Then Morris saw the father. James Trapwell lifted his feet and lowered them as if he were walking in place. He was fat and unsteady. Morris could not imagine him as a young athlete, only thirty years ago. Men on either side of him—too detached to be family—steered him toward the tent as though he were to be sentenced. Only three of his kin seemed to be with him, all of them very old, two of them women in dark hats. Other, younger men helped them to their seats. The father could not bring himself to sit, still moving his legs up and down in the harsh blue of his obviously new suit.

Morris turned at the hand on his shoulder. It was Doc, who nodded to Sullivan.

"His daddy would strip naked if he knew Harry bought that suit he's wearing."

"The old man looks like death," said Morris.

"You shoulda seen him before I gave him two injections."

"Did you ever see him play?"

"Oh, yes. He was a halfback. He was hell."

"What happened to him?"

"Failure. He never finished school. Came back from the army a bum. Harry tried to help him. Trapwell never forgave him for trying to help, a sort of sick pride. He wanted Harvey to go to Notre Dame. Why, I don't know. The old man isn't Catholic. Hasn't been in a church in thirty years, that I know about, except ten years ago to bury his wife."

"Why did Harvey decide to stay here?"

"Harry. Harry can be a persuasive man, you know that. He seemed to reach the boy somehow, beyond football. Until last week. Harry makes a ass of hisself once a week, some way. You know that, too."

The young preacher was praying. There was no other sound except the wind, high in the huge, scattered trees. The sun fell behind a wide cloud and suddenly it was cool. Sullivan shivered against Morris' arm. The young voice of the preacher rose even more earnestly.

Harry Carr looked straight ahead, his long arms directly by his sides, his thick, graying hair lifting in the November wind. The silver sea of athletes behind him bowed as if in defeat.

Morris picked out the President, thick in his coat and vest, and his man Myers, both of them somehow taller than he remembered. Walker ignored the woman between them, small and silently ineffectual in her formally cut suit. Morris was sure that she was his wife. She looked up at her husband in the middle of the prayer as if she might be expected to do something. When the young preacher finished his prayer, Walker turned and whispered something to Myers, who eased back into the crowd toward the main gate. The small woman watched Myers until he was out of sight.

Lieutenant Blake and Sergeant Redding stood on the far side of the tent, he low and ridiculously round; she trim as an athlete. To the side of them, alone, was Frank Caplin, wisps of hair blowing over his narrow forehead. Caplin loved to write funeral scenes. Especially of people he despised. It would be tougher for him, writing about a kid. But at least he was murdered. That would give him something to go on. Then he could tell the Lieutenant why he had talked with Trapwell for eleven minutes the Wednesday before he was killed. Morris looked for, but had no way of identifying, a small, blond girl who had been Trapwell's high-school friend. There were hundreds of students, their clothes brightly out of place and somehow welcome. And then he saw Trapwell's friend, Teller, tall and flawless in his suit. He might have been the young preacher whose voice was now passionately reassuring them that it was "all part of a Divine plan." The young pallbearers stood as rigid as a firing squad. Morris was surprised to hear himself whisper, "'Is football playing, along the river shore, with lads to chase the leather, now I stand up no more?'" He turned on his cane, meeting Sullivan's eyes. He could see Doc chewing tobacco without spitting.

The preacher was finished. The crowd stood, as if in punctuation, then began breaking apart, still in silence. Morris could hear the wind over the sounds of their feet.

Chapter Eighteen

The sun was down behind the river; Morris could see the old iron bridge shining with false youth. The wind seemed to blow the dark over the town. It was cold enough to use the heater in the car. Sullivan sat nearly in his lap.

"Okay, but buckle your seat belt," said Morris.

"Spoilsport."

Morris found a gap and backed into the light, before-dinner traffic. "Where do you want to eat?"

"First let's drive through the school. I always enjoy the lights on a campus. Even if I remember how awful it was to be alone in the shadows."

"I've forgotten college," said Morris. "I think it all happened one day before the Air Force."

"If I had been there, you would remember it."

The driver ahead of them daydreamed through a green light.

Sullivan blew the horn with his cane. The car stuttered and moved ahead.

"What are you trying to do, get us arrested?"

"Not with a blonde lieutenant keeping the jail. It's dangerous enough, her joining us for dinner."

"You two seem like perfect friends."

"Yep. As long as she sticks to the criminal classes. I'll even let her have Harry Carr."

"What do you know about her and Harry?"

"Of course I knew the first time—Ooohhhh!"

Morris' own head slammed back into the headrest. The steering wheel spun in his hand; before he could catch it, there was another tremendous jolt to the rear of the car. The right-front wheel jumped the curb, a fender clipping an iron pole, but he managed to straddle the gutter and work the wheel back, not jerking it, onto the road—when the car leaped forward again in a terrible collision he couldn't understand.

"Morris!" His name seemed jarred from her lungs. "A TRUCK!"

His right foot was lost in the air . . . above the accelerator.

". . . Trying to KILL us . . ."

The Chevrolet slewed toward oncoming headlights . . . when Sullivan jammed his cane onto the accelerator, the car jumped forward without a collision, the only noise leaping under the hood. Morris felt the wheel wind back in his hands. He missed the headlights in an instant, the Chevrolet running away with itself now at the bottom of the steep hill past the stadium and gunning up the incline magically on its own. His right foot searched for the accelerator and kicked away the cane Sullivan had pressed to the floor.

His eyes looked for hers. His head rang. He couldn't speak.

"I'm . . . all right," she said in a thin voice he had never heard.

Morris kept the speed coming without looking back.

"You can slow up. He turned off."

"Who turned off?" Morris cut their speed, his hands slippery, the sweat running down his sides, his legs trembling.

"The truck . . . that hit us. Morris—" She was almost crying. "—it was *huge.*"

"You're okay? No whiplash?"

"My head was on your shoulder."

Morris lifted his right arm. For the first time he felt the pain in his bicep.

"Sorry about your pitching arm." Her old voice wavered in the dark.

He put the arm around her.

"Thanks for making me fasten my seat belt," she said.

"How did you hit the accelerator with the cane?"

"I must've missed it five times. You better count your feet."

"Somebody's driving drunk. We'll go by the police station and report it," Morris said.

"Not drunk." Sullivan was shaking inside his arm. "He . . . did it on purpose. He aimed it at us . . . the bumper. I could see it coming." She buried her head in his shoulder.

Morris drifted into the middle of the town.

Sullivan was still.

"You okay?"

He could feel her head nodding up and down.

Morris did not recognize the Lieutenant until she stepped off the curb. It was the first time he had seen her out of uniform. She looked younger, or maybe more vulnerable, in a khaki skirt and vest. Sullivan rolled down her window.

"You're late," said Lieutenant Blake.

Morris checked his watch. It was 7 P.M.

"Look at the back of our car." Sullivan's voice was its old, crisp self. "This used to be a Buick."

"Good Lord, did you park it on the railroad track?"

Morris opened his door. He got his balance and stepped around to look at the damage. "The 'good Lord' had some help. Sullivan hit the accelerator with my cane, or you would be going to the morgue instead of to dinner."

"What happened?"

"Someone tried to run us down from behind in a truck. About ten minutes ago. Coming down the hill on College Street, opposite the stadium. Nearly knocked us into the oncoming traffic. It could have been a day for a triple funeral."

"Could you see who was driving?"

"No. Its lights were too bright," said Sullivan. "It hit us three times. Then turned south. It was a large-bodied truck, like a moving van. White. It looked as big as a great white shark."

"I'll get out an all-points alert. You're sure it was white?"

"Yes. And I think it broke one of its headlights."

They went inside with the Lieutenant. A patrolman took a detailed account of the incident. Sullivan described the truck as if it were a large, animate object that had attacked them. It took two cups of coffee to settle her imagination.

Within an hour, Sergeant Redding hurried into the room. His high voice climbed an octave with excitement. "Found the truck. Off the Old Atlanta highway. One headlight smashed. Looks like it was stolen, all right. Somebody broke a window, then jumped it off."

"Whose truck?" asked the Lieutenant.

"Local moving company. Henderson's. We're trying to raise 'em."

"Anything left at the scene?"

"Don't know yet. We'll get a team out to work it over."

"One thing is sure," said Morris.

"What's that?"

"It was no accident. Let me borrow a phone to call Atlanta. What happened to us is worth a few paragraphs. It's a remote chance, but it could have been an accident. I'll give it to the bureau straight."

"Yes, and it could have been our imagination," said Sullivan. "Or maybe it was just a horny truck."

Morris shook his head and dialed Atlanta. He dictated three hundred words, then called the U-Drive-It agency at the Atlanta airport. He arranged to swap automobiles the next day in a detour to Knoxville.

"Why?" asked Lieutenant Blake. "Why did someone run you down?"

"Not to scare us. To kill us," said Morris. "Something we know bothers somebody. But what the hell do we know except the word *Oberon*? I wish we knew what Harvey Trapwell was going to tell me. Or what the kid Young was hiding."

"Sparta's a small town," said Sullivan. "Where does a double murderer hide?"

"I'll have to skip dinner," said Lieutenant Blake. "If anything turns up, I'll call."

"Could you do us a favor?" asked Morris.

She brushed her hair out of her eyes.

"I'm going to Knoxville tomorrow. I won't be back until

Sunday. I'd rather not leave Honest-Julia-Sullivan here by herself. Some criminal's life might be imperiled."

Sullivan rolled her long fingers into a tight fist.

"She can stay with me." The Lieutenant balled up her own fist. "We'll start a vigilante group."

"Or have a slumber party," said Sullivan.

"I'll drop her here at the station. Tomorrow morning. She wants to visit with Trapwell's college professors. Maybe a few of his high-school teachers."

"Good. I'll help you with a list of their names. Morris? You'll see Harry . . ." She left the question hanging.

"Yes. Somewhere. At least after the game Saturday. He wouldn't know his mother before the game."

Blake's head moved forward as if she were going to say "I know," but she did not speak.

"We're off then . . . to dinner," said Sullivan. "And I'll eat it even if it's called 'supper.'"

Chapter Nineteen

Atlanta behind him, Morris began tracing a life source of two-man, 500-watt stations on the radio. Between country songs, the announcers sold gospel records and cut-rate tires. Morris began to look for the first mountains. He could remember the same drive years ago when it had been snowing and it was like two trips. An old mule, brown in his winter coat, dominated the town of Fairmont. He had perfect dignity and did not move at all, except for the shaggy ends of his winter coat, which riffled under his old belly in the cool wind. A chicken-wire fence collapsed on broken, impromptu stakes around his one-quarter acre. A ruined poster of *The Return of Frank James* was still playing after two decades at the abandoned, unclean picture show. It was a mean, past-tense town in North Georgia.

The foothills grew higher and more rugged after Murray County, but you couldn't call them mountains until you got through Chatsworth. Morris remembered a deputy sheriff there from his first trip. He had a prevention for almost every speed until you were ten miles above Chatsworth. After that, there was no doubting they were really mountains. They were always on your right, at heights which were important if you had grown up in Atlanta. Just outside Conasuage, Tennessee, past an absolutely flat schoolhouse, was tethered an old stag of a mountain, dark with November trees; then there was suddenly bright, open sky, as if the mountain were the last of a species. Morris remembered the hill beyond Old Fort, and kicked the car up to eighty. The hood fell terrifically down to the Ocoee River. The horizon was suddenly ajar and tilted forty-five degrees to the east. It was as if he had come on an earthquake. The mountains here were close to the road, and like great animals asleep. You could not see the lake behind the mountains, only the river coming between them. The year it had snowed, the river had been a running, jagged fault in the everywhere white. The earth continued to erect itself with great efforts of rocks and trees. Then the brown mountains ran out to the east. They were blue in the distance. When you got as far as Benton in Tennessee, they earned the name *Smoky Mountains*. Morris was sorry to remember that the snow had not been pretty on the mountains. They were so grown over with trees, leafless in winter, that the white under the millions of dark, bare limbs looked like a remedy on the hide of an old dog. It had been so all the way into Tennessee. The snow had been especially beautiful in other places as though to make up for its poor showing in the mountains.

If your team lost, thought Morris, you still had the trip to Knoxville.

Morris was pleased that the old Andrew Johnson Hotel was still open. Even if they had redecorated and built a swimming pool. A tall, wasted man, who was not that old, registered him without seeing him. Cheap paint and a thin carpet could not resurrect the ugly, square lobby. Morris was pleased the hotel seemed as shabby as he remembered it. Pockets of football fans gathered in the uneven light. A voice shouted, "Go Vols," but without enthusiasm. The high rollers now stayed up the hill at the new Aztec Hotel, which was built on its side like a Mayan temple.

Morris sent his bags to his room. He went out the main entrance of the hotel and turned left onto the high, dirty concrete bridge. He walked halfway across and spat into the Tennessee River. It was too windy to count the seconds before it hit. There was nothing else that could be done legally in Knoxville.

They drink. Thank God they don't sing. In the South they don't. They do in the East. They drink and they sing too, in the East. They only sing at fraternity houses in the South. Not at parties and never at bars. They only cheer when the piano player plays the alma mater. Thank God for that. We're too shy to sing in the South. We only sing individually, thought Morris. But when you can't sing individually, it's too late. Nobody ever sings the National Anthem. Except at Tiger Stadium in Baton Rouge. It's all right to hum. They always skip the third verse in the Methodist Church. Or the fourth and fifth verses if there is a sixth verse. Thank God for that. The Episcopal Church never skips any verse. We have resolution. Methodists only know we kneel. And that we drink anywhere. They don't suspect we never skip a verse. You cannot buy a drink in Knoxville. You have to bring your own bottle. If you register at the hotel, or if they know you, you can pay and they call it your bottle. Thank God for that, too. They have three bartenders. All women. But you can't have everything. Women bartenders are the hardest women in the world. They are hard on all girls who wait on tables. No man can wait on tables for women bartenders. It can't be done. You can get drunk the same. But you cannot enjoy it. You know they will call the police. They always call the police. They let you pay. Then they call the police. He heard they did. He never saw them do it. All the husbands are too heavy. In the South. Everything's different in the Southwest and in the East. He had never seen it in the West. He bet it was different in the West, too. All the husbands who have season tickets who can pay the hotel bills are too heavy. They have always been successes. Their fathers were successes. And their grandfathers. He did not know about their great grandfathers. Thank God for that. Some of them are bankrupt. Or have been. Or will be. But they are successes. It's a state of mind. American men are aging. He looked in the mirror. The light was bad. The gray did not show in his hair. Their wives were also successes. They carried themselves as successes. As all women who have looks carry themselves. Or who had them. They were too heavy, but nicely. When they drank, their faces would shine. Beside them, the young girls, thin, looked like manikins. The wives did not know it. Their husbands did not know it either. It was too bad. Morris felt a hand on his back, and someone sat down next to him. No one noticed in the near-dark.

"Got a bottle? I'll have a ... bourbon and glass," the man said.

"Are you registered in the hotel?" As it gets later, the voice of a woman bartender gets harder.

"I'm ... Secretary of the Interior," he said.

"You have to bring your own bottle here." She was throwing glasses under the faucet.

"What if I were jokin'? ... if I were Secretary ... Health, Education, Welfare?"

"Register in the hotel or bring your own bottle." She wouldn't stop or look at him.

"All women belong in their taxicabs. Why can't women stay home in their taxicabs?"

"The door is over there." She slapped down the washrag.

"It's all right," Morris said. "I have a bottle ... I'm registered ... Give the man ... a drink."

"He was also honorary pallbearer ... to Robert R. Neyland," said Harry Carr.

"It's true," Morris said, "but I remember it was you who was."

"You couldn't beat him. And you couldn't outdrink him. The only thing you could do was live after him. What kind of man is that?"

"Harry, what the hell are you doing in here? Tomorrow's Saturday."

"It's okay. The General's not alive. Don't forget. I was ... honorary pallbearer."

"Somebody'll recognize you. They'll raise hell if you lose."

"They'll raise hell if I tie ... if I spend the night on my knees."

"Whatever you do, Harry, don't trust the new President."

"That candyass."

Morris was still drunk. It was the only time he had ever called him Harry. He was enjoying it. "If they see you here, Harry, the new President would love to hear it."

"That candyass."

Suddenly, Morris was not drunk anymore. "Don't put your head on the bar," he said. Harry propped his hand under his chin; he smiled. Morris pushed himself on his feet with his cane and looked around the bar. There was nobody he knew. But there was a lieutenant colonel in the Air Force. Morris was lucky. The colonel understood immediately. He was also strong. Both of them helped Harry through a side door into the corridor and onto an elevator. Morris had the key to his own room in his pocket. They laid Harry out on one of the beds. He was already asleep in his clothes.

"Is he like this much?" asked the colonel, who recognized him.

"No. Not really," said Morris, who wasn't sure.

"I won five hundred dollars after the war," said the colonel. "I was in Berlin. I bet on him in the Rose Bowl."

"I remember the game. Against Stanford." Morris had listened to it driving around Atlanta with an older buddy who had his first jalopy, a 1937 Ford.

"Do you think he'll win tomorrow?"

"Yes. But I wouldn't bet on it. He lost his quarterback."

"Are you traveling with him?"

"I'm here covering the game. For Associated Press."

"I wish I could stay and see it," said the colonel.

The colonel was all right. He left to go back down to the bar.

Morris woke in the middle of a sound. He turned on a light. It was 4 A.M. Harry Carr was struggling to get up. When he saw Morris, he lay back on the bed. His shirt was violently open, with two buttons off at the throat. His left arm lay along the bed and his tie was on the floor under his right hand. His face was running with sweat; his hair was limp with it; the pillow around his head was dampened into a crude cameo. Harry raised his right knee, then straightened it against the bed.

He pointed to his jacket on a chair and struggled for his breath, making no attempt to speak.

Morris picked up the coat. There was nothing in the outside pockets. In the right breast pocket was a clear plastic vial. He had difficulty shaking out one small colorless tablet. Morris' mother had carried them for years. Harry did not have to tell him the nitroglycerine tablet went under his tongue.

Now Harry was running with perspiration. He raised his right knee continually and let it straighten against the bed.

"I'll call Doc Haywood," said Morris.

Harry grabbed his arm with unexpected quickness, and shook his head.

Morris wavered, then sat down. Harry's breathing began to ease. When he spoke, his voice was a bare whisper. "Dyin' drunk won't be nothin' new.... My old man died drunk and cryin'. That's all he could do, drink and cry ... the poor son-ofabitch. Momma could milk cows ... work us boys on the sorry land that wadn't ours ... churn butter at night to sell off the wagon like we wuz gypsies." He got his breath. "Shit. I couldn't run a hundred yards in a hour. But who was gonna whip my ass? I got to Ole Miss; I'da killed God to stay. I wasn't goin' back to the dirt. I still ain't. That's why I love the nigger players." He was breathing easily. "You cain't make 'em quit. Whadda they got at home? A slap screen door and newspaper on the walls. Goddamn, they'll die in the ground to stay. Same as me." He propped a pillow under his head. "Momma didn't die cryin', I can tell you that. She died in a hundred-thousand-dollar house outside Tupelo, Mississippi. You know what a hundred-thousand-dollar house woulda looked like to us in nineteen twenty-two? Woulda looked like the First Baptist Church of Atlanta. She died churnin' butter in the kitchen ... nineteen sixty-seven ... with a cook there.... But that's all right. She didn't know ... how to rest.... Just gave the butter away—"

"Harry, what the hell do you know about the murder of Trapwell?"

"Nobody can help him ... or the sonofabitch that killed him."

"Do you know why he was killed?"

"Thought I did. I was wrong."

"You were wrong because someone also killed the manager Henry Young?"

"Yeah . . . little turd . . . didn't know what he was mixed up in."

"Harry. If you can even guess who might have killed them, you had better tell the police."

"Tell 'em? I'll fix the . . ." His voice trailed off into sleep.

Morris, dizzy again with Scotch, slowly nodded into the chair. Then slept himself.

"What we need is the most important drink, the first one." Harry was up.

Morris could not bend out of the chair or find his cane through his headache.

Harry shed his clothes, pouring himself a straight Scotch from the bottle in Morris' open suitcase. He disappeared into the bathroom. The shower hit against the old-fashioned tub in an indefatigable hiss.

Harry came out wrapped in a towel, holding his empty glass. His skin sagged, but he still had the definition in his shoulders of a younger man. His silver hair was thick with false health.

Morris could not believe he was in the room with the same man. "Are you okay?" He did not offer to pour another Scotch.

Morris did offer a clean shirt. It swallowed even Harry's wide shoulders.

"If you hadn't learned to read and write, you mighta made somebody a middle guard." Harry picked a tie out of the suitcase.

"Can I drop you somewhere?" asked Morris.

"Yeah. The Aztec. How come you're stayin' in this dump?"

"It's closer to the bar," said Morris, digging out his razor.

"You got somethin' there." Harry laughed. He took the razor and whistled tunelessly while he shaved.

Morris wondered how long he had needed the nitroglycerine, and if the young coach with the look of a hawk in his face was awake at home in Knoxville.

Chapter Twenty

The stadium had 82,000 seats in a classical steel-and-concrete horseshoe. It curled against itself, fortresslike, in a long S bend in the river, as if abandoned in some other, more violent, time.

Tennessee had not won a national football championship since General Robert R. Neyland was buried. There had been certain outstanding teams. But there had been a long, careful glide into oblivion. Still, today they would need all 82,000 seats. The new Tennessee coach insisted on his hands and knees he could not produce a miracle. But that is exactly what they came to see raised up on Shields-Watkins Field in Neyland Stadium, a miracle.

You'll need one, thought Morris; wait'll you see the Hulk; he could tackle a miracle. Maybe he could have tackled the new Tennessee coach himself when he was a player here twenty years ago. And maybe not. What a thin, sudden thing he had been, the last of the great Single Wing tailbacks, his long, easy stride hardly settling on the grass, then gone insane with knees and legs, cutting the air unbreathable as he passed. Morris set his typewriter on the field and regretted the artificial perfection of the turf. He turned back under the stadium. It was a ritual he had not forgotten since his first game here twenty-five years ago. He always stopped by to see the photographs on the wall under the stadium. Morris lifted his typewriter and started up the tunnel under the still-empty seats. He stopped outside the athletic department offices. The framed, black-and-white photographs held time on the walls. They had not yet developed the photographic cliché in 1929, the year of Neyland's third great team, and Bobby Dodd, with his massive arms hanging immediately down from his leather-thin pads, and with his patchwork jersey shrunk against his trunk, was standing there like three cylinders. The General could not discipline the animation in his face. He also allowed Dodd to pass, even from behind his own goal line, when he preferred not to pass at all. Dodd did not have a pass intercepted in two seasons. In three seasons, he lost one game. Morris looked for the great end, Paul Hugg. Tennessee had taken his high-school teammate, Dodd, to get Hugg. But there was no picture of him. There was a photograph of halfback Gene McEver running directly ahead with his toes pointing at ten o'clock and two o'clock as he led with his insteps. He was never caught from behind until he ruined a knee sliding in a baseball game in the summer of 1927. Morris could not believe the photographs. There was Herman Hickman. Neyland despised a big man, but Hickman could outrun the 1931 team, except for halfback Beattie Feathers, so Neyland compromised his 225 pounds on the program roster to a more reasonable 206. Feathers was punting in a game with his square helmet down over his eyes and with a calf the circumference of a thigh raised over his head. Tennessee did not lose a game, or tie one, in 1938, 1939, 1940. The team was unscored on in 1939. The war came, so that the Major could become the General, or Tennessee might not have lost again for three more years. No wonder General Neyland would be photographed with his hands in the pockets of his jacket, looking very grim. Morris thought it was too bad they began to pose the players after 1947. They no longer only stood for the camera. They were put in artificial postures so that you could not understand them from their photographs. Wyatt, Suffridge, Cafego, Molinski, Shires, Foxx: Morris could not turn away from the pictures, but they were posed, and he could not guess anything from them, either. After the war, too many all-America teams were selected to have the same meaning. There were occasional great players at Tennessee until 1952, and again in 1956—the senior year of the new coach—but there were photographs of many players that should not have been included on the walls after 1952. They were all posed, wearing plastic Riddell helmets.

The stadium was beginning to fill. There was no wind, but when you moved, you could feel the air cool against you. The sun was high, and it was formidable if you looked directly at it, but it was as if all that light were trapped in a great mirror, brilliant, but leaving the air perpetually cool. Morris took the elevator to the press box.

The A&M players drifted in a silver line onto the field for their warmups. The noise of the fans threatened the wooden end-zone bleachers. Harry himself walked and smoked; now he was leaning against a goalpost as if waiting alone for a bus out of the past. The A&M players rolled their helmets, like silver specters, along the west sideline. There was a deliberate casualness in their manner, in the way they split up into groups for light exercises, in the effortless snaps from the center to the punter, who lifted the ball free in the air; in the way the assistant coaches strolled among the groups of players like proud owners.

Morris did not have to look to know the Tennessee players had taken the field. When the noise stopped, the absence of it was physically in the air.

"Morris. Can I talk with you?" It was Frank Caplin. His thin face was white as paper.

"Speak," said Morris, resting his typewriter on the next seat.

"I've . . . got a problem." It was odd to see Caplin so vulnerable. He alternately dug into the backs of his hands with his fingers. "Lieutenant Blake called me down to the station yesterday after the funeral. The police checked Harvey Trapwell's telephone charges. They showed an eleven-minute call to *me* last Wednesday. I *swear* I never talked to the boy."

"Was it a person-to-person call?" asked Morris.

"That's the hell of it. It was. But, goddamn, Morris, you know how my phone rings. We have five lines in the sports department. Half the time I'm talking to somebody on one line, and somebody else is waiting on another. All I can think is, the long-distance operator asked, 'Is this Frank Caplin?' I said, 'Yeah, wait a minute,' and put the call on hold. When I went back to that line, he must have hung up."

"You remember all that?"

"Hell, no. It happens every day. Somebody wants to tell me what he thinks of my last column, or wants tickets to the fucking Falcons, or wants to tell me some fact he thinks I don't know. I talk to anybody. I learn a lot that way. You know me, Morris. You worked with me long enough."

Morris laughed. Nobody in the sports department ever worked *with* Frank Caplin. It was *for* him, *under* him, that you did your work, and he never let you forget it. Morris knew the phones did stay tied up, the great unwashed public waiting to talk to the powerful Mr. Caplin. Morris did not offer him any relief. "Do you remember keeping somebody on hold Wednesday for *eleven* minutes?"

"No. I mean, I don't remember any exact call. I get dozens of them. Every day. That's what had to happen, or the phone company made a mistake. I hadn't talked to the kid Trapwell since I did a column on him last spring. He was a bore when he didn't have the ball. He had nothing to say."

"He certainly doesn't now," said Morris.

"Listen." Caplin was desperate. "You know the Lieutenant. You know how my phone rings. Tell her it could have happened: the boy could have just been left on hold. I would sure as hell have talked with him if I had known who was on the line. The quarterback of an unbeaten team has something to tell me, I'll listen, even if he is a bore. You know that."

"I think you had better try and make a list of everybody you talked with on Wednesday. The eleven-minute conversation might come to you. That's long, even for one of your conversations."

"I've tried. My mind is a fucking blank."

"*That* is hard to believe of Frank Caplin, the man who never forgets anything. Weren't you convinced? Aren't you convinced this A&M team has a drug problem? Is that what Trapwell wanted to talk about, do you think?"

"I *know* drugs are missing and unaccounted for," said Caplin. "I don't know why the boy called, *if* he called. Morris, just tell the Lieutenant the way my phone rings. It's awkward for me. I was in Sparta at the banquet the night Trapwell was killed. I was home alone in Atlanta the day the manager was killed. You know me: when I'm not working, I'm a loner. I didn't drink with anybody, eat with anybody. It looks awkward for me."

"You're right," said Morris. He could not help but feel a pull of compassion for the fear in Caplin's face. But he did not trust anything about Caplin, including his fear. "I can testify that your phone rings constantly. But I would work on that list of people I talked with last Wednesday. I'm betting you'll remember."

Caplin put his hand out as if to hold him there, but Morris moved toward his own seat.

The stadium was filled. Even if you were not making any of the noise, it was difficult to get your breath. It was as if the air had been scarred permanently. Tennessee's students had prepared a chant for Harry. They spelled aloud: B-a-r-b-a-r-i-a-n. They had a boy and a girl dressed as skid-row bums carrying whiskey bottles; and five little bums with whiskey bottles. They were all clever and could dance. Morris swung his field glasses on Harry Carr. He was furious. He stood with his arms folded and his jaw anchored in a rage.

The Tennessee students stood up in a practiced detonation, unfurling a fifty-yard-long white streamer with orange letters: BARBARIAN . Everybody was laughing, as if it were an Alec Guinness comedy. It was strange, hearing it in a stadium.

Harry walked out in front of his team, which was suddenly gathered in a circle, jerking its hands and arms to its helmets in a spasm of quickness drills, grunting HUT-HUT, HUT-HUT like a great beast.

The teams retreated to their dressing rooms before the kick-off.

The captains came out like knights for the coin toss. Harry sent only Jack Mitchell to the center of the field. All of the Tennessee seniors were waiting there in a row. Four stepped forward; their carriage and their shaking of hands with Mitchell with the solemnity of distant connections, before or after the wedding, betrayed them as unequals. Mitchell, with his hands directly at his sides, won the toss. He took the ball. And jogged casually back to the bench through the roar.

Tennessee teed the ball up to kick it. Typewriters in a row stood-and-said and stood-and-said like nervous auctioneers. The screens of the electronic Tele-Rams filled with silent, yellow words hurrying into print.

Neither team scored in the first quarter. It was a synthetic equality. Twice, Georgia A&M had first down as near as the Tennessee thirty-yard line. The first time, the new quarterback was late breaking off his fake and was behind the halfback with his pitch. The second time, a pass was thrown short and another was dropped. A field-goal attempt was short. A&M

held, and Harry tried a second quarterback. He could not make ten yards consecutively.

The quarter ended without Tennessee crossing the fifty-yard line.

Morris made notes to himself for his series on Harry, which had long since turned into an exploration of murder. The Knoxville bureau was covering the game. The burden of proof swung to Harry. As it had for thirty years.

The teams changed direction for the second quarter. Harry had his offense out in a double tight-end formation from its own twenty-yard line, with only the flanker split to the outside. The snap came off without a count directly between the spread legs of the quarterback to the halfback, who took one step backward with his right foot and swung it forward, sending a low, tumbling, end-over-end quick-kick that Tennessee had not anticipated. The ball hit, and seemed to accelerate along the artificial turf. The silver defense raced behind and ahead and among the frantic Tennessee retreat. Only the safetyman had as much as a step on the nearest silver shirt; he feared the geometry of the driven ball and allowed it to die of its own weight at the Tennessee five-yard line. Eight silver players leaned and heaved at the air above the ball until the field judge, caught equally by surprise, struggled up to blow the play dead.

Tennessee called for a dive play, and the sound at the end of it was final. The Hulk, Crawford, hit *through* the runner, driving the ball ten feet into the air. It came down under a flood of quicksilver in the end zone. The Tennessee runner did not move.

Harry stood huge in his topcoat, as if he had silenced the eighty thousands with an act of will. Through his binoculars, Morris saw the young coach opposite Harry, snatching at orange jerseys and grabbing shocked players by their face masks, screaming at them as if to shout hope back into the air.

Down seven points, Tennessee could not run the ball. Or protect the passer to throw it. The only weapon left was a punt, a good one. The greed to win in the stands now turned to rage. To hate. To *kill* the runner with the ball.

Harry did not move. He nodded in a play without unfolding his arms. The offensive line rose up as one beast and shivered the defenders. The fullback Godfrey, with legs like twin bodies, folded himself over the ball. He might have slammed into the crowd, the gasp it gave. Godfrey—all knees and thighs and lowered helmet—stomped for nineteen yards until they dragged him down. Harry gave them Godfrey again. And again. And then *seven more times*. Now you could hear the fury of the lines of scrimmage and the awful weight of Godfrey thudding against the smaller sidebacks. Even the young hawk of a Tennessee coach stopped his grabbing and screaming to watch the fine art of brutality set against his team. The crowd swallowed its noise for good and learned again the taste of defeat that Harry had taught them for a generation.

Morris drank a beer at the half. He did not watch the bands playing for their own amusement.

The teams were back on the field for the kickoff before Harry, walking stiffly, deliberately, reached the middle of the sidelines. After the kickoff, he gave them Godfrey six lethal times in a row. Morris could see the new blood on the players' faces and down their shins. And then the tall A&M quarterback faked the ball to Godfrey and passed to a wide receiver so open he bobbled the ball twice for fear of dropping it, but held on to cross the goal line alone by ten yards.

Morris opened another beer and folded away his notes. Punctuating the rest of the game were round pockets of sound from the few visiting A&M fans, delirious to rub another defeat into an old rival.

Morris watched the stadium begin to empty only minutes into the last quarter: entire rows of fans leaving trails of paper programs. The young Tennessee coach was again on fire. Morris could imagine his voice ruined in his throat. Harry stood without turning his head, never unfolding his arms.

The dressing room was a sound of random water driving itself into steam. The singing was over. Players had dressed. Managers had packed their gear. Only Harry stood in the room, a carnage of wet towels and ruined tape and bloody bandages. No one had thought to turn off the showers.

Harry smoked, leaning against the wall. "Listen to it. Goddammit, did you hear it? We drove their asses down!"

Morris was careful not to speak.

"First time we ever came here, thirty years ago, all I could smell was my own *fear*." Harry threw his cigaret on the concrete floor. "Now. I smell it on them. On their players. I smell it in the goddamn stadium. Well . . . they can *rot* in it."

Harry looked up as if Morris had just stepped into the room. "I should have known if anybody was gonna get himself killed, it would be that little bastard."

"You mean Henry Young?"

Harry ignored him.

"Why do you say that?"

"The company a man keeps can kill him."

"What do you mean?" asked Morris.

Harry ignored him.

"Why did you keep Young as manager?" asked Morris. "You must have known he'd been in trouble for cheating in class."

"Damn right I knew," said Harry. "Anything happens in this town I need to know, I know it. He was a nasty little kid. A good manager. Most of the players sell their own game tickets. Morris, you're a big boy. You know that. The NCAA knows that. It just won't admit it. *Every* college player in the country sells his extra tickets for all he can get. Or he gets somebody to sell 'em for him. Young could do it. Little bastard had larceny in his soul. He got top dollar. Kept ten percent. Knew better than to cheat on my boys. They'd break him in two pieces. Going rate at home is a hundred bucks a pair. Little bastard sometimes could double that for the Tech game. That's why I kept him."

"You tell the police that?" asked Morris.

"Hell no, I didn't tell the police that. All the NCAA needs is to read that in the paper. Then they'll jump down here like they didn't know every jock in college makes his car payments with ticket money. Nobody killed him for a thousand dollars' worth of tickets."

"Maybe somebody 'broke him in two pieces' for holding back on his sales."

"Bullshit," said Harry.

"You better tell the Lieutenant," said Morris.

"Bullshit. If it comes to that, you tell her. Our boy wasn't killed for ticket money. He met one hotshot too many, our boy did." Harry spat on the wet concrete. "One too many."

"Harry. Who killed the two kids?" Morris looked directly into Harry's dark eyes.

"One idea is *possible* . The other is *impossible*." Harry spat again. "In this business I'm in, you better believe the *impossible*."

"You believe one of two people killed him?"

Harry looked straight back into Morris' eyes. "You're the fucking reporter. Who wasn't in here?"

Morris had no idea whom he meant. Winning dressing rooms became madhouses of players and writers and—when Harry was in the mood, like today—relatives, and in the outer room, even girl friends.

"If you know something, if you suspect someone, you better tell the police," said Morris. "Somebody has killed twice already. And tried to kill Sullivan and myself."

Harry stepped on his cigaret. "Tried to what?"

"Tried to run us down in a truck. Opposite the stadium."

"The sonofabitch will get exactly what's coming to him. One of them will. Or both of them. I can't prove a goddamn thing, Morris. But maybe they don't know that."

"Harry."

Harry wasn't listening. He was lighting another cigaret. "We drove their asses down," he said.

Chapter Twenty-One

Morris welcomed the dark on the drive back. The absence of noise, the cold air whistling after him.

The lights of Sparta were all but out when he crossed the river. It was not yet midnight. Fraternity row, he knew, would just be coming alive. He steered through the empty downtown. The Georgian Hotel sagged on its wooden foundation like an old homeplace.

A folded message shook in the hand of the night clerk. "A note for you, Mister Morris."

He unfolded it: *Check Back Porch* . It was signed *Oberon*.

Morris forgot the weight of his fatigue. The note was printed, but the handwriting was unmistakable. He asked the way to the back porch. The old clerk pointed him toward the kitchen. "It's closed," he warned. "It's all closed."

Morris made his way through the dining room, between the empty tables, his cane tapping a steady code on the wooden floor.

The clerk was wrong. The door to the kitchen was unlocked. He pushed inside. It was empty and old fashioned and surprisingly clean. A cylinder of coffee stood beside a huge triple sink that looked to be marble. Morris poured himself a cup, making the only sound in the room. He carried it to the back of the kitchen. The first door he tried led into a storage room. He heard what could have been a quiet laugh. The second door opened onto a wide, screened porch.

". . . trust anyone except a journalist—I think I hear one . . ."

Morris closed the door behind him. He could see two profiles. "What is this, *Little Women*?"

"Saved you a blanket and a chair." Sullivan stood up to guide him. "You found the coffee. The Lieutenant and I kept crime under control. Of course, some of our greatest threats were out of town."

"How did you know I would drive back tonight?"

"I wrote another note for tomorrow. We were going to be on the roof."

"It's freezing out here."

"I know. Drink your coffee."

"So the team won," said the Lieutenant, her voice softer in the dark than he remembered.

"Same old Harry. It wasn't a victory. It was a massacre."

"You did . . . see him."

Somehow, Morris could not imagine the two of them together. But then it was always difficult for a man to imagine a woman with any man other than himself. "Oh yes. We had a drink Friday night. He was in rare form." Morris couldn't keep the curiosity out of his voice. "Now what's this message signed . . . *Oberon*?"

"Julia found it. She may be our next chief of police."

"Found what?" Morris sloshed coffee over the sides of his cup.

"An advertisement. From Oberon himself." Julia thumped her purse.

"Sullivan. Have you read the famous Back-Porch Murders?"

"No."

"They are about to be written. What the hell did you find?" She was all seriousness. "I kept looking at the note you took from Trapwell's locker. It didn't make sense: CHECK THE TIME . . . OBERON. What *time*? Then I realized the word *time* ran right to the end of the scrap of paper, with *Oberon* written under it. Maybe the manager Henry Young just ran off the page onto the wall with his pencil, without realizing it. He must have been holding the phone and writing at the same time. He could have run over an entire word, but I thought he would have caught that. Maybe just a letter."

Morris leaned forward in the dark.

"So, what letter was missing? I tried the whole alphabet. 'S' fit. Perfectly. It wasn't the 'time.' It was the *Times*. It threw us that all of his letters were hurried block capitals, like a child would make. The word didn't look incomplete."

"*The Sparta Times*," said Morris, welcoming the hot coffee against the cold night air.

"Yes. Sharon took me to the *Times* office. It's wonderful. Like something out of Dickens. All dark and musty and papers everywhere. Henry Young told you he couldn't remember if he took the message this past week or the week before or when. I got a copy of each issue of the *Times* for the last month. It was a helluva job. The old man there, a Mister Perkins—he has a solid white beard like Moses—doesn't keep a record of anything. It's unbelievable. I found it, Morris. In the Personals. In *this* Tuesday's paper."

"The day *after* he was killed," said Morris, who found himself standing in the dark.

"Yes." Sullivan unfolded a newspaper page from her purse.

Lieutenant Blake switched on her flashlight. Morris bent down as Sullivan read: "All's well. Home again. After eight. Oberon." She sat back with all the modesty of Margot Fonteyn waiting for thunderous applause.

"When was the ad placed?" asked Morris.

"It was called in Monday. By a man," said Lieutenant Blake.

"His credit's good. He has called in notices before. All signed 'Oberon.' He always mails the payment . . . in cash."

"If this message was for Trapwell, in Tuesday's paper, Oberon couldn't have known he would be killed Monday night." Morris might have been talking to himself.

"Or didn't guess that *he himself* would kill him," said Sullivan.

"What does it mean, 'All's well . . . after eight?'"

"It sounds like a rendezvous," said Sullivan. "Maybe Oberon had been out of town."

"Oberon calls the Athletic Center," said Morris, "so that Trapwell would be sure to look in the Personals. Why? Why all the secrecy? If he could call, why wouldn't they just talk?" Morris folded the paper. "Who *is* he? Oberon."

"I don't know," said Sullivan. "But I worked my way through the history department, asking for their reactions to the word *Oberon*. One of the professors recently brought out a book with a prestigious Canadian publisher. In Ottawa. The firm's name is *Oberon*. The professor said when the editors announced the formation of Oberon Press, they received an enormous number of gay manuscripts. They were puzzled at first as to why."

"Oberon, 'King of the Fairies,'" said Morris.

"Yes. The story's gotten around the faculty. Nothing travels faster 'underground' than word of mouth," said the Lieutenant. "Certainly not in a college town."

"How do we trace him?" asked Morris.

"If he calls the newspaper again, the telephone company is set up to trace him automatically. It's not likely he would."

"We could place an ad," said Sullivan.

"Sure. 'Wanted. Medieval killer. Alias, Oberon.' It is not a bad idea," said Morris. "If Oberon didn't kill him, he must be sweating the investigation. We've asked everybody in town what the word means. He could be a lover. Nobody has said a damn thing about Trapwell's being gay. Not even Harry. Harry's called him a 'pretty boy.' But I thought he was talking about his nose. If he was gay, Harry knew it. I'd bet on it. I wonder if that's what he meant when he first said it would be better if the reason Trapwell was killed was buried with him?"

"We go back around to everybody who knew him," said the Lieutenant, "and we ask until we find out."

"Something I need to tell you," said Morris. "Harry said I

could, but he will strangle me anyhow. The manager Young sold many of the players' extra tickets to the games. He got a hundred dollars a pair, and more. Kept ten percent off the top. He was a hustler. Kept the boys in spending money. That was why Harry kept him on as manager."

"I'll have to talk to Harry."

"Do that. But don't release it to the papers until—unless you have to. All the schools do it. But it will get Harry in deep trouble with the NCAA, which is nothing compared to murder. But Harry insists Young wasn't killed over the ticket money. He said Young 'met one hotshot too many.' Whatever that means. He also said he had two ideas about who killed the two kids, one *possible* and one *impossible*. He said in his business he had 'learned to believe in the impossible.' Whatever the hell that means. I warned him to tell the police what he knew. He said he didn't have any goddamn proof, but 'maybe *they* didn't know that.' Whoever *they* is. You talk to him, Lieutenant. Talk some sense into him. Oh. One other thing that's important: I pressed him about who he suspected. He said, 'You're the fucking reporter. Who wasn't in here?' Meaning the dressing room. I have no idea who he meant. It was a jungle of people in there after the game. Harry thinks the killer was one of two people, or maybe obviously even both of them. He must have expected one or both of them to be in the dressing room. You get to him, Sharon. Find out who he suspects."

"I'm driving him to Atlanta for his television show," she said. "I'll press him. But you know Harry. He's stubborn as Stone Mountain."

"I thought Sunday was a day of rest," said Sullivan.

The Lieutenant stood up. "See you two tomorrow. After I get back from Atlanta." They walked her to her car. Then took the elevator to their room.

"You didn't call Friday," said Sullivan, her chin on her hands.

"No. I got smashed."

"You, Morris? Come on."

"God, yes."

"Really smashed?"

"I think I may have sung by myself in the bar."

"John Morris, don't you dare ever sing without me there. I will buy all the whiskey it takes to hear you."

"I sobered up when Harry came in. He was drunker than I was."

"*That* I believe." Sullivan looked down from the palms of her hands. "Why? Why do you think he drinks?"

"He's old. His health's bad. He's afraid. He's afraid he'll die poor. Isn't everybody afraid of those things? Hell, no wonder I was drunk."

"You missed *me*, that's why."

Morris put his huge right hand around both of her wrists. "You're right. I should have called you smashed. Were you okay? You didn't dream about trucks?"

She shivered. "No. We talked most of the night."

"Tell me about the Lieutenant, when she's at home."

"Both of her parents are dead now. She lives alone in an old, frame, two-story house with a wide front porch. She has a white cat. She does beautiful needlepoint."

"What did you talk about?"

"Harry Carr. What do you think? Morris, didn't your mother teach you to knock before opening doors?"

"Not in an athletic center. I might have been any one of eighteen-thousand students coming through the door. At least they could have used the steam room." Morris squeezed her wrists. "Why did she tell you? Didn't she know I would keep it to myself?"

"I wouldn't have gotten it out of you? Ha. Sharon Blake knows better. Of course she told me every juicy detail. I think I'm jealous."

"Just wait until I'm older. I've already learned how to cuss and get drunk. Next thing, I will be ripping off your clothes in the post office building."

"I'll save all my Christmas mail until you give me the word. Which year do you think it will be?" She made fists of her own hands. "She loves him, Morris." He was amazed. She was about to cry.

"She's crazy. Harry's known more girls than lives in O'Hatchie County. He's probably known that many ex-cheer-leaders. She knows that."

"It doesn't matter. When it comes to some men, it doesn't matter."

"Where do you send to get your blood typed so you'll know?" He let go of her wrists.

"Not you, Morris. You're a better man."

"I don't want to be a better man. I want to be one of the other kind."

She took one of his arms in both of her hands. "You're *bad* jealous."

"Damn right."

"Don't you see? She wants to be the last one. It doesn't matter how many others there have been."

"Or that he has a perfectly alive wife? Jesus, Caroline doesn't deserve to be stuck all her life with Harry Carr. She's a gentle lady. I remember once—I'd forgotten all about it—she liked a story I wrote... about a boy who had stayed on the team, survived all the impossible practices for four years, and had never gotten in a game. The boy said he wouldn't trade those four years for anything. Caroline sent me a box of tea cakes. And a note. I wish I'd kept the note. She said it was good that someone cared about boys who were not stars... I don't remember how she said it. But it was a gentle note. And the tea cakes were wonderful." Morris released her arm. "Sharon may be the last girl friend. *Any minute.* Harry has to keep a nitro-glycerine tablet under his busy tongue, just in case."

"Morris."

"Sorry." He put his fist under the small angle of her chin. "The truth: I like him. I don't blame her. He's ruthless, he's old, he's doomed, he's a better man than all of us. I don't know how."

"Bullshit." She leaned across the table to kiss him on the mouth. "You can take my skirt off *on top* of the post office building."

"It's a deal. The afternoon I'm sixty-six."

Chapter Twenty-Two

The phone rang twice before Morris picked it up.

"It's the Day of Rest. But I think you're overdoing it."

"I have to sleep in the morning," said Morris. "My roommate snores at night."

"Your roommate is in the dining room repenting of her sins. Get up. We're on for church."

"Remember the sin of gluttony."

"Please. I'm having an extra Danish."

"Order me a fifth of coffee."

Sullivan sat in the corner of the long dining room. She was wearing a white, wide-brimmed hat.

"Is this the president of the missionary society? I love the hat."

"Sharon lent it to me. It was her mother's." Sullivan lifted her hand to be held.

"Gloves, too. My God."

"He's fine. He's looking forward to having you in church. I hear they have a young preacher. He's enough to make a person fall into sin. He's preaching on honesty."

Morris held out a hand, palm up.

"What's that for?"

"You owe me three dollars and nine cents. Parking. In Atlanta last year."

"Next week's sermon is on *greed*. Maybe we can stay over."

"Maybe we will be here next year, the way things are going. Are you sure Trapwell's high-school English teacher will be in church?"

"She never misses. Have some coffee and we're off."

The Methodist church was a hundred years old. Half the congregation seemed old enough to have been at the laying of the cornerstone. There was a smattering of college kids among the pews, leaving the regular worshipers looking even older, many of the women in their comfortably dated hats.

Morris gripped the hymnal when they sang his mother's once-favorite hymn. She was always such an indomitable woman, tall in her white dress, her strong voice singing the words that did not daunt her: ". . . time like an ever-rolling stream bears all its sons away." Sullivan, under her hat, did not see the brief glaze in his eyes. The preacher was young and handsome, and his blond wife sat in the front pew as if there to worship him. He preached on commitment. He was ardent in his definition, but Morris again found his mind wandering to the small Episcopal church in Atlanta and the mornings there in the strong, comfortable presence of his mother, who never made him feel he let her down when he came to the age of automobiles and girls and she went to sit alone—in the last pew on the right aisle. But then the service was over, and the worshipers rose to their feet in one great relief, as if they had earned some share of immortality.

"You're sure that's Miss Anne Hill," said Morris, looking for the thin lady in the blue suit who had sat in front of them.

"Oh, yes. Sharon described her perfectly, and she has sat in that pew all of her life, and her mother before her. Come on, let's wait for her outside."

Miss Hill picked her way carefully, someone stopping her on each step to chat. Before she reached them, she saw that they were waiting for her in the sun, which was bright in the cool air.

"Miss Hill?" asked Sullivan.

"Yes." Her voice was soft and absolutely controlled.

"My name is Julia Sullivan. This is John Morris of the Associated Press."

Miss Hill nodded with a closed politeness. "Sharon Blake called and said you wanted to see me. About Harvey Trapwell." Her voice lost a hint of its control.

"Yes," said Julia.

"I don't have to write anything," said Morris, finding himself speaking his own words more precisely. "We want to know

147

more about the kind of young man he was. It might help us understand what happened to him."

"He was...a very fine young man," said Miss Hill.She lifted her chin with an effort. She looked at Morris and then at Julia, and seemed to make a decision. "I live on the next block...that way." She pointed. "Walk with me, and we'll talk."

Morris waited for her to speak. Then risked a question as Julia carefully moved to put Miss Hill between them. "Was Harvey a happy young man?"

Miss Hill walked as deliberately as she spoke. Morris kept pace with his cane. "He was a serious young man. But no. Not happy. You know of his family life?"

Morris nodded.

"His father's failure embarrassed him. Then I think it drove him. He was so quiet and yet a very fierce competitor, in football and in the classroom. He had average intelligence, but he studied as seriously as any young man I ever taught. He was the kind of boy a teacher could cry over, a football star who would rather study chemistry."

"Did you ever cry over him?" asked Morris.

She stopped in front of a very old frame house painted an impeccable white. "This is my house. Come inside and have a cup of coffee."

Morris waited until they were seated and each of them had sipped the strong coffee. "Miss Hill. I have to ask you a difficult question. I'll respect your answer. I won't write it unless I have to. I may well have to." He gave her only a moment to gather herself. "Was Harvey Trapwell a homosexual?"

Anne Hill did not flinch. The cup and saucer were steady in her hands. "We owe the dead something. We don't owe them gossip. What does it matter?" She lifted one hand as a question mark.

"It might be important in finding who killed him," said Morris.

She sat with her hands folded in her lap. Morris could see her making an almost physical decision to answer him. "I don't know...I don't know what I saw. I could be very unfair to the memory of two dead boys."

"Did you know the manager, Henry Young?" Morris sat forward in his chair.

"Oh, no. I—" She looked at Sullivan, as if for help.

"Murder undoes our lives," said Julia. "John Morris won't write anything that would be unfair."

Miss Hill hesitated, then plunged ahead. "I want whoever did it caught and punished. It's not fashionable today to *punish* the wicked. But I prefer to be out of fashion when an innocent boy is killed. I know Harvey Trapwell was innocent of any criminal act. He never hurt anyone off the football field. He was *different*. I told you that. He was a most serious boy and a most serious student. He was obsessed with being a doctor. He would have been a good one. He was quiet. He was well liked, by athletes and non-athletes. By girls." She put her cup and saucer on the table. "He dated. Not often. He was such a student. But he took out the little Jennings girl. Patty Jennings. I think *she* took *him* out, actually. It was obvious she was very much in love with him. Oh, they went to class parties together their senior year. But the year before . . ." She closed her eyes as if remembering. "I was a chaperone at the Junior-Senior prom. The dance was at the high school. I decided to go by my homeroom and pick up some papers to grade. The hallway was dark. I turned the corner, and I could just see . . . two boys were . . . hugging each other in a way that men don't often do . . . in this country. They didn't see me. I went back to the dance. I won't tell you the name of one of them; he was killed that summer in a car accident. But the other boy was Harvey Trapwell. They were dear friends. Perhaps that's all they were. I . . . didn't think any the less of either of them. They were the two best students in their class . . ." She left her thoughts in midair.

Sullivan patted her shoulder. "They were lucky to have you as a friend."

Morris waited to see if she would continue. But that was it. "Miss Hill, does the name Oberon mean anything to you?"

"Of course," she said.

Morris looked at her in amazement.

"Shakespeare. *A Midsummer Night's Dream.* Oberon, the King of the Fairies. Why do you ask?"

Morris shook his head. "I wasted the question on a building full of history professors who failed to cite the play. We only needed to ask an informed English teacher. No ladies in Colorado read Shakespeare. We know that."

Sullivan made a mock fist.

"I don't understand," said Miss Hill.

"Someone left a message for Trapwell. The message was signed *Oberon*. There isn't such a person in the telephone book, here or in Atlanta. We had a devil of a time understanding what the word meant. Did Harvey ever use the name to you?"

"No. I'm sure of that."

Morris propped himself up with his cane. "We do thank you. What you told us will help. There is absolutely no need for it to be published, now or anytime that I can imagine. We—" He fumbled for words to ease her mind. "I promise you that whoever killed him will answer for it. It won't help much. But it will help some."

She saw them to the door; Morris turned the rented Chevrolet toward the campus.

"What do you think she saw?" asked Sullivan.

"Lovers," said Morris. "I don't think much escapes Miss Anne Hill. You'd have to say Harvey Trapwell never had a lot of luck. A failed father. The awkward hurts of learning his own homosexuality. The boy he loved killed in an automobile. He himself murdered. All of it in a sleepy, college town. By God, the world is not such a promising place, Sullivan."

She slid closer on the seat. "I should feel guilty for being so happy." She squeezed his arm. "Damn if I will."

"Let's drop in on his old girl friend. The freshman dorm is not far from the stadium. She might be in. She might know something she doesn't realize. Sharon said she could hardly talk to the police for breaking down. Maybe she has accepted Trapwell's death by now." Morris parked in a visitor spot outside the high-rise dormitory situated deep in a grove of oaks gloomy without leaves.

A young girl was drinking coffee at a low table in the lobby of the dorm. She looked up as if she expected to be asked a question.

"We would like to speak with Patty Jennings," said Sullivan. "Can we telephone her room?"

"I'll ring it for you. She always goes home for Sunday dinner. I don't think she's left." The girl flipped through a directory and dialed a number. She looked up. "Who should I say is calling?"

"John Morris, of the Associated Press."

The girl covered the mouthpiece of the telephone as if protecting it from bad news. Someone obviously answered the ring.

"There's a man . . . to speak with you," said the girl. "He's from the Associated Press?" Her voice was a question.

"May I?" Morris held out his wide hand.

The girl wavered. "Just a minute, Patty . . . I'll put him on."

"Miss Jennings." The 'yes' the girl answered was a tiny sound in his ear. "I'm John Morris. I don't want to upset you. Or keep you from dinner. I was just speaking with Miss Anne Hill. She's anxious that whoever harmed Harvey Trapwell not go unpunished." Morris decided to stretch the facts. "She felt you might help us understand Harvey better."

The girl made sounds instead of words.

"I won't keep you but a minute," said Morris. "Miss Hill said you two were great friends."

"I don't have long," said the whisper of a voice. Then she hung up.

The girl at the table was too curious to sip her coffee.

"Will she come down in the elevator?" asked Morris, nodding toward the foyer.

The girl nodded.

"We do thank you. We'll wait there."

It was not a long wait. The elevator doors opened on a small, blonde girl standing motionless, as if she were a parcel being delivered. Finally, she stepped reluctantly forward, obviously threatened by Morris' great bulk.

"I'm Julia Sullivan." She took Patty's arm. "The big block of coat here is John Morris. His job is asking questions. You don't have to answer any you don't want to. I promise."

The girl did her best to smile.

"If you like, we can talk outside. If someone is picking you up," said Morris.

"I have a car." There was a bit more substance in her thin voice.

"Good." Morris led the way, holding the door open with his cane.

Patty's white Mustang was parked beside their own Chevrolet.

"Morris, your left front tire needs help," said Sullivan. "Poor thing. All that weight."

The tire was nearly flat.

Morris shook his head, then turned to Patty. "Miss Hill was right? You and Harvey were close?"

"Yes." She looked in Morris' eyes for the first time. Her own were the palest blue. She seemed to make a decision to talk to him. "We . . . went together in high school. To parties. The movies. I asked him as often as he asked me. He was a quiet, shy, nice boy." Her voice wavered. She clenched her small teeth. "He was serious about school, about being a doctor. That's what he lived for, I think."

"He was something else on the football field," said Morris.

Patty nodded. "He seemed like another person. He was a great player. I don't know football. I know no one could bring him down in high school. Even on the university team . . ."

Morris was careful not to interrupt. But she did not finish the sentence. "Did you love him?"

The question unnerved her. She crossed her arms in her plaid sweater. Sullivan patted her gently on the shoulder. The three of them stood subdued by the huge oaks.

"Yes," she said. Now she was crying. Sullivan offered a handkerchief. She seemed to stop crying with an act of will. "I knew it was impossible . . . Miss Hill was right. He thought of me as a friend." She twisted the handkerchief. "I used to wish he would hate me instead. Then I could . . ."

Again Morris waited. Finally, he completed the sentence for her. "Forget him?"

"Yes."

"When did you see him last?"

"On campus one day a couple of weeks ago. We ran into each other. He said he was fine. He looked so . . . unhappy."

"When did the two of you split up?" asked Morris.

"It was not as if we were ever really together. But the first week of school, I picked him up at his dormitory. We went out to eat. I asked him . . . I was embarrassed, but I didn't care. I asked him how he felt about me." She stopped. She didn't need the handkerchief anymore. "He said I was the best friend he had. He didn't want to hurt my feelings. I cried anyhow. I'm not very . . . tough. But it was best. I was over it, until I saw him on campus. And he looked so thin."

Again Morris waited. She only looked down at the dead

leaves. "Did you ever hear him say the name 'Oberon,'" he asked.

She shook her head, puzzled.

"You said he looked thin and unhappy when you last saw him. You don't know any specific thing that might have been bothering him?"

"Only football. It took so much time. All he wanted to do was study."

"Could you always reach him when you called him?" asked Morris. "I mean, when he wasn't practicing football."

Patty looked around her as if she had just discovered the great trees. "He had labs in the spring and winter. He practically slept in the library. Sometimes he studied at the PKA house. I could reach him there. He stayed in the athletic dorm in the summer, took one course, and worked for Building and Grounds. He liked to work outside. Weekends, this past spring and summer—" She smoothed her straight hair. "—he seemed to disappear. He didn't often call, only once or twice during the week."

Morris pressed his cane into the dead leaves. "He never left word where he might be reached? Did he go to Atlanta?"

She was shaking her head. Then something came to her. "Last spring. He left an unfinished chemistry report in my car. I couldn't reach him anywhere. I was afraid he might need it. I went by the library. It was a Saturday. I even went by the chemistry building. No one knew where he was. I noticed . . . there was a seven-digit number with a slash, in the margin of the report. Harvey always made a slash in the middle of a telephone number. He said it helped him remember it. I dialed the number and asked for Harvey. The man who answered was *very* upset. He said I had the wrong number. I tried to explain, but he just said again I had the wrong number, and hung up."

"Did you ask Harvey about it later?"

She shook her head. "It didn't seem important . . . it was just odd how upset the man was. Harvey was happy to get the report back. I only just now remembered dialing the number. Do you think—?"

"Do you remember the number or anything about it?" asked Morris.

"It wasn't a college number. I remember that. They all begin eight two two. That's all I remember."

"The voice that answered. You said it was . . ." Morris left the sentence unfinished.

"A man. He sounded older than a student. I remember he was awfully uptight for a wrong number."

"A southern voice?" asked Morris.

"No." She shook her head. "I don't know why I say 'no.' I couldn't be sure of his voice. I'm amazed I remember it at all. It was just that Harvey seemed to disappear all late spring and summer." She looked at her watch. "I'm late for dinner. Mother will be anxious. I'm sorry I couldn't help you. I—"

"We thank you," said Morris. "You have helped."

The girl was gone in a flash of blonde hair.

"I'm glad you didn't ask her if Trapwell was a homosexual," said Sullivan.

"No. Maybe we'll have to later. But I doubt that she saw any further than his blue eyes."

"Do you think the voice was Oberon?"

"I'd bet on it," said Morris. "Interesting that she remembers the voice as older and not southern. The roommate Mitchell also said a man who called Trapwell sounded older. He didn't remember the voice as southern or non-southern. Sullivan, we had better go through Trapwell's notes and papers with a microscope, especially his chemistry reports. The Lieutenant's people might have overlooked what could be a telephone number with a slash in it. Of course, every seven-digit number doesn't necessarily belong to a telephone. Patty Jennings may have simply waked an angry man from a Saturday nap. Trapwell kept careful notes, and I bet he never threw a paper away. The Lieutenant has stored everything he owned. Jesus. She drove Harry to Atlanta for his TV show." Morris looked at his watch. "We have plenty of time to catch his act. Harry's show has run longer than Ed Sullivan's. And it's just as obscenely improbable."

154

Chapter Twenty-three

The NFL Today was a sound-and-light show, touchdowns and ten-second tapes of wide receivers juking in the end zone. Cut back to New York: The earnest young announcer was catching the world up on college football, no less, and what was happening with Harry Carr and his murdered quarterback. There was a film clip from Sparta.

"That's Sharon!"

Morris shushed Sullivan with a wave of his hand. The Lieutenant faced the lights, quite in control, and said that no suspect had been arrested.

The announcer's sidekick, a battered old professional halfback, recited Harry's former players who were active in the NFL—there were twenty-three of them. Fourteen of his old players were head coaches in college, three in the NFL. Both announcers wished Harry well. Morris could almost hear the old halfback say, "Keep on kickin' ass, Harry." He meant it if he didn't say it. There was a rush of film and the sound of a crowd and *The NFL Today* died in a crash of geometry.

"She looked wonderful," said Sullivan.

"She'll look a lot better when she has somebody under arrest." Morris switched the dial.

Harry Carr was slumped in a chair. Somehow, his physical presence was bleached out by the white lights. Facing the dead round lens of the camera, Harry had none of the power he commanded in front of a live audience. Morris knew it was an act of will and Scotch whiskey that kept him in his chair. Only when he forgot himself, at the sight of something happening on the football playback, did Harry sound like Harry.

* * *

"LOOK-AH-HERE . . ." Harry sat up. His own player went down in a tidal wave of orange jerseys. "Them Tennessee boys know sump'in 'bout blockin' and tacklin'." Nothing Harry loved better than a kill-or-be killed hit. He drank from a cup of the coffee that sponsored his show. "HOT DAMN! We hadn't run that play right since Walter Deihl was tailback in forty-seven. Saw Walter this week. Came by practice. Looked like he coulda played Saturday. Had his granddaughter with him. I'm not talkin' about no little tyke. I mean a good-lookin' granddaughter, 'bout growed up, too good-lookin' for her granddaddy, I can tell you that. Walter reminded me—LOOK-AH-HERE! Thought we knocked that boy's head off in his helmet." Harry seemed to realize what he said. His eyes searched for the camera and shrank from it. He willed himself to keep sitting there. And never said what Walter Deihl had reminded him.

Harry knew the names of his players, but a boy could letter four years and not hear Harry call his name once on TV. Hit somebody and Harry would love the lick.

"WATCH-IT-DERE, BIG BOY! . . . Piled on a little late. Official woulda got'cha *if he'd been in position* . . . I forgot to mention the black arm bands. The boys wore 'em for Harvey Trapwell. And our little manager Henry Young. I know ol' Harv' was with us in Knoxville. We got boys who love the Lord. HOT DAMN! We blew the lead block."

Morris closed his eyes, waiting for lightning to strike the set. Harry was caught up in the action.

"LOOK-AH-HERE! Caught 'em in a overshift . . . At boy's GONE. You cain't coach what he's got. Comes from the good lord. Coach Johnny Moore was in charge of gettin' us ready for Tennessee. Did a heckuva job. Always does. All our staff. They coach. I just stand around and grumble to myself." Morris knew he never called any assistant's name but Johnny's. The others, all kids, came and went with the seasons. Every young assistant wanted it in his resumé that he'd worked for Harry Carr. Harry won with any set of names his staff might have.

"OKAY! We put it behind the goal now, we can break out the seegars. Our boy'll have sump'in to remember the rest of their lives. Not many seniors can say they never lost to Tennessee. GOD! . . . There we go . . . BELLYIN' around . . . ROOSTER FIGHTIN' . . . Makes you want to VOMIT!" Harry had forgotten the white lights, the round lens; he might have been talking to three hundred drunks. "Nobody wants to give up their lives to get the ball over the goal. We go over to Jackson, Mississippi like that, they're gonna bring us back in a bucket."

Harry seemed to have taken on a rare contempt for the camera, saying what he damn well pleased. It was the nearest thing to honesty that Morris had ever seen of him on television. The film ended, and there was Harry talking, mumbling into a coffee commercial, his face as washed out and uncomfortable as Morris had ever seen it. Morris looked for Sullivan. She was sound asleep in her chair. He looked back at the screen and realized what Harry was saying:

"—and people want to kill each other in the street here in Atlanta, nothin' I can do about that. Nothin' anybody can do about it, didn't look like. But Sparta ain't Atlanta. We got first-rate police. They're doing a good job. But the law has to work *inside* the law. The law takes time. Too much time. I been in Sparta thirty-two years, my God it didn't seem possible, and I don't draw a check from the law. But you kill my boys, I'm *law enough*. I *know who you are*. And don't think I wasn't lookin' for you Saturday. I know it was a wad of people in the dressing room, and I waited for you. But you didn't come by. Your old 'buddy' Henry Young would have missed you. Well, you come to see me tomorrow, or I'm comin' to see *you*. And the law can take what's left." Harry's face dissolved into music, a march that came prematurely down on the program with no sign-off by Harry or the sponsor or anybody. Morris could imagine the producer waving his hands to get Harry off the air before he libeled the whole town of Sparta.

"Sullivan." Morris shook her awake. She jumped up in her chair as if she had been attacked by the television set.

"John Morris, you scared me to death."

"You should have heard Harry. He was threatening the killer."

"Who?"

"He didn't name him. I think if they hadn't gotten him off the air, he might have. Harry spoke directly to him; asked him why he hadn't come by the dressing room in Knoxville; said his 'buddy' Henry Young would have missed him; threatened to look up the killer tomorrow if the killer didn't look him up. 'And the law can take what's left.'"

"Harry's finally, officially, out of his mind," said Sullivan.

"I don't know. Nobody can rage on like Harry. But I've never seen him back down from anything he said he was going to do. You can poll thirty years of coaches he has put into real estate. Or anybody who ever played for him or against him. But whatever Harry knows, or thinks he knows, he had better tell the police."

"The Lieutenant drove him over. I wonder if she was watching him in the studio," said Sullivan.

"Good question." Morris dialed the long-distance operator and finally got through to the Atlanta television station. They were sorry; Harry Carr had left. No, they did not know Lieutenant Sharon Blake. Morris dialed the AP bureau in Atlanta. They had monitored the show. They always did, for the A.M. football roundup for Monday.

Morris turned to Sullivan. "Our boy Harry is going to be news again in New York."

"Was he drunk?" she asked.

"He wasn't feeling any pain. He must know something. Or suspect something. I keep wondering about Harry changing his tune? Remember when Trapwell was killed, he thought it was best if the reason he was killed was buried with him. Then, when the manager was killed, Harry began to threaten the killer. Now he's done it on television. When I asked him why he changed his attitude, he said, 'Yesterday, I was stupid.' Harry Carr has been many things, but never stupid—except when he unbuckles his belt."

"*Happy* stupid," snickered Sullivan.

"You're hopeless," said Morris.

"I wonder . . ." Sullivan paused.

"What?"

"If Trapwell had a lover on the team?"

"Maybe. Maybe Young himself." Morris didn't sound convinced.

"Maybe he was sleeping with Harry." Sullivan giggled in spite of herself.

Morris threatened to turn the chair over with her in it.

"I'll be serious. Harry first thought Trapwell was killed by a lover. But when someone murdered the greedy, surely heterosexual Mister Young, Harry changed his mind. He began to suspect one of the manager Young's alleged 'buddies.'"

"Well said. Just because you are beautiful doesn't mean you can't be smart."

Sullivan watched him closely.

"I mean, the Egyptians loved a long nose."

"John Morris, I have to talk and run. I have a date with the preacher. It's about the sin of—"

"I know," said Morris. "God is leaving all that up to me. I'm teasing you. But tell me this. Was Oberon Trapwell's lover? Or Young's 'buddy'? Or one and the same?"

"The idea of the word *Oberon* seems a romantic one to me," said Sullivan.

"And yet, it was Henry Young who took the telephone message from him." Morris stared into space. Then looked at his watch. "I know this. I've got to get to Harry. He's been news for thirty years, but now he has really gone and done it. If Sharon is still with him, God knows where they are. You can never get Harry on Sunday afternoons after a game. I remember that. But his assistant coaches always break down the Saturday game film late Sunday afternoon. They grade the players. Harry stops by at night to check the grades. He doesn't believe in film grades. But he checks them. He has a computer in his head that tells him which players are winners. That's why his old assistants so often fall on their asses as head coaches. They can take Harry's schemes. But they can't take Harry. I just hope . . ."

"What?" asked Sullivan.

"I hope the killer was not watching Harry on television."

Chapter Twenty-four

The door to the Athletic Center was locked, but the old watchman recognized Morris and let him in.

"A quiet Sunday," said Morris.

"Lord. Too quiet." The watchman glanced over his own shoulder.

"I'm looking for the football coaches," said Morris.

"Up in room two hundred." The watchman pointed the way. "The *po*-lice got the man who killed those boys?"

"Not yet."

The old man shook his head and looked again behind him.

Morris knocked on the conference-room door. He heard chairs sliding inside. The door opened. Morris could see the confusion in Johnny Moore's eyes under his gray crew cut. Other assistant coaches were smoking in the dark of the room, watching the game film. Johnny stepped outside, closing the door behind him. His wide chest was still a band of muscles in the sweater.

"I need to see Harry," said Morris.

Moore shook his head, biting his concern. "He's not here. Morris, I don't understand it. Harry's *never* late."

"Maybe his car broke down coming from Atlanta."

"Harry could get a ride in North Africa; hell, he's been there: goddamn army clinics. We've graded game films every Sunday night for thirty years. He's gone out of town maybe twice. He sure as hell told me before he went. He's been in the hospital twice. That's it."

"You think he's had an accident?" Morris could feel his own chest tighten. Still, it was impossible to worry about Harry. He was indestructible. Nitroglycerine or no nitroglycerine.

"No way. Not unless his car jumped the road somewhere in the dark. Anybody who saw Harry would know him. *Anybody* in this state." Johnny looked at his watch. "It's seven-fifteen. He should have been here forty-five minutes ago."

"What's forty-five minutes? He could be fixing a flat."

"Yeah, and he could be running for Governor. I tell you, Morris. Harry is never late for *any* reason. I got a roomful of nervous coaches in there. How about calling... you know ...her...the Lieutenant."

"Not his wife?"

"Hell, no."

"I'll see what I can find out," said Morris. "Where's a phone?"

Johnny opened the door to Margaret Stewart's office. Morris did not have to look up the station number. A voice he didn't recognize called the Lieutenant to the phone. When she said "Hello," she sounded happy.

Morris was relieved. He and Johnny were paranoid. What the hell was forty-five minutes late? Even for Harry.

"It's me. The AP."

"Hi. I was just going to call you." The way she said "Hi," she might have been a kid.

"I'm at the Athletic Center. I came over to see Harry. He's not here."

"Check the film room. He watches game film on Sunday night."

"I did. He isn't here. Look, it may be nothing. He's only forty-five minutes late. But his assistant coaches are worried. Especially Johnny Moore. He says Harry's never late. *Ever.*"

"No...he isn't." Morris could imagine her checking her watch.

"Do you have any idea...where he might be?"

There was a pause.

"Let me make a call," she said. "I'll ring you right back." She took his number.

Morris looked at his own watch. Funny. He wanted a cigaret again. It was the second time in a week. He hadn't smoked in twenty years.

The ring seemed to lift the phone on the desk. "Yes."

"No answer." She sounded older. Morris regretted it; he missed the girl in her voice.

"It's probably nothing. A flat." His own voice was not convincing.

"His health, Morris." Now she was scared.

"If he was in a hospital. Any hospital. We would have heard. Did you call his home?" Morris could feel Harry's small, plastic vial of tablets in his own hand.

"He never goes home on Sunday afternoon."

"If something . . . if he became ill, someone might have called Caroline."

"She's too ill to come to the phone, and he has an unlisted number." There was fear, but no guilt in her voice. "Wait out front. I'll pick you up." She didn't listen for his answer.

Morris opened the door back into the hall. Johnny stood with one foot behind him, propped against the wall.

"Any luck?"

Morris shook his head. "Not really. The Lieutenant's picking me up. She was with him earlier. She has an idea where he may be. Harry'll probably come lumbering in before she gets here. We'll look like a couple of fools."

Johnny held his mouth tight. "Yeah," he said. There was no expression in his eyes.

Morris found the watchman, who let him out of the building.

The campus was dark. And empty. Morris waited on the steps, his jacket collar turned up against the raw wind. He remembered the sight of Harry in his room, struggling for his breath.

Chapter Twenty-five

Headlights separated from the thin traffic and turned toward the Athletic Center. Morris waited at the top of the steps. The police car stopped. Its lights steamed in the night air. Morris came down the steps one at a time, keeping his balance with his cane. He could not get the sight of Harry, bending and straightening his leg on the bed, out of his mind. He felt none of the grip of a news story in his stomach. He felt the same unreality of seeing his aunt waiting in the long black limousine on the way to his mother's funeral. Morris could think of nothing to say. The car jumped forward before he closed the door.

She was driving too fast and too stiffly, her fists tight on the wheel.

"Where are we headed?" Morris kept his voice deliberately even.

She didn't look at him, as if she could move the car faster with her eyes straight ahead. "His cabin." Her voice was as tight as her grip on the wheel. She took the shoulder of the road to pass a slow-moving van. Morris forced himself not to flinch.

"Sharon." She turned her head at the sound of her name. "We can't help him at the bottom of the O'Hatchie River."

She cut her speed and merged into the traffic crossing the bridge.

"You heard him on television? Telling the killer he hadn't come by the dressing room in Knoxville. Challenging him."

She moved her head up and down. "He wouldn't tell me afterward what he knows. He said to 'mind your police business.' Then he wouldn't speak, all the way to Sparta. He finally said, 'One of them did it. You'll see.' I threatened to take him to the station. He laughed. I will tomorrow, Morris. I swear it. He's making a fool of himself, and me." She drove silently. "But you can't stay *pissed*—Why does he love that word?—with Harry . . . I can't." She was smiling.

"Where did you see him last?"

"At the cabin. An hour ago."

"He had a car?"

"Yes. We dropped it off there this morning. On the way to Atlanta." Talking helped. Her hands relaxed.

"Maybe he has car trouble."

"He would have called. When I dialed the cabin, the phone rang, but no one answered." She was squeezing the wheel again. "Morris. I'm afraid."

"Listen. One thing about Harry . . . Harry's a tough sonofabitch. Harry's outlasted them all."

The traffic was behind them. The Lieutenant slowed and turned onto a dirt road. She was crying.

"Help me look . . . a driveway." She cut her speed. "There." She came to a gate. It was open. A gravel drive led off to the right toward the river. Morris thought he saw a light. The trees were thick, and as they wound through them, the same light seemed to go on and off like a signal code. The drive ended in a circle around an old, huge sycamore tree. A silver Cadillac was parked in front of the cabin, Harry's. Lieutenant Blake stopped the car beside it. Her radio came startlingly alive. A Quick Mart had been held up, someone killed.

"Go ahead," she said to Morris. "I'll follow you." Her hand gripped his arm. She answered the radio call.

Morris stepped out into the cold. The thin gravel slid under his feet. He opened the door of the Cadillac. It was empty.

The cabin was old and had a stone foundation. Three stone steps led up to a screened porch. The porch ceiling light was on. There were lamps on twin tables, but they were dark. The screen door was not locked. As soon as Morris was on the plank floor of the porch, he heard a faint, rapid sound. Then it was gone. The sound and the ceiling light made him feel ridiculous. He knocked on the cabin door. It was solidly built. There was no answer. "Harry!" His breath condensed in the cold air. He called again. It seemed natural now for Morris to use his first name. There was no answer. He tried the door. It was also unlocked. "Harry!" This time his voice echoed through the cabin. Now Morris could hear a faint whirr and then a louder fluttering. A lamp burned in the front room. Coals were still alive in the fireplace. "Harry!" The live coals made Morris feel more ridiculous. He could now hear a steady whirring. There were two doors off the front room, both open. The door on the left was dark. He reached in and found a light switch. It was a bedroom. The bed was unmade. There was a coat over a chair. Big enough to be Harry's. Morris backed out of the room and tried the other door. It opened into a den. A lamp was burning on a table. The lamp stand was made from an old gun stock. A back door to the cabin was bolted. Morris opened it onto a wide, screened porch. Below, between the tops of the trees, he could see the reflection of the river, a thin, metallic script in the moonlight. The porch was empty. The other door in the den opened into the kitchen. It was surprisingly modern, with built-in appliances. A stairway led down from the rear of the kitchen. A dim light flickered on the wall above the stairs. "Harry!" Morris could hear a constant whirring and now and then a mechanical fluttering. He looked down the stairway. A reflected afterlight was leaping grotesquely on the wall. The stairs ran straight down against the back side of the cabin. Morris could see the wall below was paneled and illuminated in wild patterns of light. All the time there was a constant whirring and then a tearing flutter.

He was dead. The angle of his head on the floor was away from life. Only his thick, gray hair swung from his forehead alive. Smoke from the overheated film projector exhausted over him like incense. A stool behind him had been kicked on end. The projector whirred forward for several dozen revolutions, then an automatic playback reversed it, and the celluloid strip fluttered mortally in the hot metal track. The players went against the bare paneling of the wall. It was an old film. The low helmets were leather and not plastic. The heavy uniforms were not tailored. There were no stripes on the jerseys. All the players wore ugly high-topped shoes. It was a wonder the film had not broken. The players rose up and went against the paneling. The projector shuttered, and they were falling back in the air, without reality. The play was a run. Morris could see it was a brutal run from scrimmage. The players in postwar jerseys rose up out of the Single Wing and went against the wall. It was a power play off the right tackle. The tailback cut behind a block and threw himself across the wall, as animate as life. The players came up, leaping and grabbing each other. There was no doubt he scored. The projector shivered and sucked them back in reverse, grotesque imitations of themselves. Morris could not identify the defense. They were in dark jerseys. The offense was in white. He was sure it might be silver. By the third replay, Morris could see that the tailback making the cut was 95, the number worn by Walter Deihl, the number inseparable from the football year of 1947. He made his cut and was in the air, alive, when the film broke. The film was sucked, wildly flapping, through the projector, until the wall glared white through the smoke. Morris could not find the switch to the projector. He pulled the plug from the wall. The room was dark. There was no sound. He could still see the players as they came across the dark.

Chapter Twenty-six

"*Morris?*" *The Lieutenant* was calling from the top of the stairs. "What's happened?" She seemed to be out of breath.

Morris found a wall switch. Harry died again in the sudden light. He was curled, half on his face, his hands digging into his chest. Morris wondered if his nitroglycerine pills were upstairs in his coat. He heard Lieutenant Blake start down the steps.

"Sharon."

She stopped.

Morris took the steps as fast as his leg would let him. She was weightless against his bulk. "Harry's dead."

She did not move. She was not crying.

"Let's go upstairs and sit down."

She did not answer.

Morris guided her without effort up the steps.

There was plenty of whiskey in the kitchen. He poured a straight Scotch. A short one. She drank it at once, without emotion. After the third drink, she began to cry. The tears seemed to slide away of their own volition. Morris poured himself a deep drink. They sat together without speaking. Her breathing became less shallow. She looked at Morris. He lifted his glass. She lifted her own. She still had not spoken.

"Are you all right?"

She nodded. "What happened?" Her voice might have been a child's.

"He was watching a game film. Odd. It was an old film. From the nineteen-forties. He must have had a heart attack."

"How long has he been . . ."

"It couldn't have been long. The film broke while I was standing there. Harry had switched on the projector's automatic replay. As if he were grading the team on that one touchdown play from thirty-odd years ago."

"Morris." Her voice was as thin as the air. "Are we the only two who loved him?" There were no tears in her eyes.

"*They* loved him . . . when he won." Morris did not hide his contempt.

"He wouldn't spit on them."

"Yes, he would." Morris was glad to find himself smiling. She also smiled.

"Harry would drink to that." They both lifted their glasses. "We better call Doc." Morris put his hand on her shoulder. "Who will tell Caroline?"

"Doc and I. Morris—" She put her hand on his. "Caroline's too ill to understand. But she has money and a nurse. She'll be all right."

"Can you talk to her?"

"I'll try."

"Can I see her, tell her . . ." Morris could see Harry in a hundred places, hear his cement-damp voice shouting some sacrilege across the grass, and he could not escape the thought of writing Harry's obituary. "One of these days, Morris, I am going to goddamn die," Harry had said to him a long time ago somewhere, "and when I do, you write, 'He was a fucking good football coach.'" Yeah, he was that, thought Morris.

"Caroline wouldn't know you, Morris. I'm sorry." Sharon tried to stand. "Let me . . . see him before we call Doc."

"You're sure?"

She nodded. Morris helped her to her feet. He guided her down the stairs. He looked for a telephone in the basement room, which doubled as a sort of gymnasium. There didn't seem to be one.

"Blood!" said Sharon Blake.

Morris turned as though he were hit.

She was kneeling beside Harry. Her hand was in the air like a spoken word.

"My God, he was shot." Now she was holding both hands in front of her.

The sound of Morris' cane dotted the surface of the floor. He lowered himself awkwardly to one knee. The back of Harry's shirt was sticky to the touch. The dark fabric concealed the still-tacky blood. There seemed to be at least three separate holes. Sharon Blake was crying again. She lowered her head to Harry's shoulder.

Morris steadied her. "Easy. We better disturb him as little as possible." He felt her shaking in his arms. "I think you'd better call in. The whole state will be on fire when it gets the news."

She moved her head up and down, still on her knees.

"Damn," said Morris.

She looked at him in surprise.

"I was remembering all the things we've touched in this cabin."

The thought seemed to lift her to her feet.

"I can't find a phone down here," said Morris.

"There isn't one." Her voice was all business, as if she had gotten up as another woman. "He came down here to get away. And to do his exercises. Those that he could still do." She looked at Morris. "The phone is upstairs."

Now Morris could see the blood on the brown floor. It seemed to be smudged, as if Harry had crawled in a half circle. He must have been sitting on the tall stool when he was shot in the back. The sound it must have made in the room! For the first time, Morris' own voice had backed up in his throat;

he could see Harry in the dark, watching his first great team flicker on the wall, and no iron-headed assholes in the stands to rise up cheering as if they had paid for the glory with their own blood. "Did he often look at old film?"

"He *always* watched film. Sometimes of games played twenty years ago. I've been seeing him a year, Morris. Since he came to my father's funeral. Maybe he came because of me. I don't know. I don't think so. I hardly knew him. Of course, I grew up hearing a lot of gossip about him—I expect much of it true. It made him terribly attractive."

Morris was afraid to touch her shoulders. He did not want to shake the ice out of her voice. "Why didn't he use the screen?"

"It was broken. I'm sure of that."

Morris thought aloud: "Harry is sitting in the dark. Watching the film of a thirty-two-year-old football game. Someone comes down the stairs and shoots him in the back. Harry didn't see him. But maybe Harry already knew who he was."

"Do you think it was Oberon?" asked Sharon.

"Maybe. Harry wouldn't even hint to you what he meant on TV? Who didn't come by the dressing room in Knoxville?"

"No. He only said what I told you: 'One of them is the killer. You'll see.'"

"Then at least two people must have been absent from the dressing room in Knoxville after the game. The room was insane with people. But Harry wasn't looking for two strangers. What did he say on TV? 'Your "buddy" Henry Young would have missed you.' Of course, no matter who admits not being there, it won't prove a damn thing. But maybe someone will *lie*. That might help us. Then again, Harry may have been dead wrong about everything. Except: the killer believed him."

"Morris, look—by his shoulder!"

The Tartan composition of the floor was the same as that on running tracks and gymnasium floors, and was dark brown. There was a straight line of blood, about four inches long, at the perimeter of the messy half circle of blood now fast-drying in the cold air.

Both of them kneeled, Morris as best he could. "The line is so straight. I don't think there is any doubt he drew it," said Morris. He could not see Harry's fingers; they were clutched into fists at his chest. Morris was not ashamed of the tears in his eyes or of the long pause before he could speak again. "It could be anything. An *I*. The start of a capital letter. A number. Anything."

"No. Not anything," said Sharon. "It couldn't be an *O* for Oberon." She was just able to speak.

He helped her up the stairs. Morris felt as cold as the metallic river shining in the night, and without any mercy in him.

Chapter Twenty-seven

Sullivan tilted the bottle on end. "That's it, my friend John Morris. You better sleep. Before the Associated Press calls again. They can't pee unless you tell them how to work the zipper."

"I keep thinking about his wife. Sharon says she's too ill to understand Harry's dead."

"I know."

"What time is it?"

"Almost twelve."

"Doc will have tried to tell her by now," said Morris.

"Do you want to see the late news?"

"God, no." Morris paused. "Who told you, Sullivan? When it was Monty?"

"A stranger who stopped on the highway. He said, 'The driver's dead.' He wasn't sure about you. You were unconscious in the back seat. For me, being there . . . made it easier . . . somehow."

"Goddamn Monty, it was my turn to drive."

"Hush. Finish your drink. That was years ago."

"I should have gone with Doc to see Caroline."

"No, you shouldn't have. She's ill. She doesn't need a stranger now."

"Why did Harry have to get himself killed? Why couldn't he die of tobacco or whiskey, like every other American?"

"Morris, why did you care about him so much?"

"He was the last sonofabitch alive afraid of nothing. He said he would kill God not to go back to the dirt. But that wasn't it. What was it, Sullivan, about him?"

"All that energy. The darkest eyes I've ever seen. You could see him once and feel his hands between your legs."

"Goddamn." Morris sat up, spilling the last of his drink. "Look what you made me do."

"I'm sorry," she said. "You asked me."

"Well, you didn't have to tell me."

She scratched the top of his head. "Don't be jealous."

"No." The whiskey did not help the pain in his knee.

"Do you think Oberon killed him?" She moved closer on the bed.

"Maybe. I can't think. Or sleep either."

"You're not finished on three drinks?"

"I'm an old man and my knee hurts."

"Poor fellow."

Morris closed his eyes. "The Lieutenant is tough. I can tell you that."

"I know. So long as she's busy. When she has time to think, it won't be easy. One day she will be glad she was there to help find him. But that won't be tomorrow. Morris. Do you think Harry would ever have left his wife?"

"They were married thirty-five years ago. Harry could have left her once a week. I wonder why he never did? Or why *she* put up with *him*?"

"I wouldn't mind having a coach. But I wouldn't want my daughter to marry one."

"Don't confuse Harry with other guys who call themselves coaches. He put a generation of *them* into life insurance." Morris opened his eyes and saw the clean profile of her nose and chin above the pillow. "Sullivan . . . the daughter you, or I, never had. We're the last of a species."

"Don't be gloomy." She reached over him and turned out the light. "You're all the daughter I'll ever need." Her voice was even lower in her throat. Morris was afraid she might cry. He held her until she was asleep. With his eyes closed he could see Harry Carr's house, with the huge porch that went all the way around it. He had never been inside. He didn't know anyone who had. Doc, of course. No writers. Nor any of his coaches. Maybe Johnny Moore. Maybe not...

Chapter Twenty-eight

The third time the phone rang, Morris put the pillow over it. He knew it was New York. There was nothing new to tell them. Sullivan did not move. She could sleep through a forest fire. Morris switched on the antique black-and-white television. The face of Harry Carr as a young man filled the entire screen. Harry was talking in a younger, higher octave. The camera rolled, and he was older. He was shouting something from the bench. The camera rolled again, and he was in the distance, on his tower. The film was network quality. Morris winced at the voice-over narration. There were three minutes of carefully phrased sentiment, with a smash ending of murder and back-to-you-Tom-in-New-York. Morris switched it off, as if to kill the announcer with oblivion. It was 7 A.M. No way to go back to sleep. The phone rang again. It was not New York. It was Doc. Morris didn't talk. He only listened. Doc's voice was a whimper.

Sullivan was snoring gently, like a house pet. Morris was reluctant to wake her. He swallowed his rage for TV, for Doc, for whoever killed Harry. His voice surprised him, how natural it sounded.

"Anybody under there?"

"Go 'way." She pulled the pillow over her head.

"I thought maybe the Chicago Bears were snoring under there."

"My contract says I don't have to get up until tomorrow."
She threw the pillow at him.

"I've got to see Doc. He just called." Morris kept his voice
under control. "I'll meet you at the police station. Tell the
Lieutenant what we learned from Miss Anne Hill and from the
Jennings girl. Help her look through Trapwell's chemistry papers for anything that might be a telephone number. Remember
the number has a slash in it."

"I remember, Master. Also, it's not an eight-two-two university number. That means it has to be an eight-two-three.
That's the only other exchange in town. Go. I can't bear to
hear a man's voice before I've had a cup of coffee."

Morris threw the pillow back at her.

"Morris."

He stopped.

"I'm sorry about Harry."

He raised his cane, and didn't speak.

The elevator was full. One of the men was saying, he didn't
care what the police said, he would bet Harry was drunk and
shot himself. Morris hung back to let the others off first. The
lobby was alive with newsmen and cameramen. You could
always tell the cameramen in their running shoes. Morris spotted Frank Caplin, who for once, turned his head as if to go
unseen.

Morris followed him to the front door. "Caplin. I read your
column," he said. It had begun: "Harry Carr died the way he
lived, by violence." "I noticed you left out Harry's record. Or
maybe it got cut."

Caplin cleared his throat. Morris was sure that he was uneasy.

"His record didn't seem very important, the way he died,"
said Caplin.

Morris was surprised he did not say it cynically. "No. No,
I suppose it wasn't. The three thousand boys who played for
him might argue the point. But what do they know?" Morris
held onto his cane for equilibrium. "You quoted Harry from
Knoxville. The dressing room was impossible after the game,
players singing through the press conference. I didn't see you
. . . I don't think."

Caplin had the same odd, uneasy look. "You know me. I
always hang out around the edges and listen to the dumb-ass

questions." He began to sound like his old self. "What do you know about this Oberon business," he asked.

"I doubt I know much you haven't heard," said Morris, hiding his surprise.

"The police have been covering it up," said Caplin, "but I can fix that."

"I'll bet you can." Morris nodded and walked onto the front porch and down the wooden steps which rang under his cane. The old man was selling the morning Atlanta paper, but he wasn't calling out the wrestling results. He shouted Harry's name blankly, as if he had been killed in another country. What had Harry said about General Neyland? "You couldn't beat him. And you couldn't outdrink him. The only thing you could do was live after him." The goddamn coaches from nine states would have to work not to smile at the cemetery.

It was a short ride to Jonas Haywood's hospital. Morris was surprised at the books, many of them paperbacks, none of them medical books, in his private office. Most of them were biographies. He might have been a professor of twentieth-century history. Doc closed the door behind them. He was tubby as a pumpkin in the brown suit.

"Worst thing you can say about a university hospital, nobody's dyin' of old age. You got to cure the little bastards. Lucky most of 'em got the clap. Cain't die of that."

"Harry *was* shot to death," said Morris.

"With a thirty-eight. Serious gun, a thirty-eight. Takes a serious shot to put three holes close as a man's hand, nearly in the dark. Even at twenty feet. And that's guessin', the twenty feet. I'm allowed to do that. Long as you don't quote nobody but the county medical examiner, that old fool."

"Why did you call me?" asked Morris.

"The Feds."

"You're in trouble?"

"They don't *say* I am. They just nod their heads and ask questions. They been over my drug records. Goddamn, Morris, I'm worried." Doc cleared his throat. "I hear the hospital pharmacist has his ass in a sling. Lotta shit missin': here at the hospital, the pharmacy school, the vet school. Not enough to start a drugstore, but all it would take to feed a habit from here to Harlem."

"But you're *clean*." Morris said the word as if it were a capital offense.

"They just shake their heads and look at my records. But I know what they're thinking."

"You're scared, Doc." Morris' voice was ugly.

"Morris," Doc pleaded. "Stuff breaks, gets lost, stolen, God knows. Somebody took the whole hospital water tank. I'm missin' just the ice in the glass."

"You *say*," said Morris, his voice without a trace of mercy. "You don't carry a thirty-eight, do you, Doc?"

Morris had never seen him frightened, truly frightened. He was standing, fat, and comically dangerous. "Get out! Tell them any goddamn thing you want to. Be a newspaper hero." Jonas was white around his eyes.

"That's better," said Morris. "That's better than the good-ole-boy shit. I know they are counting every cc of anything you ever signed for. I'll help them any way I can. The man who killed Harry is going to need more than a shot of Demerol to ease *his* pain."

"The Lieutenant trusts you. You can help me . . ." pleaded Doc, turning in a fat circle, looking as if he wanted to shake hands and be old friends.

Morris waited. "Tell me: Did you see Frank Caplin in the dressing room after the game in Knoxville?"

Doc was relieved to be asked a question. "Sure. I mean, yeah, he's always in the dressing room when he's at the game. He *was* at the game?"

Doc was pleading to be able to answer the question. Morris was sure he had no idea if he had seen Caplin. But only Harry knew more of what went on in Sparta, Georgia, than Doc. And Harry was dead.

Morris could see the Lieutenant had not slept. Her face shone with energy, as if fevered. Her restless hands lit on objects, then flew back into her lap. She stood up when the phone rang. "No," she answered before anyone could have finished a sentence. Her voice was unnaturally high. She had not yet begun to shake with fatigue.

"Where's Julia?" he asked.

She seemed to wonder for a moment whom he meant. "Upstairs. With Trapwell's papers."

"Find anything?"

She shook her head. Her eyes seemed to focus more clearly. "A chemistry professor, a friend of mine, helped sort out Trapwell's chemistry papers. This quarter he was taking Qualitative..." She was staring, then suddenly looked at him as if she had forgotten him. "Qualitative Analysis. Nothing, nothing like a telephone number in the margins."

"Maybe Oberon listened more carefully on the phone than Patty Jennings thought. Maybe he warned Trapwell, and Trapwell destroyed the chemistry paper with his telephone number."

"Maybe." She didn't seem to be following his reasoning.

"Are there many papers?" Morris asked twice.

"Yes." She smiled for the first time. "We could start a library. That boy never threw a scrap of anything away."

"Do you think Miss Anne Hill saw what she believes she saw in the hallway?"

"I don't think Miss Hill has ever been entirely wrong about anything."

"Do you think Oberon was Trapwell's lover?"

She nodded, then stared at nothing.

"I was just with Doc. He's scared. They're going over his drug records with a microscope. You know that?"

She nodded, but followed him with her eyes.

"Doc wants me to influence *you* to believe *him*. He says you trust me."

"I do." She smiled again, but it did not relieve the fatigue in her face.

"Doc says the university pharmacist has drug shortages of his own to explain: from the vet school to the hospital."

"Harry was right." There was pain in her face deeper than the fatigue. "Doc can't shut up."

"Who is the pharmacist?"

"He's an old man, Grimes. Phillip Grimes. He's been here forever. I doubt he could tell you how many floors the hospital has. He's too out of it even to be afraid. You should see his records... an unholy mess." She began to tremble. She folded her arms to keep from shivering.

"I also saw Frank Caplin," said Morris.

She watched him as if from a distance.

Morris frowned. "Caplin said he was at Harry's press conference after the game Saturday, but he looked—uneasy—that

I asked. I'm sure he heard what Harry said on TV: that the killer didn't come by the dressing room. Caplin was too . . . reasonable. He should have had a nasty answer for so dangerous a question." The Lieutenant was hardly hearing him.

"It was a thirty-eight," said Morris.

"Yes." Her small chin seemed too heavy to lift.

"Some aim, in the dark."

She nodded again.

"Maybe a professional job?" Morris did not believe it when he said it. Harry didn't gamble. It was the one vice he missed. No one loved him more than the big-time rollers. They lived high, betting Harry's teams. It wasn't that so much, Morris thought, as they liked his style, his "insolence of office" to reporters, millionaires, presidents, a way no other coach could ever be. Morris leaned forward to catch her dozing out of her chair, but she sat straight up and blinked.

"I'll just run upstairs and see Julia," said Morris.

"Yes." Her eyes were bruised with sleeplessness. Morris bit the inside of his cheek to keep from telling her to go home. Harry was dead, but the life force of him swam in her paleness. So long as she was awake, they both were alive.

Sullivan sat in the middle of the floor with boxes of papers on three sides.

"What's this, the 'Great Scorer come to score against our name'?"

"Ever notice how writers always quote better writers?" Sullivan deliberately kept her eyes buried in a box as if she were speaking to it.

Morris put his hand on the top of her head.

"How's Sharon?" asked Julia.

"Dead sitting down."

"Oh, Morris. The next morning, for the first time you know it's really true."

"I know. Death doesn't keep very well in the night." He smoothed her hair. "Not finding any telephone numbers?"

"I'm going back through the chemistry papers. Patty said the number was written in the margin, remember? I unconsciously have been looking first in the left and right margins. I didn't look so closely at the top and bottom margins. Then I have to tackle all of *those*. The officers who boxed up Trapwell's papers mixed this quarter's sophmore papers with all of his freshman papers. We'll have to go through every box. It'll take time to do the job right. I know his careful handwriting so well now I hurt for him, for how hard he worked. I feel I know him; it's the strangest feeling, Morris. I *know* I can find the number if he didn't throw the chemistry paper away."

Morris checked his watch. "According to Patty's schedule, she doesn't have classes this morning. I want to ask her..." Morris picked up the phone on the one table in the room. His luck held. Patty answered: "Yes?"

Morris was sure she had answered every call she had ever gotten with a question. He identified himself and quickly put her at ease. "No. Nothing's happened. We're looking through Harvey's papers. We haven't found the telephone number you saw. Tell me, Patty, how did you know it was a chemistry paper the number was written on?"

"Please." She seemed to panic. "I told you I wasn't sure it was a telephone number. The man who answered said it was a wrong number."

"I understand. We simply want to check it. Have you studied chemistry?"

"No. Goodness, no. I'm an English major. I didn't recognize any of the formulas or whatever they were. But the paper was in a chemistry book."

Morris gave her no help.

"I remember the word... 'analysis.'" She waited, as if for Morris to confirm her recollection. "I remember wondering just what the course meant. The textbook looked impossible. The paper was in the book."

"Was the course Qualitative Analysis?" asked Morris.

"Yes. I think that was it... I'm sure."

"Were there any other papers? Or books?"

"No. Just the one book. He left it on my front seat."

"The formulas, the graphs on the paper, could they have been calculus?" asked Morris.

"I don't know calculus. The paper looked as impossible as the textbook to me."

"Thank you," said Morris. "You've been a big help."

"Please..."

"Yes."

178

"You won't. I worry about upsetting the man. You won't use my name . . . on the telephone?"

"No. Not if we can help it. There is no reason to at the moment. And thank you again."

Morris looked down at Julia. "The professor who helped you is sure he separated out all the chemistry papers?"

"Morris, you wouldn't believe how fast he went through them. Trapwell's four quarters of chemistry papers were in separate batches, but roughly together. But the professor flew through everything. I think he could have missed the Elephant Man in there."

"You know what I think?" said Morris.

"I can't wait." She propped her hands on the floor and leaned back in a deliberately appealing way.

"I think it may not have been a chemistry paper at all. It just happened that it was folded in a chemistry book. Trapwell this quarter was also taking calculus. Patty Jennings doesn't know qualitative analysis from digitalis. But she remembers 'formulas or whatever it was.' You know calculus, Sullivan?"

She smiled for a long time, and still smiling, said: "You don't think I know the difference between chemistry and calculus, do you, Morris? Since they both start with a 'c.'"

"God knows *I* don't," said Morris.

"Wonderful." She threw a handful of papers in the air. "All I have to do is find his calculus papers. And look for seven numbers written with a slash in one of four margins. Morris, I love you a lot, or I would kill you."

"We'll get you some math help. Maybe a cute lady mathematician."

"Oh, I'll recruit my own help. I'll tell you something funny. I minored in math until I gave it up for a golf bum; one just like you, Morris; you remember him well."

"He's not here to defend himself." Morris eased toward the door.

She looked wonderfully awkward getting off the floor. "Okay. I'll look through the calculus papers first." She was all seriousness. "It'll save time, if you're right."

"I have to go to a press conference. The good President of

this university—" Morris' own spirit turned to chalk in his mouth. "—is going to tell us who will be Harry for the next thirty years." There was no fun in his voice.

Sullivan hugged him with both arms.

Chapter Twenty-nine

The doors to the President's private office were open. Morris was sure the secretary recognized him, but she did not speak. She seemed older, or maybe more tired. Morris stopped to admire the early Matisse print, then stepped through the double doors. The President stood in a black tangle of electrical cords to a battery of TV flood lights. Again, in this room, Morris felt a sense of *déjà vu*. Harry might have been squinting into the same lights, waiting to speak. Theodore Walker's voice was deliberate and under control, with none of the passion of Harry Carr.

"This university has survived for one hundred and thirty-seven years. It survived a civil war. And two world wars. With many casualties. It has never had a sadder, more regrettable moment." The President paused, as if to weigh the effect of what he had said. He had said it well. Morris would give him that.

"You know his record. Thirty-two years of teams and never a losing season." Strange. He did not call Harry by his name. "Six national championships. To coach was the second best thing he did. To *teach* was the best thing he did. He taught a generation of young men how to compete." Walker raised his chin, advanced his ruined complexion brutally into the cameras. His eyes were gray circles in the white light. Why all the bullshit? wondered Morris. Harry kicked a generation of young men in the ass until they won nine out of every ten football games they played. Walker still hadn't said his name. "I played football. I know what a tough game it is. I know how his teams laid it on the line. I have been here for only one fall. I counted him as a close friend." Morris watched him; he did not blink when he said it. Morris remembered the fury on the President's face the night Harry spoke, drunk. What had Walker called him? "The last dinosaur." In truth, he had not said it viciously. But Walker had added, "He can't go on forever." No, he wasn't going on forever. Why all the shit about Harry's being a close friend? What had Harry kept calling him in Knoxville? "That candyass." But Harry had called plenty of people worse. Morris missed what Walker was saying. Something about prayers for his wife. "We can't replace him. Football can't replace him. But I am naming his longtime assistant, Johnny Moore, as acting head coach. Until the end of the season."

Walker agreed to answer questions. "Yes, a search will begin to pick Harry's successor."

God help him, thought Morris. He raised his own hand. Walker nodded. "Do you know Oberon?" asked Morris.

Walker cocked his head as if he had misheard him. "I'm sorry I didn't get that." He was sweating in the white lights.

"O-b-e-r-o-n, " spelled Morris. "Do you know him?"

Walker again shook his head. "Is that a last name?"

Other questions were fired at him.

Morris did not yield the floor. "Did you speak to Harry Saturday, after the game?"

"No." Walker fumbled with the microphone in front of him. "I stuck my head in the dressing-room door. It was even more hectic inside than usual. I saw Harry, but I didn't stay to speak. I also heard what he said Sunday on television. I have no idea who he was talking to. Who the person was who didn't come by the dressing room."

"You don't doubt Harry meant the killer of the two boys?"

Walker cocked his long head. "Harry was threatening somebody. I was going to insist he talk with the police. That's all I can say."

Questions came from every direction.

Morris did not wait for the answers. He was the first reporter to leave the room. He nodded but did not speak to Frank Caplin, who smiled as if he had inherited the earth. Jack Pruitt matched steps with Morris. He had reserved a telephone down the hall.

Morris was careful not to interrupt Pruitt until he had called in the announcement of Harry's temporary successor to the Atlanta bureau.

"Did you get any sleep?" asked Morris.

"Hardly. It's . . . been one follow-up after the . . . other," said Pruitt with his familiar hesitations. "Help's . . . coming this afternoon. Some . . . job you did last night. Morris . . . you didn't have to . . . put my name on the story . . . but . . . I thank you." Pruitt looked as worn as his bad teeth.

"If you don't mind going back in there?" said Morris. "I want to wait outside and catch Johnny Moore alone when he comes out."

Pruitt turned to go, and stopped. "I . . . quoted Harry a . . . hundred times. Never really knew him. He used to ask where the . . . hell you were living. Said once . . . he missed your big ass and 'Fessor Blake ganging . . . up on him . . . trying to run . . . his damn team. I never heard . . . him call any other newsman by his . . . name." He grinned a libel with his bad teeth: "Except Caplin. That's who . . . he meant when he said . . . 'asshole.'"

Morris was glad to laugh. The tower clock chimed the quarter hour.

Morris took the elevator; and then the long steps one at a time, down to the sidewalk blowing with leaves in front of the old main building. Students hurried under the trees, bulky in their sweaters and jackets, keeping their separate appointments. Morris found a bench from which he could see the steps. Reporters came down in pairs, and then cameramen with all their gear over their shoulders and hanging on their belts. Morris welcomed the wind cutting into his back, keeping him alert. Pruitt was the last reporter to leave. He spotted Morris and raised his hand in salute. Then the steps were empty until the clock struck the full hour. Morris stood as soon as he was sure he saw Johnny Moore, who came down the steps as erect as a major general.

Morris waited so that Moore would see him. Johnny stopped, his face rigid and suddenly old under his gray crew cut.

"You must be the only man who ever really knew him, Johnny?"

Moore stood as if at attention. "No. There wasn't a day Harry didn't amaze me. I could never guess what he would think. He never said *why*, for anything he did, for as long as I knew him. I ran the offense until I made a decision he didn't like. Then he changed it. Instantly. God knows he could be wrong, but not often. You think he was tough?" Johnny didn't wait for an answer. "He scared hell out of me, what he was capable of watching a boy do to his body. Funny. Every year some kid dies playing football, but never here. Some days I couldn't believe anybody could live through it, and Harry would have me in the middle slinging kids off the ground. God-a-mighty, Morris, I never meant to coach one day after him. If I can get this team through the last game, I'm through. I know I don't have to ask you not to write that."

Morris laughed. "You learned more than you know from Harry. Listen, what did he mean on television? Who was he accusing?"

Johnny shook his head. "I noticed he kept looking for somebody in the dressing room Saturday. That wasn't like him."

"He didn't say anything to you?" asked Morris.

"I don't know."

"What do you mean?" asked Morris, leaning on his cane.

"Harry would say something and never explain it. He was always doing it with me. I got to where I ignored him unless he had something to say about our offensive scheme. Then I waited for him to tell me what he wanted me to do."

"What did he say Saturday after the game?"

"He wasn't happy with our play selection into the short side of the field. Thought we should have pitched more into the sideline. He was right. Twice, after the dressing room was empty, he said something I didn't understand. I thought about it after the television show. Twice he said, 'Who the hell could have believed it would be either one of them?' Or something like that. I didn't pay any attention, but I did notice he kept looking for somebody Saturday. It wasn't like him. He didn't give a damn what senator came walking up to him after a game. Or millionaire. He liked to shake hands with the old players he believed in. He didn't fake any interest in old players who hadn't laid it on the line. We didn't have many of those who stuck around..."

"That was all he said?" Morris asked. "Nothing else."

"That's all he said, twice." Moore held his shoulders square, as if to get through the rest of the season on sheer will.

"Did you tell Lieutenant Blake?" asked Morris.

"No. I haven't talked with her. But you can tell her for me. I don't have any idea what Harry meant, if anything."

Morris offered his hand. Johnny's grip was solid as oak.

Coming toward them was the President himself, Theodore Walker. He walked directly to Morris. "You had a telephone call, just now in my office. From Julia Sullivan. She said it was very important. She left the telephone number of the police station. I'm sorry I don't have it—"

"Thank you," said Morris. "I know the number." He started toward the administrative building, and stopped. "Doctor, you have a good man in Johnny Moore. The best."

Walker tilted his head and shoulders. "I know that."

Johnny did not speak or even smile, his shoulders stiff as iron.

Morris took the steps with his cane, not letting himself imagine why Julia was calling him out of a press conference.

There was a small office just inside the front entrance. Morris asked a secretary if he could use the telephone, a large hand already on the receiver. The lady nodded without taking her fingers from her typewriter.

The police switchboard put him through to Julia's room. She answered before the second ring, breathing the word *yes* as if she had run up two flights of stairs.

"What's up?"

"Morris." Her words did not wait for a response. "I found him, I talked with him; he's terrified." She caught her breath.

"Who?"

"Oberon. I said the name. He was hysterical. He was crying. It was his number—you were right—on the calculus paper. The man is terrified. But he admitted who he was."

"You just spoke with him."

"Not ten minutes ago. Morris, he wants to see us. Before the police. He begged me. It was pitiful."

"When? Where?"

"Now. I could hardly understand him. He was in his apartment. I'm sure for lunch; I was afraid of his apartment. You couldn't believe how he cried and begged. Morris, it was awful. I said no, we would meet him in a public place. I could hardly understand him. But he said the library. Something about he

184

does research, has a small office there; he'll meet us on the front steps."

"Where's the Lieutenant?"

"She left an hour ago. Exhausted. They had to drive her home. She hasn't slept in two days. Morris, I promised him we would meet him at the library."

"That's all the way across the campus from here. You have your car?"

"Yes."

"I'll see you there—Julia! What's Oberon's name?"

"I'm not sure, he was crying uncontrollably; I think he said 'Doctor Brewton.' He couldn't talk. But he'll be waiting for us. Morris, he didn't sound dangerous. He sounded . . . terrified."

"Tell that to Harvey Trapwell. And Harry Carr." Morris' own voice was like dry ice. "Doctor Brewton has reason to be terrified."

The hike to his car seemed longer than Morris had remembered. Then he couldn't spot the Chevrolet in the huge parking lot. He looked at the tag on the keys to the U-Drive-It to remember the color of the Chevrolet: gray. Every car in the lot seemed to be gray. Finally, he was sure he saw it. The license matched the number on the keys. His own hands were sweating in the cool air.

Backing out, the car seemed to lurch under him. Morris shifted into Drive, and the Chevrolet nearly veered into the rear of a Buick. He opened his door and propped himself up on his left leg. The front left tire was flat. He had forgotten it needed air. And now the tire was dead on the rim. Morris sat down and closed the door and pushed the gearshift back into Drive. He wrestled the wheel in his big hands as the car moved erratically forward. He gritted his teeth against the sound of the now-ruined tire.

Every car in Sparta seemed to be coming down College Street. Morris feared he would lose control entirely if he attempted to dart into the traffic. At last there was a brief gap, and he kicked the Chevrolet forward. He made a desperate left turn as the front end threatened to slew out from under him. He could feel the left tire bunching and writhing. The street pitched down toward the stadium, and the tire went, the hood sinking to the left and toward the oncoming traffic. Morris lifted the car with his huge hands and turned it on its one tire into the curb, where it jammed. He braced himself for the traffic behind him and *felt* the sound of squealing tires like a physical impact. He sat braced, amazed at the stillness.

A student in a plaid coat was rapping on his window. "You okay?"

Morris nodded his head. Then looked at his watch. Julia might already be at the library. He opened the door and tried to get out. It had been years since he had forgotten his stiff leg. His cane had pitched onto the floorboard. It was an effort to retrieve it. Then he stepped out into the lines of cars which had stopped in both directions, making an impossible traffic jam. Students left their cars to see what had happened. Now horns were sounding in the distance. Morris looked again at his watch. "I'm sorry," he said to the student in the plaid coat, as if he were a cop, "I've got to leave the car here. I've got to get to the library. Someone's in trouble."

Morris started down the hill toward the library, which was more than a mile away. There was no hope of getting a ride. Cars were stymied in both directions. Morris swung himself down the sidewalk, his left knee already stiffening from the pace. All the way down the long hill and then up the other side, he had to will himself not to look at his watch. He settled into a pace and kept it, ignoring the knee, putting as much weight as he could manage on the cane. He could feel the cool wind on the sweat in his hair; the cane was slippery in his hand. Finally, he could see the library building, massive, up ahead of him. The long steps seemed to retreat in front of him, and then he began to gain on them. Between breaths he looked for Julia. Students were moving and standing, even a few sitting, on the steps. Morris walked the length of the building before climbing the steps, making certain Julia was not waiting on them.

The silence inside stopped him again.

It was a huge library. Morris felt the weight of his cane in his hand. He searched the faces of the people standing at the main desk. None of them was Julia's. Now he saw a building directory near the elevator. The reading room was on the first floor. He turned, narrowly missing a thin woman with a re-markable armload of books and a pencil between her teeth.

The reading room was long and full and noiseless. Morris stopped at each table. Faces lifted at the sound of his cane. No

Sullivan. He was sure of that before he was halfway down the room. Still, he checked each table. Then the open stacks around the tables.

Morris plunged back to the front desk. The thin woman had put down the armload of books.

"Excuse me. I'm with the Associated Press. I'm looking for a woman, Julia Sullivan: tall, slim, brunette, attractive, mid-forties. Came here maybe fifteen minutes ago. Looking for a . . . Doctor Brewton."

The thin librarian turned her palms up at the number of people going in and out of the building. "I'm sorry. I just came on duty." Her attention wandered. She turned to the stack of books behind her.

"Do you know a Doctor Brewton who does research in the library?" asked Morris.

She shook her head. "Sorry." She bent toward the books.

Morris checked his watch.

"Did you say, *Doctor Brewton*?"

Morris turned at the sound of the name. An older woman, short, quite heavy, with round eyes, looked up from a stack of books she was checking out to a girl who was young enough to be a freshman.

"Yes," said Morris.

"Are you sure you don't mean Doctor Brewer? He was with a woman much like the one you described. She left a note." She turned her back to retrieve it. "For 'John Morris.' Is that you?"

"Yes." Morris struck the desk with his cane, reaching for the folded note. The woman stepped back with fright, holding her throat with one hand.

"I'm sorry." He willed his voice level. "The note is terribly important."

She handed it over reluctantly.

Morris read the two lines at one look: *Dr. Brewer is upset. We are waiting in his office, Room 1027.*

Then the name struck him—*Brewer*. "That son of a bitch!"

Now both librarians were frightened.

Morris did not comfort them. "Did they go up on the elevator?" he asked the heavyset woman.

She was nodding her head yes, but did not speak.

Morris pushed himself forward into the people waiting for

the elevator. A tall, older man with a mustache looked up at the size of him with annoyance. No one spoke. The elevator came down filled. But without Julia. Morris watched the face of each man getting off as if to read his past in his eyes. He did not give a damn for Dr. Marvin Brewer and/or Oberon. He wanted to see Julia Sullivan.

Morris wedged himself into the near corner of the elevator. It stopped on six of the ten floors. Only he got off at the top. The narrow hallway was empty. He had hoped there would be a security guard, but there was only an empty table.

He swung his stiff knee under him. Room 1027 was the third room on the left. The door was open. Morris turned inside without stopping, the noise of his feet and his cane startling a thin, bald man at the one small desk.

Morris gripped his cane as if to attack him. "Where's Brewer?"

The thin man tried to speak. He could only nod his head yes.

Morris leaned on his cane, surprised that he needed to catch his breath. "It's bloody important."

The man found his voice. "I share the room with Marvin. He has it afternoons. I'm usually finished . . . he was here just now . . . Are you Mister Morris?"

Morris put his fist on the desk. "I am."

"Marvin was . . . he could barely talk. There was a lady with him. I offered to leave. Marvin was too disturbed to sit down. Do you know what's the matter? My name is Doctor Paul Melton—"

"Where the fuck are they?" Morris was ready to drag him over the desk.

"I'm sure there is nothing improper." Melton sat far back in his chair. "They asked me to tell you to meet them on the observation walk—"

"The what? How do you get there?"

"The stairs at the end of the hall. They lead to the roof."

"The roof?" Morris was out of the room without thanking him. He felt nothing climbing the stairs, not even his stiffening leg. He pushed the glass door against the wind, which was colder than he remembered.

Chapter Thirty

The observation walk circled the air-conditioning works in the center of the roof. No one was in sight. The brick wall was chest high. He started counterclockwise around the roof. His cane rang on the cement. He was surprised at the noise the wind made. He did not look down at the campus. He was sure it was not the wind he now heard. Someone was crying. Morris pushed forward on the rough concrete. Around the turn was a man's back. Bent forward. Shaking. His two arms hidden in front of his huge body. The wind blew her long brown hair over his elbow. Still the sobbing. Morris lifted the great back straight up with his hands and arms, lifted until the waist was as high as the top of the wall. The sobbing became a scream.

"Let her go. Or I'll drop you, you sonuvabitch!" Morris was amazed at the terror of his own voice.

The man shook uncontrollably in his arms.

"Put him down!" The face was Julia Sullivan's. Tearless. "John Morris, he's already scared to death."

Morris lowered the man to his feet, his own arms trembling with effort. And turned him against the rim of the wall. Brewer was wide but soft. His eyes were closed. Tears poured down his face into his heavy beard.

"So, *Counselor*, you only met Harvey Trapwell '*twice in your life*,'" Morris said. "The last time, I suppose, was when you killed him."

Brewer's mouth faltered in his beard. His eyes opened, blinking as if they feared the light. Sullivan bent to pick up a pair of round wire glasses that, amazingly, were unbroken on the concrete.

Brewer put them on, huge tears smearing the lenses.

189

Morris spoke to Sullivan as if Dr. Marvin Brewer were not standing on the roof of the library between them. "You always invite killers up to the roofs of buildings alone?" Morris' own fear sounded like anger.

"We waited for you. It was awkward, so many people in the library. The research office he shares was occupied. Doctor Brewer's in shock. And where were you, Morris?"

"The damn tire. I had to leave the rental car in the street."

"I won't say I saw it was going flat. Thank goodness you're here, Morris. Doctor Brewer's in terrible trouble."

"Murder is a nasty habit," said Morris, holding on to the iron in his voice. "What was Trapwell to him?"

"They were lovers." She did not say it brutally. "He panicked when the boy was killed. He wants to clear himself. He says."

"He's about three murders late."

The man raised his chin in an effort of courage.

Morris felt only the cold wind blowing in his face. "Let's get off of here and talk. Before we see the police."

Brewer opened his mouth at the word *police*, but could not speak.

Morris ignored the front desk as they left the library. The librarians could read about Oberon soon enough. He felt their eyes follow them through the door. Students on the steps were still going from group to group with the latest rumor of the death of Harry Carr. And who might have killed him. And who was replacing him. Brewer passed unseen among them.

The lunch crowd was thin at Jake's on the edge of the campus. One of the small private rooms was empty. Suddenly, Morris was hungry. He ordered a ham sandwich, and Sullivan, unusually quiet, nodded the same. Brewer couldn't eat. Each of them had a whiskey. Brewer wiped his mouth and beard carefully with his napkin. Morris could see the drink helped. He was not prepared to believe anything the man answered.

"Did you kill Harvey Trapwell?"

Brewer bolted the rest of his drink. "No." He held onto the glass with both hands. "I loved him." He did not avoid Morris' eyes.

"How did you know he would . . . respond?" Morris was glad to hit on the verb *respond*.

"I didn't. It was a simple progression: from counselor to friend to . . . lovers."

Morris gave him the word *simple*. "Why did you call yourself Oberon? Is it the code word of a group . . . or a cult?"

Brewer was shaking his head. "Not to my knowledge. I don't belong to any . . . group." He did not touch the word *cult*. "It was just a name I picked. My field is medieval history." He was almost whispering. "My work is important to me."

"Did he have other lovers?"

"I don't know."

The answer came too easily. Too quickly, thought Morris. "When did you see him last?"

"Harvey stayed at my apartment Sunday night. I lied when you called me . . . about the note in his locker. I wanted to tell you when you came to my office. I couldn't. I've been terrified since. When the phone rang today—when she said the word 'Oberon,' I almost—killed myself."

"Why did you call in an ad to the paper on Monday if you had just seen Trapwell Sunday night?"

Brewer did not hesitate. "I called from Atlanta Monday. I was doing research at the Emory University library. I didn't know when I left if I would be gone one day or several. I saw I could finish Tuesday. Harvey was so upset when I left. He had quit the team. I didn't try to talk him out of it." He looked at Morris. "That man Carr treated him like an animal. Now he's dead, too—" Brewer's voice faltered. He did not look up to see how his story was being taken.

"Don't forget the football manager Henry Young. He took your message on the telephone. He's dead, too. When did you leave the message?"

Brewer clicked the ice in his glass thirstily against his teeth. "I never . . . I didn't know who was on the phone. It was two weeks ago. Harvey had been depressed with the whole football scene, but he wouldn't quit. I was tired of hearing about it. When I got to Atlanta, I knew I was wrong. He had to talk it out. I took a chance and called the athletic dormitory. Then the Athletic Center. I panicked and left the note from Oberon. I tried to pass it off on the phone as a joke. I put one word in the Times: 'Sorry.' Harvey laughed about it when I saw him. Suddenly, we were both taking too many chances."

Sullivan lifted the one-word ad from her purse.

"Did you charge the two phone calls from Atlanta?"

"Yes. To my hotel room. I have copies of the hotel bills. I have a grant for part of my research expenses."

"Where were you after Harvey's funeral . . . about six forty-five P.M.?"

Brewer did not speak until Morris repeated the question. "I was in my apartment. I almost didn't make it through the funeral."

"You were alone?"

He nodded.

"Where are the coat and tie Trapwell was wearing the last Sunday afternoon?"

Brewer needed another drink. He was tugging again at his beard, his eyes wide in his glasses. Morris did not signal the waiter. Brewer cleared his throat. He said into his hands, "I should have thrown them out, but I couldn't."

"For an innocent man, you're frightened of everything. Even the clothes of a dead boy." There was no mercy in Morris' voice.

"You know why I'm afraid." Brewer sounded more pitiful than angry. "My life . . . my job. Even if they don't—This is a state university in Georgia. Not Harvard. You don't think they would have kept me a minute if they had known . . . even before Harvey was—" Brewer ran out of anger. His hands scrambled from the table to his lap.

"Do you know Paul Teller?"

"Barely. Just a friend of Harvey's."

"Did he know you two were lovers?"

"For God's sake don't involve the kid. You'll destroy him."

"Maybe Teller was jealous. Maybe he killed Trapwell."

"No." Brewer shook his head. "He's just a kid, a bright kid . . ."

"What about the clothes Trapwell died in?" asked Morris.

"He kept a few things in my apartment. A pair of his trousers are missing, and a blue shirt of mine."

"Didn't you think the shirt would be traced to you?"

"It was new. I had never worn it. I bought it in Atlanta." He did not blink.

"Lucky you," said Morris. "I had an appointment with Trapwell for Tuesday morning. Why did he come to my hotel room Monday night?"

"I don't . . . he . . . Harvey said Sunday he was going to see a reporter. He was sick of football. He was sick . . . of his life. Everybody feeding off of him . . . Harry Carr, the drunken fans, his teammates, all of them bloodthirsty . . . He even found someone in the dressing room stealing drugs . . . He wanted someone to tell his whole life to . . . I warned him . . ."

Morris slid both palms down on the table, careful not to raise his voice. "When was someone stealing drugs?"

Morris nodded for the waiter to bring another round.

Brewer seemed to gather himself. "It was during Saturday's game. Harvey had gone to the dressing room, with his nose broken—not that anyone gave a damn." Brewer was truly angry. "He told me someone was going through the team medical supplies. Someone who had no business being in the dressing room at that time. Harvey said he took the bottles away from him . . . He said he even took his key to the dressing-room door. Harvey hurt his nose again, and the man left—"

"Who was he?" Morris did not take his eyes from Brewer's face.

The drinks had come. Brewer drank greedily. "I don't know. He never said. Harvey wanted to tell his whole life story to a reporter. To *you*. He wanted to write a book. He was obsessed about it. Even tell that he . . ."

"Was homosexual," said Morris.

Brewer nodded. "I warned him. I begged him. No medical school would ever touch him if he did—"

"And so you killed him," said Morris.

Great tears came again in Brewer's eyes. He shook his head above the glass. "I could never have hurt him . . . no matter what he told."

"What happened to the key?" Morris gripped his cane with his left hand. "If Harvey took away the thief's key, where is it?"

"It's in his coat pocket, in my apartment. Stuck in bloody cotton, Harvey's own blood from his broken nose. He showed the key to me." His tears ran into his hands.

"Drink up," said Morris. There was no malice in his voice. He looked across at Sullivan. "Are you the lady at this table without a tongue?"

"He told me much of it on the roof. But not about the key."

"We had better wake the Lieutenant," said Morris.

Brewer looked up from his empty glass. "I don't suppose there is any use in asking...if my name—"

"No," said Morris. "Don't ask. You lied from the beginning. To me. To the police." Brewer did not deny it. "Your reputation isn't much beside three murders."

Brewer's jaw seemed to shrink in his beard. The fear in his eyes increased Morris' anger: Harry shot to pieces in the dark, bloody with regrets. Not Harry, who was he kidding? Bloody with hate, maybe. Morris almost smiled. "What did you say you teach?"

The professor did not look up. "Medieval history."

"Sure," said Morris.

"What will happen to him?" asked Sullivan as if Marvin Brewer were not sitting at the table.

"It's not going to be fun and games, even if he's telling the truth. If he killed Harvey Trapwell or Harry Carr or Henry Young, or all of them, he's going to sit in that long line waiting to see if they ever again switch on the electric chair."

Chapter Thirty-one

Morris waited in the back seat of the car with Brewer. Neither of them spoke. Brewer's hands never stopped moving in his lap. Julia Sullivan came through Sharon Blake's front door carrying a thermos. Sharon was right behind her in a fresh uniform, with a coffee cup in her hand. Her eyes were swollen, but the absolute fatigue was gone from her face.

Cold air blew into the car as they opened the front doors.

Morris waited until Julia had started the engine. "Lieutenant Blake, this is Doctor Marvin Brewer of the history department. He has a complicated story to tell you."

"Wait." The Lieutenant's voice was not unfriendly. She told

Brewer his legal right to remain silent. He shook his head. "Go ahead," said the Lieutenant.

He began to tell her all that he had told them. He forgot the key, until Morris reminded him. Brewer then told of the key and remembered one thing he had forgotten. "'You can't trust *anybody*,' Harvey said."

"He was surprised at the identity of the thief?" said Morris. Brewer nodded and resumed his story. His voice held up remarkably well. Sullivan kept the car running and the heater on in front of Brewer's old frame apartment house until he was finished.

The walls inside the three rooms seemed to be held up by books, including the kitchen walls. But everything was in place; even the stacks of papers on his table-desk were squared and cornered.

The Lieutenant warned them all. "Don't touch anything."

Morris stayed within a step of Brewer, who stood awkwardly, as if he were a stranger in his own apartment.

The bedroom contained only a chair, a lamp, a bed, more books, and a closet.

"Is this the closet with his clothes?" asked the Lieutenant.

"Yes." Brewer said the word as if it were a confession.

The Lieutenant opened the door with her handkerchief.

"The blue coat," Brewer said without hope.

The Lieutenant touched the slight bulge in the coat's left flap pocket. She reached inside with her handkerchief, revealing a ball of bloody cotton and the tip of a large key.

"It's a door key, all right," said Morris. "Do you think it might carry a fingerprint?"

The Lieutenant shook her head. "I doubt it. If the blood is Trapwell's, the key will probably have his prints, if any. Keys are tough." The Lieutenant turned to Brewer. "Anything else of Trapwell's here?"

He led them back into the living room to a modest stack of books and papers. "These," he said.

The Lieutenant was careful to touch nothing. She lifted the phone with her handkerchief. Morris could hear the high voice of Sergeant Redding answering. The Lieutenant repeated herself. Morris remembered that the Sergeant only understood sentences that were repeated twice. He was to wait for them on the back porch of the police station. The Lieutenant hung up.

Sullivan drove them past the police station before turning behind it.

Morris counted seven television vans parked out front. "I don't think TV left anybody in Atlanta to read the weather."

"They don't have weather. This isn't Colorado." Sullivan sounded like her old self. Dr. Brewer in the back seat had not spoken since they left his apartment. Still, Morris could not suppress a certain cheerfulness.

The Sergeant was waiting on the back porch.

Brewer walked reluctantly up the steps without looking left or right, as if approaching his own execution. Morris could not retrieve the hate he had felt when he had held the man's weight in his two arms.

The Lieutenant led them inside.

Brewer was too terrified to speak.

The Lieutenant's voice remained not unfriendly. "Doctor Brewer, please follow Sergeant Redding." He turned his soft, heavy body through the door without hope.

"So that is Oberon?" said the Lieutenant.

"Yes," said Morris. "And he denies killing anybody."

"Do you believe him?"

"I believe he's Oberon."

"Come on in the kitchen." The Lieutenant put her arm around Julia as if the investigation were their own personal conspiracy.

Coffee simmered on the stove. Morris poured three cups.

"We'll take his story again, from the top," said the Lieutenant. "And we'll keep taking it until we have everything he can possibly tell us. We'll check his telephone calls from Atlanta, and all of the facts we can run down. What do you think of his story?"

"I don't know," said Morris. "But I don't trust him. He admits he hated Harry. He talked to the manager Young, who was greedy enough to get himself murdered. But I can't see Brewer killing the boy Trapwell. Then again," said Morris, "*all lovers* are more dangerous than bullets."

The Lieutenant blushed away the fatigue under her eyes.

Julia took both of her hands. "John Morris writes well enough. He only sounds like a fool when he says something."

Morris resisted the urge to apologize. Lieutenant Blake was the first to look away.

"Will you release Brewer's name?" Sullivan's voice did not hold out much hope.

"We'll read him his rights again and keep taking his story and comparing it with what he has already said. But we can't suppress his name. Not after three murders. And his lies to us. We called him early in the investigation of Trapwell's death. He lied to the Sergeant." Her hand lifted to the top button of her blouse. "Morris, I'm releasing a statement about myself and Harry . . . But I'm still on the case. Until the city tells me differently."

Morris put a heavy arm around her shoulder. "Sure you are." He could not help but ask: "What will Harry's wife feel about your statement?"

Lieutenant Blake shook her head. "She's not well enough to read it or hear it."

"When will you release Brewer's arrest?"

"Not for a couple of hours. I'll call you at your hotel and give you a thirty-minute warning. We wouldn't have Brewer without your help."

"Will you release the fact that Trapwell and the professor were lovers?"

"Everything. We'll have to."

"But not the key that Harvey took," suggested Morris.

"No." She shook her head. "Not that. Who could it have been, Morris?"

"Anybody. That dressing room was supposed to be empty *during* the game. Not even Trapwell was supposed to be in there. Unless he had had a broken leg instead of a broken nose. Perhaps Doc saw whoever it was."

"Perhaps Doc wasn't surprised." The Lieutenant bit her fingernails. "Anyway, thanks both of you."

Sullivan hugged her like a sister.

Chapter Thirty-two

Morris wrote the story in his mind while Julia drove. She was careful not to speak until she parked in front of the Georgian Hotel.

"I'm worried about Sharon."

"You can bet it will be nasty," said Morris. "But she'll survive . . . if we catch the killer."

"You don't think Oberon did it?"

"Maybe 'catch' is the wrong word. Maybe 'convict' is a better one."

"What about the key?" asked Sullivan.

"It could mean anything. Brewer could have planted it."

"With Trapwell's own blood in the cotton?"

"We'll see. I've got to reach Pruitt. I'm sure he's waiting back at the police station."

"You go up to the room. I'll bring some ice," said Sullivan.

Morris had been right. Pruitt answered the page at the station.

"Jack. This is Morris. Something you should know: Lieutenant Blake has a suspect. Certainly a material witness to Trapwell's murder. She's going to release his name in a couple of hours." Morris could imagine the way Pruitt opened his mouth without speaking. "His name is Doctor Marvin Brewer. Of the history department. He was Trapwell's academic counselor. He also used the code name *Oberon*. He and Trapwell were lovers."

"Jesus."

Morris heard Pruitt scrambling for his note pad.

"Listen," said Morris. "The Lieutenant is going to ring me here at the hotel before she releases Brewer's name. She'll give us at least a thirty-minute warning. I agreed to hold back a fact or two she doesn't want printed. Get over here with your Tele-Ram. I'll draft a story."

". . . Yes." Pruitt managed to hesitate, pronouncing the one word.

Sullivan came into the room with ice.

Morris mixed two drinks. "I was scared to death at the library," he said.

"I know."

"It was worse than seeing you go down one of those Colorado ski slopes like a falling bird. I thought I might never see you again."

"I'm sorry."

He handed her a glass. "I should have had more confidence. You could see he was not dangerous."

"I think I might have been a fool. Who knows how a killer looks? Maybe they cry, too." She lifted her glass. "Thanks for being afraid."

There was a knock on the door. It was Pruitt, smiling through his bad teeth.

Morris sat in front of the still-unfamiliar computer. The story wrote itself. He edited it ruthlessly on the Tele-Ram screen, as if all the characters were expendable, himself included.

A drink later the telephone rang. It was Lieutenant Blake.

"Go ahead and release your story, Morris. There must be a dozen newsmen here. I can't protect this man. I don't have the right to."

"Everything except the key? Even that they were lovers?"

"Yes."

"Are you holding him? Have you charged him?"

"At the moment we're holding him as a witness. For his own protection, as much as anything else. I don't think he was bluffing . . . about killing himself. We haven't charged him yet. Morris, I know you aren't writing it, but the key does fit the stadium dressing room. It's not a copy, either. It's an original key. It had only one partial print, Trapwell's. We also did a quick test of the blood. There was enough to show that it's Trapwell's type."

"So our boy Oberon was telling at least as much truth as he knew we could prove."

"Yes. Morris, he also remembered that Trapwell said, 'Doc had better count his keys.' He swore he didn't know what Trapwell meant. Do you think Doc is involved?"

"Or maybe Brewer is looking for a suspect to take his place in the electric chair, should the juice ever come on again. Does Brewer have a police record?"

"Nothing obvious, that we've turned up. We're making a thorough check. Morris." Her voice was suddenly tight. "This will destroy him, even if he didn't kill anybody."

"Yes. In this town. He can't live here. But remember this—" Morris swallowed his own concern. "He could have told the truth. No one lied for him. When are you releasing his name?"

"In half an hour."

"See you at the press conference. And, Sharon—"

"Yes."

"Hang tough. Don't let the questions about Harry get to you."

"No." Her voice was not steady.

Morris hung up. Sullivan touched his arm. Pruitt stood at the window trying to look as if he had left the room. "Call the story in and let it ride," said Morris. "All of it. Insert . . . the police are holding Brewer as a material witness, but they haven't charged him. Yet. As soon as the story clears we'll go down to the station. It won't be dull."

Frank Caplin did not ask her, he accused her. "So you slept with him an hour before he was killed." He smoothed a ragged few strands of hair across his thin, bald head.

"I didn't *sleep* with him. I made love with him." The Lieutenant gripped her shoulder bag with both hands. Her voice did not falter. The laughter in the room was aimed at Caplin.

Someone said, "That's the only four-letter word Caplin can't spell."

"He can come closer to *spelling* it than anything else."

Laughter broke out again.

"Did you share drugs with him, Lieutenant Blake?" Caplin's thin hands shook with anger.

"Yes." The room was quiet. "Aspirin. He had a headache. I believe it will show up in the autopsy. Now, if there are any other questions regarding Doctor Brewer?"

Cameramen switched off their lights. Reporters began jockeying for the few telephones.

"Well, I'm not finished . . ." Caplin's hand trembled at the end of his tie.

"Well, I am." The Lieutenant turned and left the room.

"Finished is right," shouted Caplin.

Morris could not resist. "Careful. You'll bust an artery. Then you'll be interviewing Harry again, and you remember how Harry never told you anything."

"What I expect from the AP is service. Not bullshit."

"You got it, *asshole*. The Oberon story has been on the wire for nearly an hour." Morris said it with twenty years of feeling.

"You can expect a call from New York. I want an apology."

"Be sure and identify yourself as *asshole*. So New York will know who's calling."

Caplin was too angry to answer him. Morris laughed. Too bad Harry was not there to laugh with him. Morris walked through the confusion into the kitchen. The Lieutenant was not there. He found her on the back porch. Shivering in the cold. She looked up as the door slammed.

"You held your own," said Morris. "Even with the assassin Caplin."

"I don't know. I'm afraid he'll write me into even more trouble." She shook in her light jacket.

"Sure. And he'll have me fired, too. Caplin's been looking for something all his life. Money. Power. Whatever he's found hasn't been enough. If he's looking for a friend, he doesn't have one in any zip code in Georgia. He gets to keep his job because he can write sentences, and because every newspaper needs a sonofabitch. The only people who will be there to bury *him* are those who'll want to be damn sure he's dead. Forget him. Now come on inside before you freeze." Morris followed her back into the kitchen. He poured coffee while she sat down. "It's a lousy time to mention it, but has anybody talked with Harry's wife?"

"Doc. She's too ill to be interviewed. I know her live-in nurse. Mrs. Carr hasn't been out of the house in nearly five years . . ."

Sharon left it unsaid. Harry's wife could not have killed him.

"Brewer has a lawyer?" asked Morris.

"Yes. A good one. I saw to that. His problem is, he can't prove where he was Monday night when Trapwell was killed, or Wednesday night when the manager was killed, or last night—" She left the sentence unfinished. "Brewer *says* he was in Atlanta Monday, and at his apartment the other two nights. But he has no witnesses. We'll have to charge him. Sooner or later."

Morris nodded, the cup warm between his hands. "You'll never convict on what you have."

"No. But we've just started looking." The Lieutenant's face was without charity.

Chapter Thirty-three

Sullivan sat in the same chair at the same table. It might have been the first day she got to Sparta. The same young bartender was still out of place in the old bar.

"Give the lady a Scotch and companion," said Morris.

"No wonder you're single, Morris. You never forget anything. No woman can put up with that. Still want half of my chicken salad sandwich?"

"Is it the same sandwich? Are you the same girl? I think I'll go out and come in again."

"Just say 'girl' again, and you'll be a hero. Hush and sit down and tell me what's happening."

"You would make someone a bully bureau chief." The bartender leaned against the table. "One Scotch. One vodka tonic." Morris covered both of her hands with his one hand. Then picked up half of her sandwich. "What with Oberon, I think I forgot to tell you about the President's press conference. Harry's assistant Johnny Moore has Harry's old job. Temporarily. The phony President made a phony statement."

"Why phony?"

"Because I don't know him well enough to call him fraudulent. Now that Harry's dead, it seems he was actually Saint Francis of Assisi. And a noble teacher. Up until then, he was a drunk who won enough football games to appoint his own President. Harry couldn't stand the sonofabitch Walker. Neither can I. Don't ask me why. Something else: He said a lot of bullshit. But he never said Harry's name. That was Harry's trick."

"I like ugly men." Sullivan ducked her head between her shoulders and shivered. "But something about this President . . ."

"I thought you went for us glamour types." Morris reached for the other half of her sandwich.

She fended him off with a spoon. "You pretty boys get us in trouble and can't remember our names." She offered him a bite.

The drinks came. "New York is going berserk over Brewer, alias Oberon. Trapwell. Lovers. Everything. The Lieutenant did the right thing. She couldn't withhold anything. You believe the professor, don't you?" said Morris.

"I think I do. He's terrified."

"He has a right to be. Listen, I've come to a decision."

"To do what?" She sat up.

"To pledge PKA. Can I trust you one more time on fraternity row?"

"You know me. I'm an independent. Do you think that boy . . . what's his name?"

"Teller. Paul Teller. Do I think he knew Oberon? Remember, he asked me: 'What's that, a constellation?' Let's ask him again."

This time a maid answered the door. Yes, she would look for Mr. Teller. The fraternity house might have been up for sale; it was that empty. Morris did not hear even the thump of a stereo set inside the rooms. "Where do they go on Monday afternoons?"

Sullivan shook her head. "Wherever it is, I bet it's not legal."

Teller came into the room by himself. His flannel trousers were beltless. He needed a shave. He was frowning. He looked much more tired than the creased and barbered young man they had seen six days ago.

"You look like midterm exams." Morris kept his voice neither friendly nor unfriendly.

Teller's hand went to the stubble on his chin. "Yes... I've been studying..."

"Can we sit here?"

Teller looked around as if he were lost. "Yes."

Morris deliberately sat opposite him. Sullivan sat on the long couch with the boy.

"I think you better tell me about Doctor Marvin Brewer. He's under arrest. He's telling the police he knew you. How long have you known he was Oberon? Why did you lie about him to me and to the police?" Morris could see his hands tremble in his lap. "Or do you still think of *Oberon* as a 'constellation'?"

Teller started to speak and swallowed the words.

"You can join him at the police station. He lied, too," Morris said, without pity.

"I don't... I hardly knew him. I only met him a few times. Has he said something about me? Is that why you're here?" Teller's voice rose; he seemed barely able to speak.

Sullivan reached out as if she expected the boy to pitch over onto the floor. He sank back on the couch.

"Paul. I think you better tell me what you know about Harvey and Doctor Brewer."

"I... are you... going to write—"

"I'm going to listen. No promises."

Teller tried to stand, but couldn't. "You don't understand ... My name... How tough it is to get into medical school."

"No one ever made it from the electric chair."

Sullivan managed to keep from holding the boy's hand.

"I was... I have nothing to hide." Teller passed his hand through his brown hair. "I knew that Brewer—Doctor Brewer—called himself *Oberon*. When he wanted to get in touch with Harvey." He ran out of air with his mouth open. He no longer looked like a young Errol Flynn.

Morris waited.

"I'm—" Teller was crying. Sullivan abandoned her resolution and put her arm around his shoulders.

Morris checked to be sure they were still alone in the front room. "Paul. You're a bright young man, with a future. If you didn't kill anyone, or help kill anyone, you will be all right. Now tell us what you know."

His breathing slowed. Sullivan's touch seemed to help. When he began to talk, his voice was strangely calm. "Harvey loved him." He did not look away from Morris. "They met a year ago. Brewer was helping Harvey with his schedule. He was older. Sure of himself. Harvey could be honest and open with him. I—" He faltered.

"Were you jealous?" There was no contempt in Morris' question.

"No." Teller paused. "Yes. I . . . I didn't kill him. It was over between us a long time ago. We were just friends . . . but it hurt."

"You didn't see Harvey again after he left your room Sunday?"

"No."

"Careful before you answer: How was Harvey going to pay his way through school? Without football."

"With *you!*" Teller looked directly at him.

"*Me*? I never saw him alive." Morris was surprised at his own anger.

"He was through with football. And with Harry Carr. He was . . . he was going to come out of the locker room. He was going to tell his life story. He needed a writer. He hated the locals, but you were a national writer. He couldn't wait to talk with you."

Morris squeezed the handle of his cane. "The AP doesn't pay for stories. Certainly not that kind of money."

"He wanted someone to help him write a book. About his whole life. Everything! He was sure he could sell it. His name was on every television channel. I told him if he did, he could forget medical school. But he had made up his mind."

Morris' hand relaxed on his cane. The long room was still empty except for the three of them. "You think someone killed him to keep him quiet?"

Teller crossed his arms as if against a sudden wind. "I begged him. I offered to help him get a job. In the lab. He wouldn't listen."

"Who did the key belong to?" Morris watched Teller's face.

"What key?" His eyes were puzzled.

"The key with Trapwell's blood on it. The key wrapped in cotton."

"Oh." He remembered something.

Morris waited without speaking.

"I swear I didn't know it was a key. Harvey had a bloody ball of cotton. He put it on the dresser. I thought his nose had bled on it. I was going to throw it away."

Morris watched to see if he would invent anything.

"Harvey put it in his coat pocket, dried blood and all. He said . . . he said . . ." Teller strained to remember. "He said, 'I need this. There are people I'm going to bleed all over.' I had no idea what he meant."

"Did you mention the cotton to anyone?"

"No." He shook his head.

"Not to Brewer."

"I haven't seen Doctor Brewer in months. I was jealous. I admit it. I—"

Morris pressed his cane against the floor, waiting for him to say "I couldn't help myself." Instead, Teller began crying again.

Sullivan held his head on her shoulder. It took him a long time to be able to speak. "I felt . . . guilty when I heard he was dead. I was home free. If I didn't blow my exams. Medicine is all I ever wanted. I couldn't help it. I was glad he was dead."

"That's enough, Morris." Sullivan eased the boy's head onto the back of the couch and stood up. "He shouldn't talk anymore, not without a lawyer."

"I—" Teller held his head in his hands.

Morris stood, his bulk dominating the room. He waited until the boy looked up at him. "Take a walk. Get yourself together. Call Lieutenant Sharon Blake. Don't go down there. The police station is full of reporters. Tell her to meet you somewhere. At Jake's. Tell her what you told me. Leave off the bullshit about you were 'glad.' I can't say what she will do. She will do everything she can to not hurt you."

"Sure, the way she 'protected' Doctor Brewer. He's in jail." Teller's voice had regained some of its confidence.

"She couldn't help him. He was too close to what happened. He waited too late to speak up, after he lied. He can't prove where he was during any of the three murders."

"I was here the Monday night Harvey was killed. Studying.

Someone had to see me. There was a lot of noise. There always is during Monday night football. I complained about it. Last night I was tutoring athletes; I can prove it." He stopped to get his breath.

"Good," said Morris, hoping that he could, in truth, prove it. He took Sullivan's arm. "I won't write anything unless the Lieutenant releases it. Including your name. You're in a spot. The truth will help. Don't shade it."

The boy nodded. He was still sitting when they stepped outside into the late afternoon wind.

Chapter Thirty-four

"You drive." Sullivan kept her hands in her pockets and looked over her shoulder.

Morris wondered if she would always look now before getting into an automobile, and flinch if a truck was coming. There was no traffic.

They rode without speaking. Sullivan turned on the heater. "That boy is terrified. He's more frightened than Brewer."

"Whoever killed the three of them had better be terrified." Morris caught himself looking in the mirror. Sullivan did not miss it.

"I just don't think Paul Teller could hurt anyone," she said. "I can't imagine his driving the truck that hit us."

"No. But I wouldn't bet my life on it." A small truck passed them. Morris caught himself bracing against the steering wheel as if the car were about to be hit from behind. "He could have been *with* Trapwell in my room. Could easily have gotten close enough—"

"Don't say it." There was no fun in Sullivan's voice.

"Sorry. But Teller's also a good athlete. He played football

207

against Trapwell, he said, in high school. He looks fit enough to have surprised the manager." Morris left it there. He reached over and squeezed her leg. Until she smiled. "Tell me, Sullivan. What do *you* think happened? Why did anyone kill the three of them?"

He drove all the way through town and parked in front of the Georgian Hotel. Still she hadn't spoken. Morris led the way back to their table in the bar. He ordered beers. Sullivan did not speak.

"Of course, in the beginning they only meant to kill Trapwell," said Morris.

Sullivan looked at him as if she had just awakened. "Why *they*?"

"Somebody killed Harvey Trapwell, and whoever did it used Henry Young to help him. Henry knew too much afterward. I think, if you will excuse the expression, he got in over his head."

"Morris. You will have to answer for that in the next world." Her voice had its old ring of fun. Then she asked solemnly, "Why did someone kill Harvey Trapwell?"

"That's the question. Was it a lover? Brewer? Teller? Someone else whose homosexuality is still a secret? Mitchell? The 'Hulk'? Perhaps our Lieutenant killed Trapwell to protect Harry. It sounds crazy, but then what's logical about love and murder? Maybe Harry killed him to protect himself? And that is the ultimate insanity. Maybe the true reason is the key in the roll of bloody cotton. Did somebody wreck our hotel room looking for it? Whoever had the dressing-room key was stealing drugs, and Harvey caught him at it. If we can believe Brewer."

"Why didn't Trapwell tell Doc, or someone, right then?"

"His face was a mess. Harry was raging at him. He was sick of football. He actually left the dressing room before the game was over. Maybe he was going to tell it all to me. Remember, Trapwell told Paul Teller there were people he was going to 'bleed all over.'"

"Maybe he was protecting Doc?" said Sullivan.

"Maybe. Doc's missing drugs. And his medicine supply should have been with him on the sideline. But who did Harvey catch going through Doc's bag? If Henry Young, or Doc, was the accomplice, who was the thief?"

Sullivan began to speak as if she were dictating: "Trapwell

came to your hotel room. Someone followed him. Trapwell was drinking. He wasn't thinking too clearly. He wanted to see you. He couldn't wait until morning to see you. To begin to tell you *everything*. Maybe he was afraid." She let that sink in. "He called your room on the house phone. You weren't in. You were still at the banquet. Someone *else* had to be sure you were still at the banquet, someone older than Henry Young who wouldn't have been conspicuous among the older men in the room: the thief."

"Did they mean to kill Trapwell?" Morris felt the chill of the beer in his hand.

"The thief did. Young may have thought they were going to frighten him, to keep him from seeing you."

"Or Young was into the drug market too far to turn back," said Morris.

Sullivan closed her eyes with concentration. "Young could see, even hear, Trapwell call your room and obviously get no answer. He watched Trapwell waiting in the lobby, about to be sick."

Suddenly Morris gripped the beer as if it might spill of its own volition. "Young pages the thief at the banquet. Tells him Trapwell is waiting in the lobby to see me and that he is sick drunk. The thief leaves the banquet, which is just getting started. He can open my hotel door with a sponge. The next time Trapwell calls my room, the thief tells him to come up. Trapwell doesn't know me, and is in no condition to guess voices. The thief leaves my door ajar and waits down the hall to be sure Harvey is nearly helpless. Harvey is a giant of a boy. But now he is really sick. He opens my door and runs for the bathroom. And our thief—"

"Becomes a killer," whispered Sullivan.

Morris began to imagine the faces of everyone he had known or met in Sparta, Georgia.

"The banquet was a drunken madhouse," he said. "It would have been tough to page anyone. You could hardly hear your own name—" Morris slid his open palm over the smooth table. "A name. A funny name. Being announced. Everybody laughing. Drunken laughter. Not a name I ever heard before. Or since. What the hell was it . . ."

"Short name? Long name? What letter did it start with?" asked Sullivan.

Morris had not realized he had been thinking out loud. "Damn, I almost had it." He finished his beer and began drinking hers. "Something to do with radio. Broadcasting. Batteries. Dial. Shortwave. Static. No! Network. Portable. General Electric. Transistors . . . No, no . . . *old* radio. Tubes. Benny. Allen. Atwater. Goddamn! Atwater-Kent Radio, the old Depression model. *Atwater Peacock* was the name of the sonofabitch who was paged at the banquet. Just before Harry was introduced." Morris was standing, holding the empty beer bottle.

"Who left?" Sullivan signaled to the bartender for another round. "What a wonderful name, Atwater Peacock."

Morris sat back down. "Nobody left. Everybody looked to see who would get up. I thought it was a joke."

"Later? Anyone could have slipped out of the crowd?"

"God, yes. Four hundred drunks in and out of the room. The name could have been a code. They could have had a procedure for getting in touch with each other." Morris gripped the empty bottle. He could hear the laughter at the sound of the odd name.

Sullivan took a sip out of both beers before handing him his. "Come on, Morris. Codes, no less. I thought this was possibly a crime of passion. Not an international assassination. Trapwell may simply have found out the number of your room on the house phone. Asked by number for the key, which the harassed old clerk innocently gave him. Then Trapwell went up to wait for you. His lover followed him and stabbed him in your bathroom."

"I thought you ski bunnies were all body and no brains," said Morris. "It could have been that simple. But it wouldn't have taken two geniuses to think up a paging code of two words. Brewer's passion didn't keep him from being careful enough to invent the code name *Oberon*."

"Back to the banquet. Wouldn't you have to be a member of the club to get in?" asked Sullivan.

"No. All it took was ten dollars. Not many younger men were there. Teller, or even Brewer, might have felt out of place. But who would have noticed anybody in that crowd, unless he was sober."

"Who else in the banquet room could have been the thief and the killer, if they were the same man?"

"Well, there were four hundred men in the room. All of

them temporarily insane with Harry and football. Doc, of course, had plenty to lose. Harry himself left in the elevator, in a tangle of arms, a good half hour before I got to my room. The President, Walker, left the banquet room before that, and he was seething. Or he made a show of being furious with Harry. Maybe Walker has addictions of his own. And his chauffeur, Myers, I saw outside the hotel before the banquet, baby-sitting the antique Packard. I didn't see him at the banquet. Walker says Myers is a sick man, but he's big and well enough to carry a knife. Then there is Frank Caplin and his 'missing' eleven-minute telephone call from Trapwell. Brewer said Trapwell 'hated' the local writers. Yet, he called Caplin—person-to-person—in Atlanta, the Wednesday before he was killed. Caplin denies they talked, insists Trapwell must have been kept on 'hold' . . . for *eleven minutes*."

"You told the Lieutenant it *could* happen, at the newspaper."

"Sure, it *could* happen. And the great Caplin *could* be on drugs himself. Perhaps he was going through Doc's bag, and it was he Trapwell took the key from. All four hundred men at the banquet were on the drug of alcohol. A fourth of them played for Harry in the last thirty years. Nobody ever played for Harry who didn't hate him sometimes. Yet, all of them at some time would have died for him. Maybe one of them killed for him. I don't know why it sounds so absurd to say so out loud."

"If we only knew what Harry knew," said Sullivan.

"He knew enough to get himself killed. You and I almost beat him to the cemetery, old girl."

Sullivan shivered and drank her beer.

"Harry wasn't bluffing on television," said Morris. "What did he say to the killer? 'You didn't come by.' He meant the dressing room in Knoxville. He said, 'Your old buddy, Henry Young, would have missed you. You come to see me tomorrow, or I'll come to see you.'"

Morris drank from his own beer. "Harry told Johnny Moore, 'Who the hell could have believed it was *either one of them*?' Whom could he have meant? That was after Henry Young was killed. And after Harry changed his mind as to what had happened to Trapwell. Harry thought a lover had killed Trapwell, until Young was murdered. Then he changed his mind. Then Harry said he had 'two ideas' about who killed the two kids.

'One possible. One impossible.' And that he had 'learned to believe in the impossible.' Goddamn, Harry, you're a big help." Morris did not let himself think how Harry had looked, or hear the roll of his voice.

"Do you think Henry Young was blackmailing Brewer?" asked Sullivan.

"It's possible. But I don't think so. He wouldn't have left the message from Oberon to sit in Trapwell's locker for weeks. Especially after Trapwell was killed. Young was scalping tickets for the players... with Harry's blessing. I think our boy was also selling harder stuff than tickets. The money was good. But the death taxes were high."

"Don't throw your cane at me," said Sullivan. "But what if Harry had one drink too many, on top of the medicine he was taking. And saw Trapwell get on the elevator after the banquet, and followed him to your room and killed him. And later killed the manager because somehow he knew too much. And someone found out and killed Harry. Maybe even the Lieutenant. She loved him enough."

Morris shook his head in wonder. "Sullivan. I don't know how your imagination works at ten thousand feet. But at sea level it's illegal." He continued to turn it over in his mind. "You could be right, though. Harry was old. He was not sober. He was probably dying. Trapwell was his chance to go all the way with a last great team. Trapwell quit. And Harry killed him. Simple as that. Now all I have to do is believe it."

Sullivan rubbed her eyes. "I'm sleepy. Will you promise to attack me if I take a nap?"

"No promises. The Associated Press plays no favorites. You go on up. I'll drop by the station. See what's happening. I have three messages to call New York. You know what I'm going to miss most about this job? The fun of not calling New York."

She handed over the last swallow of her beer.

"I won't be long. I'm scared to leave you alone with that imagination."

Sullivan threw her napkin at him.

An old truck, lapsed on its frame, one of its wheels turning out of round, pulled away from the police station; Morris turned into the parking place, between two rival television vans. Both empty. He hesitated before opening the door. He could feel the wind against the Chevrolet, even parked. He should have worn his topcoat. He sat with the heater running.

The front door to the station opened, and a television cameraman backed through, followed by a clutch of men in business suits. Another cameraman kneeled in the door. The business suits gathered in a circle on the porch, as if the cameramen were going to attack. The wind seemed to blow the circle apart and down the steps. Morris saw the Lieutenant coming through the door. Now the cameramen spotted her and jockeyed for shooting positions. She seemed confused. She gripped her shoulder bag with both hands. Morris opened the car door and stepped out on his stiff left leg. He pushed his right hand, not lifting it, on the horn. The noise fractured the cold air. One cameramen shielded his head with his free arm as if he were being fired at. Morris released the horn.

"Sharon!" His one word started her moving. He sat back in the car, reaching over to open the other door. The Lieutenant, her head down, broke into a disarmingly girlish jog. Morris started the engine before she closed the door behind her. Now the cameramen were shooting them backing out and pulling away—from what, Morris wasn't sure.

The Lieutenant was trembling. She made no effort to speak.

Morris drove through the campus. The students seemed even younger, hatless in the sharp wind and wearing brightly colored jackets. Morris did not look at the stadium or the practice fields. He concentrated on his driving and the youth of the students.

"I've been fired." She sounded like a small girl sent home from school.

"For what? They can't fire you without a hearing."

"Suspended. Same thing. For conduct unbecoming a police officer."

"Harry?"

She nodded.

"Not the silly column Caplin wrote this morning?"

"Who knows?" Her voice was a closer imitation of her old self. "The university. The town. The media. Everybody wants blood." She pushed her hand through her hair. "So do I." She held her chin up.

"Buy you a beer."

"Why not? I'm off duty. Forever."

"It gets here sooner than you think." Morris pulled behind Jake's. The parking lot was half empty.

By the second beer, he had replayed every possibility, including Sullivan's: "... so maybe *you* figured out the first two murders. And it was Harry. And you killed him. To save him." He was careful not to quote Sullivan.

The Lieutenant looked awkward drinking the beer. She held the bottle as if she were not sure which end to pour from. "I loved him enough. And you're right: Harry was capable of almost anything. But not of killing someone for no reason."

"Anger?"

"Nobody could hate like Harry," she said.

Morris flinched, as if the words had come from his own mind without his consent. Then he remembered thinking them a week ago, before he left New York. She looked at him curiously. "I'm sorry. What did you say?" asked Morris.

"You were off somewhere... I said, Harry only stayed angry when it paid for him to be angry."

Morris signaled the waiter and paid the bill, then led the Lieutenant back to Sullivan's rental car. "Every time I think I'm in Harry's mind, some face eludes me. Who didn't come by the dressing room? What did he mean, 'How could it be either one of them?' Who was 'possible' and who 'impossible'? I think I know something and I don't. But I know this: Harry knew. Tomorrow, I want to go to his cabin again. I want to read every letter Harry Carr dictated in the last three months. I want to talk to Johnny Moore. I want to talk to you. I want to see a rerun of Harry's TV show. Of every TV show he did this year. I know to a point what he understood. We've got to know what Harry *knew*."

"Turn here." The Lieutenant pointed left at the intersection. Then Morris remembered 'Fessor's house, and where it stood.

"I'll sit down and type every scrap of conversation Harry and I had this fall that I can remember," she said. "But I won't have a badge to help you with."

Morris stopped. Her house was vintage Sparta, with three stories of Victorian gingerbread and a wide porch under the trees.

"I'll call you," he said, "and we're going to start over, and we're going to see what Harry saw."

Chapter Thirty-five

Empty, without windows, no sound, no light, only the wind moving on the wall in the dark, moving backward in the air... Morris was awake. The room was cold. He shivered under the covers. He was glad to see the streak of light under the bathroom door. Sullivan's pillow was empty. He felt until he touched her deep under the blanket, curled up like a ferret, asleep. How did she get any air under there? Again, oddly, Morris wanted a cigaret. He sat up: *Smoke*, he remembered, like incense over Harry, in the dark. Watching a goddamned film of a football game he had won and the whole fucking world had forgotten thirty-two years ago. It was as if he had gone back to see his life begin again, with Walter Deihl carrying the ball in the air like a ghost. Shooting him then was like killing him at his prayers, saving Harry from all his sins. If Harry had had the choice, he would have chosen a touchdown play to die on. Morris switched on the light. He looked at his watch. It was 3 A.M. Sullivan did not stir. He dialed the Lieutenant's number. The fifth ring, she answered.

"Take a minute and wake up," he said.

She mumbled.

"Don't even look at the clock. You'll feel worse. This is Morris."

"What is it?" She was still drowsy.

"You awake?"

"Yes."

"You know how to operate a film projector?"

"Yes. Why, Morris?"

"Did you ever operate Harry's? At the cabin?"

"Sure. Harry was a film-aholic. He filmed practice drills. I often watched with him. I even ran the projector."

"When we found him, you said he sometimes watched films of old games?"

"Once in a while. He would take a play from a game that happened twenty years ago, and use it. He had a huge film library of every game his teams had ever played."

"I wonder . . ." said Morris.

"What?"

"I wonder why the film he was watching when he was killed happened to be stopped on that particular play?"

"Probably he wanted to use it Saturday. Harry's projector had an automatic replay so that he could look at any piece of film over and over, without manually running the projector back and forth. He just switched on the automatic replay."

"When?" Morris rubbed his swollen left knee.

"What do you mean?"

"Did Harry switch on the replay *before* he was shot?"

The Lieutenant paused. "I don't know. I assumed he did. He was shot so badly, I don't think he could have . . ." Her voice wavered.

Morris squeezed the telephone. "I don't think Harry was taking an offensive play from thirty-two years ago. Twenty years ago, maybe. But thirty years ago he was running the Single Wing and not the T formation. His hands were bloody, Sharon. If he touched that replay switch *after* he was shot, he had to leave blood on it. Did he?"

"I don't know. There was blood smeared on the projector and the table, where he tried to catch himself when he fell. The replay switch is concealed; it's hard to see."

"Where's the projector now? And the film?"

"Both were fingerprinted. Only Harry's prints were on the reel, Morris. A few of mine showed up on the projector. I was told that when I was suspended. But the projector and the film, after they were dusted for prints, were taken to the radio-TV department at the university. They were going to splice the film back together today. You have to be very careful with film that old. It's brittle."

"Can you get the key to the radio-TV department?"

"Now?"

"Now."

"I'm suspended. You keep forgetting that."

"Maybe the janitor hasn't heard."

"They've already got me for conduct unbecoming an officer. You want them to get me for breaking and entering?" The Lieutenant sounded plenty game.

"If the film was being spliced, then you haven't shown it to anyone: Walter Deihl or Johnny Moore?"

"No. I talked to both of them," said the Lieutenant. "Deihl's the one in the film who wore number ninety-five. A strange number for a back, wasn't it?"

"Not then."

"Deihl had to leave this morning on business. I tried to describe the film, but he couldn't remember what game it might have been. He's going to see it when he gets back Wednesday. Deihl and his granddaughter saw Harry at practice last week. Remember Harry mentioned them on his TV show. Deihl said they only talked about his granddaughter."

"What did Johnny Moore say about the film?" asked Morris.

"He said it could be almost any game in nineteen forty-seven. If it *was* nineteen forty-seven. He said Walter Deihl scored against every team they played. He couldn't imagine any real reason Harry was looking at a film that old. Except that Deihl was Harry's all-time favorite player, and he would get out an old film of his sometimes when he was drinking, to see him play again."

"Maybe that was it," said Morris. "But I want to be sure Harry wasn't trying to tell us something. Where's the radio-TV department?"

"Do you know the Communications Building?"

"The ugly, six-story job east of the stadium?"

"That's it. I'll meet you there . . . in half an hour."

"You might wear your uniform," said Morris.

"I thought I would go stark naked. It would be less illegal than impersonating a police officer."

"That's the Lieutenant we know and love."

She hung up.

"If there is going to be any loving 'east of the stadium,' you'll have to put me and this bed in the car." Sullivan sounded as if she were speaking from the bottom of nearby Lake Lanier.

Morris trapped the covers around her with both arms, holding her in a ball like a giant pincushion. "She lives! Do you know what time it is?"

"Must be late. It's dark under here." She came up for air. "Morris, where are we going?"

He switched on the table lamp. "To look at a film."

She touched his arm. "You know something?"

"I should. But don't ask me what."

Even the lights in the fraternity houses were out. No one was on the street. Near the stadium a pair of headlights slowed, then passed them.

"Campus police," said Sullivan. "Where were they when we needed them?" They topped the same hill they had been coming down when the truck hit them.

Morris turned between two enormous oaks, their dark limbs bare of leaves under the street lights.

Morris was careful not to park in front of the old six-story building, which was square and ugly even in the dark. He turned into a service alley and hid the car against the thick growth of a cedar tree. He held his door open for Sullivan, who slid across the front seat rather than tackle the sticky cedar limbs. They picked their way in the shadows toward the front of the building, where a single outdoor light burned opposite the entrance. A flashlight beam hit them both. Morris lifted his cane instinctively.

"I think we better stop for an electrocardiogram," said Sullivan. "My heart quit."

"Sorry." The Lieutenant lifted a six-cell light. It gleamed in the dark like a piece of artillery.

"I couldn't find a watchman, and the janitors haven't come in. But my funny keys work on this old lock."

A side door stood open.

"Sharon. We can find our way from here. You might—"

"No." She was adamant. "I know the room."

She led the way with the flashlight. The heat was off in the building, and it was cold.

The Lieutenant turned into a stairwell. "One floor up. Let's walk. We don't want to get stuck on an elevator."

She stopped the light on a room number. One of her keys fit the lock. The long, dark room was filled with shapes like animals. Sharon switched on the overhead light. "We're safe.

There aren't any windows." Morris could see the room was a film-editing lab.

"Do you see Harry's projector?" asked Morris.

"I'll know it." The Lieutenant moved among the arms of the machines. She stopped. "Here it is." She stood away from the projector as if it might speak of what it had seen.

Morris pulled over a chair and sat beside the machine. He could see dried smudges of blood across the outside of the projector. "Where's the main 'on' switch?" he asked.

The Lieutenant came closer and pointed. "There."

Morris looked carefully at the switch. "Let me see your flashlight." He shined the beam against the switch. "No sign of blood. The projector was running before Harry was shot. Now, where's the replay switch?"

The Lieutenant bent over. "Under there."

"Here?" Morris was careful not to touch the switch inside the mechanism.

"Yes."

Morris did not need the flashlight to see the crust of blood.

He waited to form the words. "Harry wasn't trying to catch himself when he grabbed the projector. He was dying. He wanted to stop the film on one play. I want to know why. Where's the fucking film?"

"I left it in a red metal box," said the Lieutenant, grit in her voice.

The three of them scattered through the lab. Reels of film wound over the tables. A few were mounted in projectors.

"Like this?" Sullivan held up a red box that might have held fishing tackle.

"That's it."

Morris opened the box. It was empty.

The three of them turned through open reels of film on the tables. None of it was football.

"Maybe it's already in a projector," said Sullivan.

"Not likely. Not much protection for old film." Morris held up a reel of film to the light without much hope.

A projector jumped into life, and Walter Deihl rose on the screen.

"Goddamn, Sullivan." The white jerseys came up leaping and grabbing in the end zone. "Run it back," said Morris.

"I can't," she said.

The Lieutenant fumbled with the switch. The projector had no automatic playback, so she worked it manually. She reran the scene, and then again and again, careful not to overheat the film. The players were much clearer on the white screen than they had been against the basement wall. Still, Morris could not identify the team in dark jerseys opposing A&M. He had been sure his subconscious would call up their uniform of 1947. He closed his eyes and saw the colors of all the southern teams. There was a time he could name the '47 starting lineups of every school, beginning with the great Charley Trippi of Georgia, Travis Tidwell of Auburn, Gilmer of Alabama... "Sharon. Run it back to the beginning. Let's see the whole film." Morris sat leaning forward on his cane, willing his mind to concentrate.

"Here we go." The Lieutenant started the film forward and took a seat. The film turned in a fit of numbers and patterns and then focused on a playing field. Opposing lines of players crouched for the kickoff. The camera panned the stadium. It was *huge*. An enormous range of hills came into the frame, and then one line of players ran forward... "Goddamn!" Morris was standing, pounding the floor with his cane. "Run it back. Run it back."

The Lieutenant turned over her chair getting out of it. The sound might have been the two teams colliding on the screen. She ran the film back to the beginning.

The camera panned again.

"Once more."

The camera moved across and over the stadium, and the line of players started forward to the ball.

"Sonofabitch." Morris let the film run without seeing it. "I'm supposed to be a reporter."

"Do you want me to reverse it?" The Lieutenant sounded afraid of speaking, of breaking the spell.

"No. No. Let it run to the end." Morris sat back in his chair. He fixed his eyes on the left side of the line of dark jerseys and did not speak until Walter Deihl was in the air, as animate as life. "That play! One more time." He watched it again. "Yes. Goddammit, Harry. You candyass. You *knew*." Morris could see the line of his own blood that Harry had drawn *toward* the play moving on the cabin wall. He felt his eyes stinging. "Sure. 'Who could believe it was either one of them?' Maybe

220

that's why Harry waited too long." Morris looked over his shoulder as if someone were standing behind him. The film ran through a geometry of crazed patterns and then onto the reel, leaving a white light burning on the white screen.

Morris sat without speaking.

The Lieutenant switched on the overhead lights.

Sullivan's hands tightened on Morris' shoulders. He looked straight ahead at the blank screen.

"Morris?" Sullivan said his name like a question.

"So neither of them came to see Harry in the dressing room. Not the *possible*, or the *impossible*...killer. Henry Young's *buddy*, Harry called one of them. Henry was scalping tickets to the 'Big Mule' alumni. He was also peddling dope, and one of the two men was using it, or both of them. Harry didn't trust either of them. Harry made a lifetime of mistakes, but not many of them judging people. What time is it?"

"It's after four A.M.," said the Lieutenant.

"I need two hours' sleep. Then we'll separate the possible from the impossible. Or bury them in the same box."

"John Morris, there will be four murders if that's all you're going to say."

Morris began to tell them what he had seen on the screen.

Chapter Thirty-six

Morris laid the knife carefully on the plate. He did not trust himself to hold it. He nearly buried it in the table. He signed the check and picked up his cane and binocular case. There was only an old man holding a small dog in the lobby. One step through the door, and he could see his breath in the air.

Sullivan waited on the steps.

"What are you doing up? After he got to his office, I promised I'd call."

"I believe everything you say, Morris, until you promise me something." The wind blew her hair. The cold renewed her skin. She looked as if she had slept for ten hours. "Do you think either of them . . . suspects?"

"After three murders, a killer has to fear everybody, unless he's not human." Morris opened the car door for Sullivan. "It will be to his advantage this morning . . . if he's *not* human."

He walked around the Chevrolet. The town was awake, but not yet on the street. The few cars that passed had patches of frost on the windows.

They drove without speaking. The heater warmed them through their clothes. Morris pulled off onto the shoulder of the road, but kept the engine running.

"What does he drive?" Sullivan took her walking glasses out of her purse.

"Most likely a black sedan. But there's at least one other car."

"Do you think Sharon can convince the police to come?"

"Sure." Morris was not sure at all. She had better.

"There's a car." Sullivan pointed as if it were a fox coming through the trees. Morris lifted his binoculars. It was a small, red Ford. The driver was a woman.

"Who is it?" asked Sullivan.

"The wife, I think. I'm sure."

"I can't imagine a killer being married. That's so *normal*."

The red Ford turned past them toward town, the wife only glancing their way. What does she know? wondered Morris. Or guess? His thoughts might have invented the black automobile in the trees, moving slowly along the same winding drive. Both occupants were in the front seat.

To Morris' amazement, the long sedan also turned onto the road directly toward them. He dropped his binoculars and leaned across Sullivan as if taking something from the glove compartment. "See if he slows down." Morris did not say the word *stop*. He found an Avis map of Atlanta in the glove compartment. He could feel Sullivan holding her breath. Then blowing it out in his hair. He straightened up. He could still see the black sedan in the rearview mirror.

"They looked . . . right at me." Sullivan folded her arms to keep from shaking. "Do you think they recognized us?"

"I doubt it. It doesn't really matter. It's just the two of them together. No houseguests. That's what I wanted to know." What if Harry was wrong, thought Morris, about both of them? Or if the film meant nothing; it was only an accident he stopped it where he did. Well, he'd know soon enough. "What?" Morris asked.

"We'd better go," Sullivan repeated, checking her watch.

"Who did Sharon say would be on duty?"

"I didn't ask her. She wasn't . . . fully awake," said Sullivan, looking again at her watch.

Morris felt strong. As if he'd slept for a day. "Do you think she may have dozed back off?"

"I . . . have a key. I'll get things moving in time."

"Why did they turn this way?" asked Morris, guiding the Chevrolet back onto the road. "It's much farther to the university."

"It's a pretty drive." Sullivan folded her arms.

That's too fucking normal, thought Morris, blocking out the fragments of doubt in his mind.

"Do you think he's insane?"

Morris shook his head. "That's a legal term. The judges don't know what it means. The body count is three. I'd rather not see it go to four."

They drove across the campus in time to hear the clock chime the half hour.

Morris stopped in the Lieutenant's driveway. The house was still. Sullivan looked at him, her eyes uncertain without her glasses. "Don't forget your cane." She didn't smile, but tapped him on the arm. Morris lifted it in a salute. He watched her all the way onto the wide front porch, then turned the car around, making sure she was safely inside.

Morris parked beside the west stands of the stadium. A great old sycamore tree survived as an island in the asphalt, powerful even without its leaves. Strange it had not been cut down when Harry expanded the stadium and the parking. Maybe it was an accident. No. Nothing Harry did was an accident. Morris waited. Then walked to the end of the stadium and looked down on the now-brown grass of the field, the yard stripes fading with the season. The air was chilly, but there was no wind. The chimes sounded the quarter hour. Morris' own watch and the tower clock were identical: 8:45. He turned toward the heart of the campus. Students, deep in their sweaters and jackets, hurried past him. A few, already late for class, broke into a jog. Morris climbed the steps and pushed open the high door. It felt good to be out of the cold. He waited until the last of the stragglers were safely in their classes. Not many courses were actually taught in the building. There was a time when they had been. He stepped on the empty elevator.

A nervous young man, who might have been an instructor, leaned against a fire-alarm box outside the office suite as if trying to get up enough nerve to go inside. Morris pushed open the door. He checked his watch once. He was a minute ahead of schedule.

Morris ignored the secretary. Her name went through his mind without effort: Morgan, Elizabeth Morgan. She seemed too surprised to speak as he walked past her desk. She turned her dark hair and heavy chin, and followed him with her eyes. Something about the innocence of the Matisse cutouts on the wall brought a sound to Morris' throat. He carefully lifted them off their mounts with his cane. The glass frames smashed on the floor. Morris turned the knobs of the high, twin doors and kicked inward with his foot; they slammed back against the wall of the large room as if they had been thrown open by the sound of the breaking glass.

Walker stood, both palms down on his desk, talking to a startled Myers. Morris did not speak or break his stride. He shifted the cane to his right hand and smashed Myers to the floor, not flinching at the sound of solid wood against his head. The width of the desk bothered Morris. But he kept moving until he was against it, and then pitched himself forward from his waist, his right hand making its own fist which went against the face with the sound of bone against bone. He was right. The desk was too wide. It took some of the force out of the blow. Not enough to save Walker's nose. Only the wall behind him kept Walker from falling. Morris came around the desk, dragging everything, pen, clock, books, telephone, on the floor, kicking it all across the carpet. Walker's nose lay over one cheek. Acne scars filled with blood. His eyes watered. He blinked them into focus, not taking them off Morris. Walker made the first sound, his mouth open as if he were strangling.

He reached with both hands for his desk drawer. Morris put the fist this time deep in his chest. But the scream in the room came from the woman at the door. When he swung, Morris could not keep his balance, even with the cane. He felt his stiff knee sliding out from under him. They both breathed raggedly for the same air. Walker jerked upward with a knee. Morris could not move; the back of his head caught the desk. He felt the sound in his eyes. He drove his cane into softness; the scream in the room was not the woman's. Morris touched an upper tooth sticking through his lip. He drove the cane with power; this time the scream was all air and no sound.

With his cane between his two fists, Morris pinned Walker's throat to the floor. An alarm bell raged through the building.

"One of you killed Harry." Morris did not recognize his own voice. He sprayed blood off his lips.

Walker could not answer. He struggled feebly for his breath. Morris eased the pressure.

Walker sucked for air under the cane.

"Take off the coat. Roll up your sleeves." Morris again eased the cane. He prepared to crush his throat at a sudden move.

"You're—"

"Shut up!" said Morris.

Walker began to squirm out of his coat.

"Easy." Morris' blood dripped onto Walker's already bloody face.

Walker twisted free of the coat. He held his arms awkwardly over his head. Cramped on the floor behind the desk, he began peeling back his shirt-sleeves.

"Both arms," said Morris.

The arms were long and still firm, with no needle marks.

Walker's voice had more body behind it: "You're mad."

"You . . . or your man's a junkie . . . and killed three people."

"Russell?" Walker's voice shook for air . . . "Has his troubles . . . never drugs, that I know of . . ." Walker did not sound so sure of himself.

"We'll know soon enough. Harry knew."

"Harry? You *are* mad. Let me up."

Morris shook his head. He realized the alarm had stopped. But no police.

Walker lifted his leg and kicked Morris against the desk.

The noise in the room was not the desk against his head. It was a gun. The bullet cut into the wall where Morris' head had been.

"Russell!" Walker rolled to his knees. "We don't need the gun—"

The shot took Walker in the chest and slammed him to the floor.

Morris threw himself, the cane in both hands, across the desk. The heat of the gun-blast fired past his face; the iron head of his cane slammed into solid bone. Russell Myers was on his hands and knees like an animal that couldn't stand. His right cheek was crushed, pouring blood down his face and neck.

Morris struggled over the desk, holding the cane, looking for the pistol he could not see.

Myers stood, seeming to draw strength from each breath. He ran backward out of the room, as if to keep Morris away with his eyes. Morris came after him without speaking.

The woman dropped the phone at her desk, her fist in her mouth.

"Get an ambulance. He's shot." Morris spat blood on the carpet. He could only think: Kill Myers.

The hall was confusion, no screaming; secretaries looking out of doors; a heavy professor with an armful of maps, amazed at Morris' face; two students running up ahead. Myers, bloody, stopped at the top of the stairs.

The Lieutenant, in blue, climbed toward him with one hand in her shoulder bag.

"He's crazy! Trying to kill me!" Myers backed away, blood running, pointing to Morris, who came on with his cane. The blood on both of them stopped everyone in the hall.

The Lieutenant's pistol appeared in her hand. Leveled at Myers.

". . . Crazy. You're all crazy." A coed froze beside Myers, unable to scream. He grabbed her and slung her into the Lieutenant, who caught her, dropping the gun between them. Now the girl could scream, wavering on the stairs.

Myers bent toward the pistol when Morris swung the cane. Myers' shoulder saved what was left of his face; the metal handle glanced into his ear; new blood shot down his neck. Myers stood up in the mob of noise with the gun pointed at

Morris. Myers was breathing, sobbing, until he squeezed the trigger.

Morris saw the black hole of the barrel: the fire that never came. Silence. The dead gun was limp in Myers' hand until Morris grabbed it, snapping one of Myers' fingers in the trigger guard. Myers' scream might have been the girl's on the stairs at the feet of the Lieutenant.

"Morris. My God!" The voice was *not* the Lieutenant's.

Her uniform amazed him. Her brown hair, not blond. Her face was Sullivan's. He then heard Myers' feet hit the stairs going up.

"The Lieutenant . . ." Morris slurred his words, too much air escaping between his teeth. He wiped his mouth, painting his hand red.

"I didn't wake her . . . ruin her life. I called from here . . . police *aren't coming* . . . wouldn't listen to me."

"I heard a bell."

"Fire alarm. I turned in a false alarm."

His face was numb. He handed her the dead gun. Patted blood on her hand. "Go to Walker's office . . . He's shot badly. The police will come now, by God. What about Doc?"

"On his way. Morris." Sullivan grabbed his arm. "What happened?"

He spit a tooth like a nail. "One or both . . . killed them all." Morris slurred the words. He pushed toward the stairs, dragging his stiff left knee. The stairs leading up were half as wide as those leading down. Morris was sure there were only four floors in the building. Above had to be the attic. The narrow stairs ended at a closed door. Morris jerked the handle, expecting it to be locked. It opened easily. He stepped inside and closed the door behind him. The only light spilled from narrow, dirty windows. Morris leaned against the door, getting his breath. His eyes began to adjust. He could see the long space was stacked with old furniture. Something bumped. And then slid. Morris started toward the sound without thinking. He could see better. There seemed to be one path through the desks and chairs and old cabinets.

"Crazy sonofabitch! What-are-you-doing? I'll *kill you*!"

Morris let the blood slip quietly out of his mouth without answering. The voice was all fear and terror. Morris deliberately turned over a tall, empty book shelf. It smashed into a row of metal chairs, as if a platoon of men had knocked them over. Feet scrambled ahead of him, near the front of the building. Morris heard a sound like whimpering, then he could see something going *up the wall*. He hurried forward, careless of the noise.

He found a ladder, straight against the wall. And a light switch. Morris ignored the switch and started up the ladder. It gave under his weight. He stepped up with his right leg and pulled his left knee after him. The cane was no help, but his hand held it of its own volition. He heard the sound again, worse than strangling, above him. The ladder disappeared into a black hole. Morris tapped the edge of the ceiling with his cane. A grunt and a wooden door came down with a shock, but not before he stabbed his cane into the opening. Dust choked down on him. Morris coughed and gagged. It was the first sound he made.

"Get away! *I'll kill you!*" There was the same strangle at the end of the cry.

Morris braced himself near the ceiling and raised up in one movement with all of his back and shoulders against the trapdoor. Lifted it suddenly in the dark with the man's weight against it. Again a grunt, and something, a shoe, drove into his forehead. But Morris was rising up the ladder, his cane slashing against a scream. He could not grab anything and hold his balance. Footsteps went up over his head. Light stained through the filth of a window. A narrow stairway went up, doubling back against itself, into the tower.

Morris spat blood without worrying about the noise. He climbed the stairs, not thinking of his leg or of what was above him. A sound came from far below but meant nothing. Something swung in the dark; he covered his face. Now it was swinging again. And again. He could barely see it . . . a chain. A great chain. He climbed the last steps up to a tiny room with something sounding in the dark. A bell. A figure stood over him, his arms raised. Morris lifted his own cane with both hands until it was shattered between them. Pain down his left shoulder lit up the dark; he could not raise his left arm. He gripped with his right hand through the bones of his fingers into Myers' flesh, and the animal in the air was the sound out of his own throat. They went backward into a larger shadow moving quicker than sound, gears whirling in the dark, a wild *striking* in his ears, snatching his hand empty of anything, jerking the tower with screams. A bell sounded as if the inside of his head had been struck with a hammer.

Then it was quiet.

Chapter Thirty-seven

Light shrank the tiny room. Morris shaded his eyes against the naked bulb that had come on as if in horror. His left arm hung down painfully. He picked up his left hand and stuffed it behind his belt. The pain eased.

The clock sounded steadily in the light. The head might have been a man's. One of the eyes hung down his cheek. Blood ran from both of the sockets. His face was crushed at an angle, as if it were being seen in a carnival mirror. The body hung from the chime gears like an obscene puppet. All the time the clock sounded over him.

A voice called from below. Someone was on the ladder. Morris picked up the long wrench that had broken his cane and, he was certain, shattered his collarbone. It was painful to bend over. He was sure he heard his name. By the second shout, Morris recognized the high, frightened voice, which added, "Police!" It sounded comical in the narrow tower.

"Come on up. It's over." Morris was unprepared for the weakness in his own voice.

"If you have a gun, throw it down." Sergeant Redding sounded closer, but still afraid. Morris did not like the fear in his voice.

"A wrench. That's all I've got." It irritated Morris that he could not speak more clearly through his broken teeth.

"Throw it down." The Sergeant's voice might have been a teenager's.

"Careful. Here it comes." The heavy wrench thudded down the steps.

"Where's the man Myers?"

Now Morris could see the top of the Sergeant's hat. "He's here. Dead. See for yourself." Morris needed to sit down.

"No. You come down here. Slowly. Both hands showing."

"I can't raise my left arm. The collarbone's broken."

"Just come slow. One step at a time." The fear seemed to be rising in the Sergeant's voice.

Without his cane, with one hand in his belt, Morris had to lean against the wall. By the third step down, he could see the Sergeant's gun. Pointed at him.

"You don't need that," said Morris. "He's dead."

The gun did not waver. Morris stumbled, but caught himself with his good hand. The gun lifted higher. Morris had to spit but swallowed the blood. "Put the gun down. He killed Harry. He killed them all."

The Sergeant did not answer. Another cop appeared below him. Morris recognized his face but did not know his name. "He killed three people. He shot Walker. Now he's dead." Morris felt as if he said the last of that in his sleep. His head was light. He was sure it was shock. He had not lost that much blood. He was afraid to fall with the gun pointed at him. ". . . I've got to sit . . ." The jolt of the steps heightened the pain in his shoulder. He closed his eyes, waiting for the sound of a gunshot. When he looked up, Sergeant Redding was standing in front of him, his gun still in his hand but pointed awkwardly down at his feet.

Suddenly, Morris was aware of how his own face must look. He lifted his arm to wipe the blood out of his eye. His sleeve was filthy with dust.

Now three cops stood on the narrow steps. One of them lifted something that shined in the dull light. Morris could see it was a pair of handcuffs. "You don't need those. Get me out of here."

"You sit," said the Sergeant, his voice normal but still high in his throat. "Don't move. I'm going up there."

The other two cops had their guns in their hands. Morris had never seen the youngest one. The narrow space in the tower seemed to make them both nervous.

"Great God a'mighty!" The Sergeant's cry was a mortal

squeal. He himself might have been crushed in the chime gears of the clock. He came down the stairs backward, afraid to turn his head on what he had seen.

"Goddamn, Morris, what happ'm'd to you?" The head and voice of Doc Haywood took Morris' eyes off the guns. "Put them fool guns up before you shoot each other," said Doc.

The three cops gave way to Jonas, still holding their revolvers barrel down, not sure what to do with them.

"Lemme look at'cha, Morris...I seen worse...but not much worse. What's the matter with ya arm?"

"Collarbone. Broke, I think."

Doc felt it. "Sure as hell is." His hands moved to Morris' face. "Lost a few teeth. Some blood. That all?"

"Ain't that enough?" Morris imitated him. It hurt to talk. He was sick to his stomach. "What about the President? Walker? Is he dead?"

"Naw. Not dead. Not far from it. Bullet in a lung. He's in good shape for his age. His ass oughta live. What about his man, Myers?"

"He's feeling worse," said Morris.

"He's dead?" Doc lost his good-ole-boy accent.

Morris only nodded.

Doc eased up the sleeve on his good arm. Morris had not noticed the small bag he was carrying. "I may miss your damn arm in this light." Doc slid the needle in without a quiver. "That'll feel better," he said.

"Count it on your fucking records," said Morris.

"He's up there?" Doc lifted his head.

"Check his arms for needle marks." Morris lisped, but kept the doubt out of his voice.

The Sergeant handed Doc his four-cell flashlight. He and the two cops waited, their guns now in their holsters.

Doc came down the stairs without a word. Then he said, "You're right, Morris. His arms look like pincushions. He dudn't need a doctor. He needs a clock maker. What the hell happened?"

"He killed the two kids. And Harry. Over drugs. I didn't know if it was Myers alone or Walker too. It's a long story."

"Come on, let's get this man outa here. And look out for his left shoulder." Doc helped him to his feet.

Whatever shot Doc had given him, it did the job. Morris

felt no pain. Doc made a sling for his arm out of a belt. One of the cops went down the ladder below him, and the Sergeant came down behind him. Morris managed the ladder with one hand and their help. He only became dizzy when he tried to stand at the bottom.

Chapter Thirty-eight

Morris woke up. The room was too white. The bed was too hard. He started to sit up. He couldn't move his left arm. It was strapped to his chest.

"If you tip the bartender here, he mixes a mean vodka and tonic."

Morris tried to speak. His mouth felt like a brick.

—Sullivan buried her face in his good shoulder. Her hair smelled like a spring shower.

She sat up and reached in her purse. Out came a vodka miniature and a bottle of tonic water. Then a bottle opener. The tonic spewed when she opened it. There was ice in a plastic bowl on the table. She topped the vodka off with just a splash of tonic. "Voilà." She produced a straw.

Morris raised the glass. What he said sounded like "Colorado." At first he might have been drinking air. Then he could tell it was wet. Then he closed his eyes and counted it the greatest drink of his life. He did not mind the burning in his mouth. He tried again to speak. First he grunted. He started over. "How's Walker?"

"I think I like the lisp. People will believe you're French. Maybe a Count. Walker's fine. They got the bullet out. He's awake. Eating. Morris, they think he was shot with the same gun that killed Harry."

"What time is it?" He was managing his words better.

"It's tomorrow. They had to put a pin in your shoulder."
She squeezed his good arm.

What if Harry had been wrong? thought Morris. Goddamn Harry, he was never wrong.

"What are you smiling at with those broken teeth?"

"Sullivan?" He raised up. Then lay back. "The Lieutenant. How did you get her uniform? And her gun? Why?"

"I always wanted to be a cop. You know how wild men are for a uniform."

"Seriously." With his missing teeth, he didn't do much with the word *seriously*.

Her face was suddenly all too serious. "Sharon was in enough trouble. Suspended. I faked the telephone call to her. She was still asleep when I got to her house. She had given me a key. I didn't wake her."

"You also lied to me."

"It's the company I keep. But I never really *said* I called her. I said I would 'get things moving.' The uniform fit me perfectly. No badge, so I wasn't really impersonating an officer."

"You have a permit—" He had to spit in his glass, just a stain of blood. "—to carry a loaded pistol?"

"It wasn't loaded." She said it as if that fixed everything. "I called the police from the administration building. I told them there was a terrible flap in the President's office; they had to get there before someone got hurt. They wouldn't believe me. They kept asking for my name and address. Then I said it was a matter of life and death. I thought I was lying, Morris," she said accusingly. "Now I know what you mean when you say you are going to make a 'scene.' In some countries it's called a war."

He held her arm. "You steal a uniform. The police won't help. You signal the fire department and come after a triple murderer with an unloaded gun."

"I unloaded it. I wasn't sure which end to shoot."

Morris held on to her arm. "Harry could have won another thirty years... with eleven like you."

His strength came and went. He waited to feel regret, but he didn't feel it. He had a headache he hadn't noticed.

"Have the police talked with Walker?"

"Yes. He woke up this morning. He's innocent, Morris. He had no idea Russell Myers was a drug addict."

"He hadn't seen any difference—" Morris butchered the word *difference*. "—in him?"

"Yes, he had. Myers seemed less nervous. More at ease. Walker thought he was almost ready to be back on his own. Now he knows Myers had picked up a major drug habit. Maybe at the VA hospital. Talk with him, Morris. Walker blames himself. For bringing Myers here. For not being aware of his condition."

Blame him, I wish I'd killed him. Morris was amazed at his own thoughts. He almost *had* killed him. Nothing would put Harry back on his tower, cursing the fate that gave him a slow tight end who would die in his shoes for him. I should be regretting the deaths of the kids, but I knew Harry; there was only one Harry, the son of a bitch. "Where's Doc?"

"Somewhere in the hospital. He was here until he was sure you were all right."

"Sharon?"

"Waiting outside. With most of America's reporters. She's furious with me, and with you. For letting her sleep. I told her you had nothing to do with it. I don't think she believes me."

"What did I tell the police?" Morris remembered only a haze of questions.

"What you told Sharon and me two nights ago. After we saw the film. You were sure Harry first thought a lover had killed Trapwell. Harry even wanted the investigation dropped. Until the killer also murdered the manager, Henry Young. Then Harry knew Trapwell had been killed for another reason. Young scalped tickets to rich alumni, for the players. With Harry's blessing. Harry had obviously seen Myers and Young hanging around together. Harry must have thought they were scheming to sell tickets. After Young was killed, and Doc's drugs were missed, Harry realized the manager had been stealing them to sell to Myers."

"Harry called the killer Young's 'buddy' on TV," said Morris. "He reminded him he didn't come to the dressing room in Knoxville. Walker later told me he looked in the dressing-room door, but didn't go inside. Myers must have been outside with him."

"Doc's drugs were missing," agreed Sullivan. "Young, as

a manager, had all the necessary keys and opportunities to steal them. Myers was looking for the dressing-room key Trapwell took from him when he wrecked our hotel room. He also wanted to frighten ûs. Then he tried to kill us with the truck."

Morris nodded. "I think Oberon can be glad Myers didn't learn his identity before we did. I have a feeling Myers would have arranged a convenient suicide that would have confused us all."

Sullivan shivered, and added, "Harry wasn't sure if Myers was in it alone. Or if he was stealing drugs for Walker."

"Harry's 'possible' and 'impossible' killers. It must have puzzled him why a college President would bring a sick, dangerous man all the way across the country with him. If he didn't need him to get his hands on his own drugs. But that was before Harry got out the game film of nineteen forty-seven." Morris rested his torn lips.

"Julia, I'm not thinking that clearly," Morris said. "Let me sort it out in sequence for the old Associated Press.

"Harry threatened the killer on television. Either come and see him . . . or Harry would look him up. Then Harry did what was natural for him. He got out an old game film to scout Theodore Walker, see what kind of guts he had." Morris finished his vodka and tonic through the straw, and Sullivan was ready with a second one.

"When Sharon and I found Harry dead, he had been looking at a thirty-two-year-old film. I recognized Walter Deihl from nineteen forty-seven. Sharon said Harry often took plays from twenty-year-old games. But when we realized that Harry had set the replay on the projector *after* he was shot, it hit me that he couldn't have been interested in using that particular goal-line play. It was run from the Single Wing, which he had long ago abandoned." Morris pulled on the straw until his face hurt.

Julia took up the narrative. "When we looked at the film from the beginning, and the camera panned the stadium, it was *huge*. You knew it couldn't have been in the South. That's why you hadn't recognized the opponents' uniforms. Then the camera panned the *mountains* outside the stadium. It had to be the Rose Bowl. A&M's nineteen-forty-seven game with Stanford."

Morris pressed the cool glass to his face. "Seeing the film, Harry discovered something he almost surely didn't know: Russell Myers was also on that Stanford team of nineteen forty-seven. He played on the same side of the line as Walker. In the film, Myers was hell: ripping, slashing, piling on ball carriers. Walker was not much of a killer, even as a player. Harry stopped the film—after he was shot—with Walter Deihl scoring, and Harry *having sent two men to double-team Russell Myers*. Harry left us a piece of film, and to him it read like a telegram: It also told him why Walker had ever bothered with Myers: He was an old teammate, however ruined he might have been. Harry would have understood that absolutely."

"You think he guessed which of the two was truly the killer?" said Sullivan.

Morris rubbed ice on his cracked lips. "I think he guessed. But there was no way for *me* to be sure both weren't involved. All I wanted to do was rattle the furniture around Walker's office and see if anything interesting turned up. It did. My teeth. And Myers."

"I almost got you killed." Sullivan's voice shook.

"I doubt the police would have responded any sooner if the Lieutenant had called. To tell you the truth, I was hoping they wouldn't."

Morris cupped his hand in front of his face, remembering the sound of the clock's great chain sliding in the dark.

There was a tap on the door. Sullivan opened it.

Sharon Blake seemed younger in her brown, two-piece suit. She looked down at Morris, not speaking to Sullivan. "You look terrible." She balled a hand into a small fist. "That's what you get for not waking me up."

"Listen. We could have used you. For sure." The "sure" escaped between his broken teeth. "Sullivan was worried about your job and keeping you out of jail." Morris held out his good hand. Finally, she took it.

Sullivan hugged her with both arms. "I was pitiful, Sharon. I dropped the gun."

Morris lifted one hand over his face before he could stop himself; he saw the dark hole in the barrel pointed at his eyes. He rubbed the stitches in his lips and swallowed his panic. "Where the hell's Doc?"

The door closed. Doc had been standing there listening. "Who said you were ready to take on *two* beautiful women?

236

They're gonna have to draw straws." Doc flashed a penlight in Morris' eyes and took his pulse. "You're a ugly devil."

Morris felt the tape in the middle of his forehead.

"You got kicked, or sump'in. Lucky it was in the head."

"What have they found out about Myers?" lisped Morris.

"Don't he sound sweet?" said Doc. "Myers didn't have a vein he hadn't shot to smithereens. They found drugs planted all over his bedroom. He had his own kitchen at Walker's house. Even had stuff frozen in ice cubes. I just got a call from a 'friend' of Sharon's." The Lieutenant lifted her head. "Walker was shot with the same thirty-eight that killed Harry. No doubt about it. Only a junkie would blow a man away and keep the gun in his car trunk with a box of shells. You're all luck, boy," Doc said to Morris, "that he didn't break your head with a wrench. He shot a man in fronta you, and a wall behind you, and kicked you in the head on a ladder. You better find a saint and light a roomful of candles." Doc dropped his accent. "If I had kept up with my goddamn medical bag, maybe none of this would have had to happen."

"I don't know," said Morris. "Sooner or later Myers would've killed somebody. He must have pushed Young too hard to steal from you. Maybe Young balked. This time Myers took the chance himself. Trapwell caught him stealing drugs from your bag and took the dressing-room key away from him. Then Trapwell made an appointment with me, the Associated Press. Made no secret about it. Said he had solved his money problems. Said he was going to write his life story, tell *everything*. Henry Young surely heard enough of it to be frightened. He knew where Myers got the key. He warned Myers, who must have been sure the kid was going to the police sooner or later. The two of them had been stealing drugs all fall. Neither of them was concerned with Trapwell's homosexuality. Or knew Oberon. They feared Trapwell intended to destroy them and Harry if he could."

Morris rested his aching jaws. Then said, "Sullivan, I'm sure it happened the way we imagined it: Young followed Trapwell to my hotel. Myers had driven the President there, and had a ticket to the banquet. Walker sat at the head table. Harry was drunk. The room was drunk. Young paged Myers with the name 'Atwater Peabody.' He told Myers he was sure Trapwell was calling my room. Harry hadn't begun his speech.

Myers knew I was there to hear him. He slipped down to my room. When the phone rang again, he told Trapwell to come on up. Myers left the door open and waited down the hall. Trapwell was sick with alcohol. Couldn't protect himself, big as he was. Maybe Myers meant to question him. Or frighten him. When he took out his knife, it was too late not to kill him."

"Then Myers had to get rid of the manager," said Sullivan in her smallest voice.

Morris felt his lips crack when he spoke. "Oberon threw us all . . . his message, everything. It had nothing to do with what happened to Trapwell. But if we hadn't found Brewer, we wouldn't have known that Trapwell took the dressing-room key from the killer."

"Poor man," said Sullivan. "We wouldn't have found him if Trapwell hadn't written Brewer's telephone number on his physics paper. But it would have helped Brewer if he had told the truth."

"Doctor Brewer's out of jail." All of them turned to look at Lieutenant Blake, who had not spoken since she sat back in her chair. "I talked to Brewer's lawyer and to the judge. The judge let him out on my recognition." She slumped back in her chair. "Damn Harry. He had to go on television and get himself killed."

"Bad luck that Myers was watching," said Morris. "Harry hit too close to him and Henry Young as 'buddies.' Harry had missed Myers and Walker in the dressing room in Knoxville. Myers always came by with the President. And then the film showed Harry he had picked out Myers as a deadly force thirty-two years ago." Morris sat back on the bed.

Doc left the room with a wave of his hand. The Lieutenant bent over the bed and kissed Morris on his broken mouth. She stood and hugged Julia, then hurried out of the room, unable to speak.

Sullivan sat on the edge of his bed. The quiet sounded good.

"Let's get it over with. Send America's reporters on in," said Morris.

"All of them? What about that man Caplin?"

"Send the bastard in. I may never have to see him again. But send in Pruitt first."

"Still the AP man."

"One last time."

Morris padded down the hospital hallway, the unfamiliar cane awkward in his hand. Julia had saved the pieces of his old cane to have them put back together. A nurse directed him to Walker's room, on the same floor. He was propped up in bed, his chest strapped in bandages. The two chairs in the room were empty. Morris waited until Walker saw him and nodded him inside.

"If you'd rather not see me, holler." Air whistled through the gaps in Morris' teeth.

"You're not much to look at," said Walker, his own voice shallow as a whisper.

"I could have saved us both a pint of blood . . . if I had known it was Myers."

"And not me," said Walker.

"And not you."

"I hate it about Myers."

Morris nodded. He did not sit down.

"I always wondered . . . what he was like . . . before the War. He went in at seventeen. He served in the Pacific. He had a bad time of it. Later, nightmares. Fevers. He only lasted two years at Stanford. We were roommates. He hated school. I must have done half his assignments. He finally quit. I kept up with him. Or *he* kept up with *me*. I got him out of a few scrapes. No felonies. Helped him draw veteran's benefits. Myers nearly killed a man in a brawl two years ago. It wasn't altogether his fault. There was an argument in a bar. The man hit him in the head with a bottle. I got the charges dropped, and had Myers placed in a veteran's hospital. He seemed to get better. *Much better.* But it must have been drugs." Walker lay back and got his breath. "Harry would have loved him. He was a helluva football player."

Morris put aside the weight of his own anger. "Can you imagine what it must have been like, shooting Harry in the dark with your own past shining on the wall . . . But why did he shoot you?"

Walker lay back with his eyes closed. "Every time Russell ever fucked up, I was there to get him out of it. He must have despised me for his own weakness. The one time he was lost for good, to drugs, I was too busy trying to run a university to see it. I can't believe I never suspected him . . ."

Morris took a deep breath. "No way I can excuse hitting you without a warning." He pronounced each word separately.

Walker opened his eyes. "It reminded me of playing against Harry's team. Nobody asked any questions. Just knocked you on your ass and left you there. Morris—"

Morris lifted his head.

"They can find another President easy enough. I can't stay here. Not now. But as for Harry . . . I liked the sonofabitch."

Morris lifted his cane in salute.

Chapter Thirty-nine

The old hotel seemed to have lapsed on its wooden foundation. The old man in front was selling his papers, calling out the wrestling results.

"Listen, you're not driving with one hand." Sullivan walked him around the front of the car.

"I forgot."

"I believe it. Have you counted your feet?"

Morris looked down before he could stop himself.

Sullivan backed the rented Chevrolet into the street and guided it into the thin traffic.

"Morris?"

He looked at her careful profile.

"Did you know Georgia was one of the original thirteen states?"

"Yes." He waited.

"If it had been the first one, I think they might have abandoned the idea."

She stopped for a traffic light.

"What's going to happen to her?" Morris asked.

"The Lieutenant?"

"No." They were passing the police station. Sullivan slowed. The Lieutenant was not on the steps or standing on the wide front porch. They had not seen her in two days. Since Harry's funeral. Since she got her badge back. The Chief had better get over his heart attack; she was now a folk hero; after all, she had slept with Harry Carr. Morris was surprised at his own disappointment.

"No," he said. "His wife. Harry's wife."

"I thought he died rich."

"Yes. But if she's that sick, who's taking care of her? What has Doc told her about Harry? Turn left here."

Sullivan swung the car through the light. "Where are we going?"

"To Harry's. I want to see her."

"Doc said she was—"

"To hell with Doc."

Morris had her turn one block too soon. "Sorry, it's the next street."

She looked at him without speaking.

Morris knew the great magnolia tree, its branches weighted to the ground. The huge old porch wrapped out of sight around the house.

"Can I come in?" Sullivan had her hand on the door handle.

"I was going to ask if you would. I'm scared. I don't know what to say."

The sound of his cane on the porch reminded Morris of the Georgian Hotel. There was no bell. The door had an old-fashioned brass knocker. It was well polished. He lifted it and dropped it, the noise echoing into the house. They waited, Sullivan holding his good arm. Morris pounded three times with the knocker. Sullivan flinched at the sound. They could hear footsteps behind the door. It opened, surprisingly wide.

"Oh." The thin, graying woman seemed to have been expecting someone else. Now Morris remembered seeing her. At Harry's funeral.

"I'm John Morris. This is Julia Sullivan."

The woman nodded but did not identify herself.

"We were friends of Harry's." Morris edited out the Associated Press. He did not want to alarm her.

The woman only nodded.

"We want to say goodbye to Mrs. Carr." Sullivan smiled as if they had always done it.

"I'm afraid . . . Mrs. Carr isn't well." Her arm had not moved, but she was bracing to close the door.

"Doctor Haywood knows," lied Morris. "We won't stay."

"He knows . . ." The woman sounded surprised. "I don't understand. I wouldn't want . . ." She turned to look back over her shoulder.

Sullivan walked quickly past her into a square, high-ceilinged living room. Morris stayed half a step behind. They stopped on a rich and intricate oriental rug. Light flooded through the tall windows over the Sheraton chairs.

"I'm afraid there's been a mis—" the woman began.

"Papa!"

Morris turned toward the door to his left. She was wearing a brown jump suit with a soft yellow blouse. Her gray hair was cut appealingly short, to the bottoms of her ears. Her face was unlined. She stepped through the door. And stopped. She looked at him as if he were an imposter.

"You're not Papa." Her voice was as deep as a woman's.

"No. But we're friends." Sullivan slid her bag off her shoulder and held it between her hands, like a guest come to tea.

"Did you bring me something?" She walked a step closer, turning her head like a small boy.

"Caroline." The woman reached out a thin arm.

"Yes," said Sullivan without hesitation. She opened her bag. And turned through it, pulling out a silver whistle.

Morris was amazed.

Sullivan held it by its thin silver chain. She waited so patiently, the woman—or nurse or housekeeper or whatever she was—seemed to relax.

Caroline walked a step this way and a step that way, advancing toward the silver whistle turning on its chain. When she was close enough, she took it with one movement and hid it in her pocket. "Do you want to see my bears?" She went through the door without looking behind her.

Sullivan followed without asking. Morris close behind her. They went through a long hall with a twenty-foot ceiling and an elaborate chandelier. Even Morris recognized the Westbury clock. He turned through a door and stopped on the yellow floor. The wallpaper was also yellow, and the soft, upholstered chairs. Sunlight seemed to grow in the room and leave through the windows. All around the floor and in the chairs were stuffed animals. Many of them bears. One of them almost as tall as she was. There were also a lion and cubs, a pony, a plaid monkey, a long happy snake, red, and animals without names that might have been in books. She went from one to the other touching them as if she expected them to walk. She sat on the floor and blew the whistle once, suddenly. Then looked around to see the expressions on the animals' faces. "Papa promised me a giraffe." She put the whistle back in her pocket.

"Yes. I know," said Sullivan. "He didn't forget. It takes time to find a giraffe."

"The right one," Caroline said.

Morris tried to imagine Harry, surrounded by the animals and games and yellow light.

Now she was talking to the lion as if she were alone. Then she walked over to a long table. Morris had never seen such music boxes. All of them antiques with animals on them, some carrying trumpets. She wound the largest box carefully, touching the carousel of animals as if to wake them. Turning, shining in the yellow light, the bears and dogs and cats circled the solitary tinkling. She was winding each box in its turn, Brahms' "Lullaby" breaking all of their sleep, spinning their separate notes in the air. Sullivan watched like a child.

Morris felt a thin hand on his arm.

"Please." The woman seemed even more anxious.

"Yes," said Morris. He nudged Sullivan with his bound shoulder. She started as if she had been in a dream. They did not speak as they left the room, looking back once, seeing her bent among the music boxes in a sea of yellow notes.

The woman closed the front door without speaking.

Chapter Forty

Her police car blocked their own in the driveway. Lieutenant Sharon Blake was standing at the door of the Chevrolet.

"I just missed you at the hotel. They said you had checked out. You wouldn't believe the last two days. All the legal folderol."

"How did you know we were here?"

"The nurse, Mrs. Hodges, called me. She was afraid."

Sullivan bit her lip.

"She either calls me or Doc Haywood. Doc was out."

"What happened? How long has she been this way?" asked Morris.

"It started thirty years ago. Harry never knew why. He took her to doctors everywhere. Even to Switzerland. She kept retreating into her childhood. Her parents died young. She grew up with her grandparents in Memphis. He met her when she was twenty. She was *different*. But happy. I would like to have known her then. I wonder . . . if she had never met Harry? Her grandparents only lived a year after they married. They were never really married."

"How did you find out?" asked Morris.

"He told me. Only Doc knows. And one other friend in town who is old and ill."

"He must have trusted you a great deal," said Sullivan.

"Harry was . . . not well. He didn't expect to live long."

"He must have trusted you even more."

"What will happen to her?" asked Morris.

"Nothing. She doesn't change. She's happy. Mrs. Hodges has no family. Harry left a great deal of money."

"And you?" asked Morris.

"I'm a friend." She opened the car door for them. "Of yours, too. Both of you. I hope."

"Only if you come to see us."

"I owe you—"

"A visit," said Morris. He kissed her on the mouth.

"Tell her—" Sullivan looked toward the house. "—that we are hunting. And we'll find the right giraffe."

"We'll send our address," said Morris, "when we get to Colorado."

Chapter Forty-one

Just outside Winder, Georgia, Madam Tina's faded sign of the zodiac flashed past, barely visible in the weeds. Morris watched it disappear.

"Are you sure," asked Sullivan, "that she can find us in Colorado?"

"Yes."

"No more Associated Press?"

"I'll leave the computers to the next generation; go back to the typewriter. I gave them a month's notice."

"Can we talk about Harry?"

"When we get to Colorado."

About the Author

John Logue, a former wire-service reporter and sports writer, is presently Editor-in-Chief of Oxmoor House Publishers and Creative Director of *Southern Living Magazine*. Formerly the College Football Editor of the *Atlanta Journal*, John Logue is the author of *Follow the Leader*. He lives in Birmingham, Alabama.

MURDER...
MAYHEM...
MYSTERY...

From Ballantine

12   TA-43